YA
KON
Konigsberg, Bill

Music of what happens

THE MUSIC OF WHAT HAPPENS

Also by Bill Konigsberg

Openly Straight

Honestly Ben

The Porcupine of Truth

Out of the Pocket

BILL KONIGSBERG

THE MUSIC OF WHAT HAPPENS

ARTHUR A. LEVINE BOOKS

An Imprint of Scholastic Inc.

LCCN Number: 2018016859

ISBN 978-1-338-21550-2

10 9 8 7 6 5 4 3 2 1   19 20 21 22 23

Printed in the U.S.A.   23

"Song" from OPENED GROUND: SELECTED POEMS 1966-1996 by Seamus Heaney. Copyright © 1998 by Seamus Heaney. Reprinted by permission of Farrar, Straus and Giroux.

First edition, March 2019
Book design by Nina Goffi

To Chuck, my love, my life, who sacrifices
so much so that I can write these books
and still eat food occasionally

CHAPTER ONE

MAX

There's this thing my dad taught me when I was a kid. One time when I was eight, and he was swinging me around the living room by my ankles. Man I used to love that, flying free with that centrifugal force, knowing that if my dad let me go I'd go flying. He got a little wild this one time I guess, and my head thwacked against the armoire where we keep board games.

The world went spinny and a sharp pain radiated across my skull. I was shocked too. Which I guess is why I didn't cry right away. But then I did.

"This is when you warrior up," he said as my tears fell. "Pain doesn't mean that much."

I sat on the floor crying and rubbing the spot on my forehead that would soon turn into a purple bruise in the shape of Texas just above my right eye. Kept wailing and waiting for my mom to come and make it all feel better. But I guess she was out buying groceries, because she didn't come. For the longest time. And Dad turned on the TV and ignored me. He wasn't the perfect dad while he lived with us, but he was right about this one thing. My tears dried, my headache went away, and I sat down next to him and watched the end of the Cardinals game, and when he cracked a joke about how Kurt Warner's wife looked like a boy,

I laughed a little. I came away realizing I had powers I didn't know I had.

I was a freakin' warrior.

That's the lesson I'm thinking about, nine years later, as I stand here at the Gilbert Farmers' Market with my mom, freaked out about whatever the hell last night was. I'm thinking about the shit show that went down when I skulked in at six in the morning to my mom standing there, arms crossed, brow furrowed fierce. As I look around the market, I'm realizing that I could freak the fuck out about everything, or I could warrior up. I force a smile, choosing the latter.

And when my mom's enthusiasm for grass-fed beef makes her start saying creepy things she probably doesn't mean to the seller guy, I decide it's time for this warrior to wander off on my own.

"I can't wait until I get your beef in my stew," she says, and since she's my mom and that's disgusting, I say, "Uh, I'm gonna hit the food trucks."

She glances my way and says, "You watch yourself, Maximo. No more trouble, you hear?"

Cumin. Creosote. The bleating of cicadas and my heartbeat, pounding. No. Nope.

I nod, gulp, and hurry away. The fine people of the Gilbert Farmers' Market do not need to know my business.

I love the Saturday morning farmers' market. I know it's weird and I'd never tell Betts and Zay-Rod, but I dig the friendly people, the parade of cute dogs, the booths giving free samples.

Organic cotton candy is like, really? I pass them up because sugar is sugar, organic or not. I like the hot sauce guys, Homeboys. Anything spicy is good to me, and they give you chips to sample the sauces, so. Double win. I'm a closet foodie. The Amigos don't know, but at home I will sometimes cook dinner. Mom's the tamale queen, but I like to cook Asian, Italian, French. It's fun to experiment in the kitchen. Give me some garlic, soy, and sugar, and I can whip up some magic with just about any protein.

I try a few samples and head to the food trucks, because everything tastes better coming off a truck. I've sampled them all. There's a kettle corn truck, a waffle truck—my favorite—a burrito truck, and one that makes ceviche. And then there's this new one at the end of the aisle.

The exterior is dirty and faded white, and it says *Coq Au Vinny* across the top in bloodred Comic Sans lettering, which looks a little amateurish. There's an angry-looking cartoon chicken standing there with its arms crossed and its eyebrows raised, like it's about to peck someone's head off. Above it is an upside-down fryer, held by a short, squat Mario Brothers kind of guy. He's using the fryer as a chicken catcher, like he's about to capture the angry bird.

I walk closer to check out their menu. That's when I see the skinny kid who sits in the back of my AP Language and Composition in the ordering window, looking like he'd rather be anywhere else in the world. My chest tightens.

The kid is just—striking? It's a weird word but I don't know what else to call him. He's rail-thin, super quiet, with a strong nose and a triangle mouth with narrow lips, all angularity and sinew. Sometimes in class I find myself staring at him and thinking about how he's all simple lines, no extra anything. When he did his oral report a few weeks ago on "This I Believe," he stood up and lazily ambled to the front of the class and it was almost like a dance, the way his long limbs moved. I couldn't take my eyes off him. I remember wondering what it would feel like to be that spare.

And then he spoke. They were maybe the first words I ever heard him say, and apparently what he believed in was yogurt. The logic went something like this, as best I can remember:

I believe in yogurt because it's creamy and a good use of milk that would otherwise go sour. Think about it: Where does all the sour milk go? That goes for people too. Not that we ferment, though I guess we do lactate, but everyone has skills and desires that go unused and unmet, and they sour. How can we make yogurt of these soured attributes? How do we make something delicious, how do we salvage them?

I was like, dude, how in the world did you manage to bring human lactation into your oral report? If I ever said anything half that creative, half that unusual, my best friends would divorce my ass. How can a guy be so comfortable with being weird?

The kid is behind the ordering window, his chin on his hands like he's uber bored, staring off into space. He's wearing a maroon V-neck T-shirt that highlights his almost alabaster, toothpick-thin arms, which take up almost the entire windowsill. He has dark emo hair that covers his eyes.

I walk up to him, and he turns and sees me. I smile, and his eyes go wide like he's shocked, like I've found him in his secret life as Food Truck Guy.

"What up?" I ask. "You go to Mesa-Guadalupe, right?"

He gulps and looks around nervously, and I immediately feel sorry I said anything. "Oh hey. Yeah."

Acne blemishes dot his cheeks, and his eyebrows look man-scaped, raised up at the ends. It makes him look a little bit like the angry chicken, or maybe just like he's questioning everything and everyone. Not sure if he's gay or not, but anyway, he's that kind of emo kid who hates jocks. I can just tell.

"I'm Max," I say.

He looks behind him. There's a large blond woman frantically scraping off the grill with the edge of a metal spatula. Maybe his mom?

He turns back to me. "Jordan," he says, kinda monotone.

"Nice to meet you. And you work on a food truck. That's cool."

"Is it?" he mumbles, raising an eyebrow, and I nod my head because, yeah. It totally is. I'm about to be sentenced to a summer at State Farm Insurance with my mom as punishment for a night I wish didn't even happen, and I'd much rather do this than that.

I point to the truck and read the name. "Coq au Vinny?" I ask.

"Yup," he says, like he thinks it's embarrassing. "Coq au Vinny. Um. 'We do Italian things with chicken.'"

I laugh. There he goes again, saying shit I could never get away with. "Italian things, eh?"

He raises his eyebrows twice in quick succession. It just makes his face more angular, and it's like I can't look away. "This ain't exactly Florence. Well, it's almost Florence, *Arizona*, I guess." His voice is soft, a little high.

"Ha. So nothing too fancy, eh?"

He looks back at the hefty woman for a moment and then turns toward me, rolling his eyes. "We fry chicken fingers in oil and put Italian seasoning on it. Or sometimes mozzarella cheese and marinara sauce."

"Man. That shit be Italian, yo," I deadpan, and Jordan's face animates for like a split second before he glances over his shoulder a second time, as if he's afraid of hurting the woman's feelings. When Jordan looks back at me, he's grinning again and it's nice, and then, like he's not used to smiling, he drops it. It's like he's panicked about how to keep a conversation going.

"I swear there's years of soot caked onto this damn thing. We should be condemned," the woman says, not turning around, way too loud given she's trying to sell food from the very truck she's condemning. "This is hopeless, Jordan. Hopeless."

Then she turns around, and she sees me, and she blushes.

"Oh shit," she says. "I was kidding. It's plenty clean. I'm just. I'm hopeless. That's all. Me. Hopeless mess."

"Mom," Jordan says, very chill-like, like he's used to calming her down. "This is Max. A kid from MG."

"Oh!" she says. "Hi. Lydia. Lydia Edwards. Worst chef ever. Nice to meet you."

"Hey," I say.

"We just took this thing out for the first time in a long time today, and it's. It's a lot." She runs her hands through her hair and widens her eyes at me. They are lined like she hasn't slept in a week. "Hey. You want to be our first customer?"

"Um, no thanks," I say.

"Oh, I was just kidding about the—come on. On the house. I'll eat one if you eat one. Okay? Come on."

It's weird because I don't owe Jordan or his mom anything. He's a cute boy from my comp class who I don't know that well. But I don't exactly know how to walk away. I instinctively reach into my pocket for my phone, like I just got a text, but then I pull my hand back out. "Sure," I say. "Okay. Thanks."

This gets Lydia Edwards to smile at me for the first time, and when she does her face energizes. There is something kind of—charismatic?—about her.

"What can I get ya?" she asks.

The menu is printed on a whiteboard with orange marker. The handwriting looks like a third grader's, and I wonder which one of them wrote it. There are four items. "Can I try . . . the chicken parm hero?"

Her eyes light up and she says, "Oh my God, you're going to love it! Love it!" She rushes to the back of the truck and I look at Jordan and I almost laugh, because his expression is like—have you ever seen one of those TV shows about people behind bars in prison? He looks like he's serving two to four years. Something about that miserable expression next to the freaky chicken drawing cracks me up, but he's not laughing and I don't want to piss him off.

"So this is like a family thing?"

He nods. "My dad. He used to run it. But he—"

I wait for him to finish and when I realize he isn't going to, I say, "Oh. Okay. My dad lives in Colorado Springs, so I get it. My folks divorced six years ago."

"Died, actually," Jordan says, looking down at the stainless steel window counter.

My throat catches. "Oh," I say. "Sorry, dude."

He shrugs like it's no big deal. "Four years ago. This was his, and today's actually our first try without him."

"Oh, wow," I say, and I feel bad for thinking of his mom as a mess.

"Shit," she yells from behind Jordan. "Ow!"

Jordan turns around and his mother starts hopping up and down, holding her wrist. "Ow ow ow ow ow!"

"What happened?" he asks.

"Damn grill. I'm such a . . . I can't do this, Jordan. I can't. I can't I can't I can't." She's still hopping, and Jordan looks quickly back at me like he's mortified that I'm witnessing this, so I turn around and pretend to look at my phone.

I hear the rest of the conversation, but I don't see it. "It's okay, Mom," he says, his voice quiet and controlled. "We can do this."

"Can we, though? Do novices just jump in and excel at food truckery?"

"We'll make it work. I promise."

"Four months of back mortgage by July fifth? We're gonna be homeless, Jordan. Homeless because I'm an idiot and—"

"Mom. Stop. Please. There's people."

"Oh!" she says, suddenly realizing that her mini-meltdown is being watched. Not just by me—I turned around, I had to—but by a handful of other people who have come to witness the crazy. People are terrible. I'm a little terrible too, I guess. It's like how traffic slows around an accident, and you kinda know everyone is hoping to see a dead body.

Jordan's mom buries her head into his bony shoulder, and Jordan turns his head to see all of us watching. He catches my eye, his jaw hardens, and he turns back away from us. He tries to speak softly, but somehow I can still hear him.

"We're gonna be fine. I'll take care of it. I promise."

"Oh Jordan," she says. "Here I am, screwing everything up,

and I don't deserve you. I really, really don't. What would I do without you?"

I blush for Jordan just as he says, "Mom!" and she launches into this kind of funny, mock-official voice: "Sorry. Sorry. Ignore, fine people of the Gilbert Farmers' Market. Ignore. Nothing to see here." Then she hugs Jordan and drops the voice. She says to him, "Oh God. Public meltdown. Sorry, sweetheart. I know this is not cute. The worst. Ugh."

Things get quiet, and most of the dozen onlookers go on their ways. I should too. I know it. Mom is probably wondering where I wandered off to. But I stay, because, well, I feel for Jordan. Tough draw in the mom department.

He and his mom end their embrace, and she sees me standing there. "Sorry. No sample. I'm hopeless on the grill. Vinny used to —" She covers her face with her hands and I'm like, *Please don't. Please don't pull me more into this. I'm just trying to be a good dude.*

And I am a good dude. Obviously. Because I say, without thinking too much, "Can I help?"

She looks up from her tears. "Can you grill?"

I laugh. "Um. Yeah. I'm all right."

She wipes her tears away. "Need a job? If you know anything about food, you've got it."

I'm like, *Um. I wish you hit me up an hour ago*, because that's when Mom gave me the news. The Summer of Max was over before it began, she explained. Full-time at State Farm until senior year starts up. Doing data entry. Which will kill my soul.

But then I think: *Maybe Mom would let me go if I actually got another job?* So I ask, "Are you serious?"

"Am I serious," she deadpans. "Have you seen me in action? I'm a YouTube viral video waiting to happen. This is clearly not happening with me in charge."

"What would I do?" I ask. I look to Jordan, and I can't quite tell from his expression if this is good or not. And then I remember the homeless comment, so I figure it's probably not a bad thing I'm doing from his way of thinking.

"I mean . . . run the truck. You and Jordan. Figure out how to make this thing work."

Hearing it put like that is all I need. Because, hell yeah. I almost don't care what they pay me. It's like the perfect job. Take a food truck, make it work, save a family and their home. Failure not an option, which is when I'm at my best. I'd be like a superhero, really.

In a world where a family's last hope is a food truck with a limited menu, Max Morrison isn't just a Good Samaritan, he's a Great one. He'll save the day, as he always does.

And a superhero not working at State Farm, so. Yeah.

"I'm in," I say, and Jordan doesn't react, and his mom lets out a dramatic sigh.

"Thank God!" she says, and we make plans for me and Jordan to meet up the next day, as I have to get back to my mom and tell her the news.

"You're my savior," Lydia says, and I think, *How hard can this be? To save a food truck?*

CHAPTER TWO

JORDAN

When we get home Mom goes back out almost immediately, thank Goddess, and I head straight for my notebook.

I sit at my desk, push aside a lava lamp, and start writing whatever comes to me.

> Here's a boy who has failed
> To take care of his mom
> Like he was asked
> He should double die
> Once for the sin of failure
> And
> Once for the sin of lameness
> Because I can't I can't I can't I can't do this
> I can't I can't
> I can't I can't I can't I can't do this
> I can't I can't

I shut my journal, amble over to my waterbed, flop down on my stomach, and as the waves undulate, I wonder what would happen if I stuffed my face into my pillow until I couldn't breathe anymore. Would I stop myself?

That makes me roll my eyes.

I don't want to die. I just. I don't want it to be my responsibility, I guess, whether or not we're going to be homeless.

In what world am I going to know enough about how to operate a grill to successfully run a food truck? In the summer, when it's a hundred and ten out every day? I was already dreading that when Mom talked me into it, but now it's totally on me and a virtual stranger my age? How's that gonna work?

What's a shelter like? Do we wind up in a shelter?

Should I learn to sell my body?

That one makes me laugh. Yeah, right. Like anyone's buying this.

I can't I can't I can't I can't do this.

I want my dad.

My dad. Yes. I really need to talk to him. Even if he can't answer.

I go into my mom's bedroom. Her sheets are tangled up like she's just been in a fight. A half-full Diet Pepsi rests on the bedside table, next to three Ring Dings wrappers, a bowl of grapes that appear to be well on their way to becoming raisins, and a bag of Sweetos, which are, apparently, the sweet version of Cheetos. Gross.

I momentarily sit down on her unmade bed, which is still warm from her body and still smells like her blueberries and shea butter bodywash.

Mom. What am I going to do with you? I close my eyes. Her room is like the room of someone who works super hard and can't afford a maid. My mom doesn't work anymore. She used to be a dental assistant, but after my dad died, she never went back to work. We've basically been living on my dad's insurance payout, which wasn't like huge, but was enough to live on. Which is fine. She's fragile, and I get that.

The thing that upsets me is the histrionics. The *herstrionics*, as she called them, that one time when I said, "Enough with the histrionics" and she said that she didn't understand the gendering of that particular word. It's just that I never know when she's going to embarrass me by becoming Crazy Mom. And yeah, doing it in front of Max the Dude Bro from school was, as she said, not cute.

I love my mom. I love the Lydia Edwards who loves to do self-made scavenger hunts where, if we find everything in two hours, we get a treat. Who loves to wrestle on the floor with Dorcas, our goldendoodle. Who insists we start off every Christmas by walking the neighborhood in ugly pajamas, singing Christmas carols with all misheard lyrics. But the unhinged woman who sometimes forgets to shower, who is too delicate to run a food truck, who spends her days binge watching *Beast and the Beauties*, her favorite reality show, while reclined on our faded and torn leather couch, shouting obscenities at the contestants while freebasing Muddy Buddies? I love that mom too, but she scares me.

I promised my dad four years ago, right before he died, that I would take care of her. And I'm trying so hard. When Mom melts down, I do the best I can to cook meals and I let her cry on my shoulder and I do the shopping. And when she morphs into normal, awesome Mom again, I don't even mention the other stuff because I'm so glad she's back. But I guess doing all that isn't good enough.

Until two days ago, I had no idea we were running out of money. She pays the bills. Or I thought she did, anyway. Now I know: We owe five thousand dollars in back mortgage. We have to pay it by July fifth or we lose our house. And Dad's insurance policy has dried up, I guess, so it's now on me until she finds a job, which she says she'll look for but no way will she find one and make that kind of money in a month.

I tap the bed, then punch it. The tap part is me sending love into the twisted sheets, hoping that she'll be okay. That we will. The punch is the part of me that knows it's hopeless. We soon won't have a place to live. Then I stand, walk over to her closet, and step inside.

The interior of the closet smells faintly of the fruity perfume Mom wears, even though I've told her a million times: no. I've told her I'd take her to the mall and get her something better. But she won't allow me to do it, so parts of our house, this closet included, smell a little like overripe melon. Nauseating.

Odor aside, what's great about the closet is that it's the one place where my dad still exists.

She refuses to throw out his cowboy boots. They are brown with a white, embroidered diamond design running up the leg. I sit down on the closet floor, pull his boots to me, and close my eyes.

The first year after he died, I used to come in here sometimes, turn on the light, close the door, and sit with them. Which sounds creepy, maybe, but it's what I have left of him and even though Dad was nothing like me, I loved him with every fiber of my being, and I know, deep down inside, that he loved me too, even if I'll never be manly like he was. His gravelly voice, gentle and strong, always made everything okay.

The leather feels smooth and warm as I rub it with my

fingertips, like it's just waiting to be worn. If only my feet were as big as my dad's, I'd wear them. Even though cowboy boots are in general horrifying and a major don't, I'd wear them proudly, because they're *his*.

I rub the leather and imagine he's here with me.

Dad, I think. *What the hell am I supposed to do? Mom is falling apart, Dad. I don't know how to put her back together again, and I'm so sorry. I'm letting you down, because I should know how to do this and I don't, Dad, I don't.*

Dad, I think. *This kid Max, who we used to call Guy Smiley in AP Comp because he is one of those dude bros who is always smiling because life is perfect? He's gonna help, I guess. Because I know how much you loved that truck. And him helping is so random, and I don't even know how to talk to boys like him, and are you ashamed of me for that? That I'm not even a real, true boy?*

And Dad, I think. *What if we wind up on the street? Are you disappointed in me for not taking care of Mom as well as you would have?*

I know it's just my imagination, but I swear I hear his voice respond. It floods through my veins, from inside of me right up to my inner ear.

No, Jordan. Of course absolutely not, never. His usually rough voice is soft, like marshmallow.

I sit this way for a long time, not moving. It's almost like I can't. Finally, I take a deep breath, kiss the leg of my dad's right boot, stand up and turn off the light.

I open the closet door and my mom is on her bed, reading. She glances up at me, and she doesn't seem the least bit surprised to see me emerge.

Her eyes are glassy and pink-tinged like she's been crying

again. She smiles weakly. "I need some snuggle time. Mini-snuggle?" she asks.

I melt. I can't help it. I always do. Because she's so fragile, like a bird, inside, like her supple largeness is inadequate to protect her brittleness, and it's my job to make sure she doesn't break. Because she's my mom, and she was married to Dad. Because I would still jump in front of a train for her, despite the fact that she sometimes makes me furious.

I sit down on the bed and she turns away and I settle into my outer spoon position.

I say, "Sure."

CHAPTER THREE

MAX

"Do you know how I know you're gay?" Betts asks as he jerks his controller to make Ezekiel Elliott juke past a defender on the big screen in front of us. "It's because you had gay sex with a gay guy last night."

I crack up and say, "Do you know how I know you're straight? Your T-shirt."

Zay-Rod, who is sitting on the other side of the couch from Betts with me in the middle, cracks up and says, "Aw, snap." Betts is wearing some cheap-ass white shirt his mom bought him at Costco. It's gone through the laundry so many times that now it's more like gray white.

"What's wrong with my T-shirt?" The Three Amigos are on hour four of our Madden Football Fest in Betts's TV room. His Dallas Cowboys are huddling up. They're trailing Zay-Rod's and my Arizona Cardinals by three in the fourth quarter, but this drive could give Betts's 'Boys the win. He breaks the snap and the Cowboys head to the line of scrimmage. Big third down.

I say, "Dude. That shirt is so straight it watches *Tosh.0*. That shirt isn't even bi-curious. You need a shirt upgrade."

"For real though," Zay-Rod chimes in as Betts hikes the ball. "You go out in that and the ladies be like, yo. That shit needs some Downy."

Zay-Rod's Cardinals blitz, and Betts says, "Crap," as he tries to help his quarterback evade the rush. Fail. Seven-yard loss.

"Clutch, dude," I say as Zay-Rod slaps my raised hand. "Clutch."

"Gang up on the white guy. Nice," Betts says, and he crosses his right leg over my left one at the ankle. It's an unspoken thing with the Three Amigos. We're very physical with each other. Telling them I was gay didn't change anything at all; it's just what we do. His Cowboys get in punt formation and Zay-Rod hands the controller over to me. I'm playing the Cardinals' offense.

"So, what actually happened when you disappeared last night, MAXIMO?" Betts asks as he punts. He says the last part real loud and slow.

I shoot him a quick-but-deadly look that he doesn't see because his eyes are on the screen. I hate being called my birth name. Imagine naming a human baby Maximo Ashton Morrison. Hell to the no. "None of your damn business," I say as my returner catches the punt and goes literally a yard before he's swarmed by Cowboys. "Do I ask you what you do with the ladies? Not that you don't tell us anyway."

"You're too secretive," Betts says. "That's not normal. I know something happened."

"Don't worry about it," I say. "Seriously don't sweat it. You're way too up in my business. Makes me think you're interested. And if you are, don't even, because I'm out of your league, dude."

Zay-Rod snorts. We call him Zay-Rod because his name is Xavier Rodriguez and, like Alex Rodriguez—A-Rod—was, Zay is a third baseman. The baseball team coined him X-Rod and we tried that for a while, but Zay is here to stay.

Truth is, yes, something went down last night. And maybe if it went better, I'd spill. I'm not shy. But this isn't the motherfucking *View*. We don't sit around and talk about our feelings. We play varsity baseball at Mesa-Guadalupe High School. We fiend on Madden. We eat Poore Brothers jalapeño potato chips by the bagful. We're the Three Amigos, and I'm so lucky, because I have the most loyal buddies in the world. They'd do anything for me. I'd do anything for them. I don't want to change that.

"Stop running out the clock. What kind of punk-ass shit is that?" Betts says.

I say, "Right. Wanting to win is punk-ass. Like you didn't do the same thing with the Pats?"

"Shut your hole, dipshit," Betts says. "Like you should have done last night."

"Snap," says Zay-Rod, and I shoot him a look, like, *Aren't we teammates here?*

He flips me off. Apparently all is fair in trash talk, even among teammates. Good to know.

"You know this kid Jordan something?" I ask as I finally bring my Cardinals to the line of scrimmage. "Skinny dude with lotsa acne? Emo? Black hair hanging over his face?"

"You just described twenty percent of my homeroom," Betts says.

"I don't know how to explain him. He's . . . I'm gonna work on a food truck with him."

"You're wha?" asks Zay-Rod. "I thought this was the Summer of Max. You were gonna wake up at noon and shit? You were gonna binge watch Cartoon Network and hang in the pool all damn day."

I bit my lip. "Yeah. Rosa was not down with that."

Betts laughs. "Since when does your mom lay down the law?"

"Since I came home at six this morning," I blurt, and then I'm sorry I said it.

Betts hits the pause button on his controller just as my running back takes the handoff from Carson Palmer. "Hey," I say, annoyed he's stopped the action.

"I knew it. Soon as you said you had to jet last night. I was like, *No way that dude's going home. I knew it.*"

I grab my phone out of my pocket and see what's up on Snapchat. Nothing.

"Yup," confirms Zay-Rod when I don't say anything. "That whole 'I need to get up early' shit was weak. Where'd you go? Was it this Jordan kid?"

"Relax. I've only been with like five guys."

"Did you hear what I just said?" Betts asks. Looking up and to my left and right, I see him and Zay-Rod looking at me funny. I smile and laugh, as if one of them just told a lame joke.

"Shut up," I say, and by habit I pick up my phone again and then put it down. "And no."

Betts says, "Holy shit. Max Mo got some, yo! Max Mo got some!" and Zay-Rod cackles.

"Yeah he did," Zay-Rod says. "What was his name? This some Grindr hookup and shit? Pitch or catch?"

Betts laughs like crazy and I say, "Shut the hell up." I pull my leg from under his.

"Oh, come on. You can tell us," Betts says.

"So anyway, I'm gonna work on this food truck because Rosa

20

was not having it when I came home in the morning. She texted me like twelve times and I had my phone off. I'm fuckin' stupid."

"Was Stupid his name?" Zay-Rod says, laughing, but he stops fast, because I'm not laughing.

"It was either get a job over the weekend, or Monday morning my ass was gonna be at State Farm with Rosa."

Betts gives Zay-Rod a look that I think means *We'll talk later.* "Whatever, dude," he says. "Don't tell us."

"That's the plan," I say, and he shrugs, and picks up his controller and un-pauses, and because I'm not exactly ready, David Johnson gets hit for a loss. "Ass," I say.

"That's what happens," Betts says back.

"What do you think you got on your podcast?" I ask Zay-Rod, as we huddle up once again. It was the final in AP Composition, which was Thursday.

He shrugs.

"You're so modest," I say. "You know you're gonna get an A."

He doesn't answer, and Betts says, "You know why he's not answering? Because he doesn't want to make you jealous, and you're not very smart. And not-very-smart people are sometimes jealous of smart people."

I say, "That awkward moment when a kid in remedial everything tells you that you're stupid even though you're in four AP classes."

"There's other kinds of smarts," Betts says. "My obdulla oblongata is bigger than yours. I promise."

I snort. "Medulla oblongata. And all that would prove is that you have a large organ that controls your heart and lungs."

"You said big organ," Betts says. "Which is funny because you have a micopenis and tiny munchkin biceps."

I punch him in the bicep and he drops his controller midplay. "Asshole," he says, rubbing it.

"If you had bigger biceps muscles, that would hurt less," I say.

CHAPTER FOUR

JORDAN

My wives take me to the Chandler Mall food court because it's Saturday evening and that's what we do.

I want to tell them about my impending employment issue, though I still haven't told them about the potential homelessness motif and I don't plan to now. It seems like a downer for a Saturday evening. Getting their full attention proves challenging. As usual.

"Did you see how she looked at me?" Pam asks as she just about slams her tray down opposite mine. She is staring at the Panda Express station, and her expression is typical Pam—defiant and dramatic in a way that is too big for the space, and most probably the situation too.

"I have my own life, Pam," I monotone. "Not everything is about you, Pam."

She sits down with a huff. "I swear to you she just gave me side-eye for no damn reason. I asked for an extra soy sauce and she was all, 'I'll give you that soy sauce' reeaall sllooww, and 'Here, have this side-eye too.' You know they're a bunch of racists over at Panda." She raises her voice now as if she's yelling back at the Panda Express girl, but her voice is way not loud enough to reach. "Yes, you. Side-eye. I swear I'm gonna boycott this racist-ass mall."

"That doesn't even make sense," Kayla says. She is on day three of her typical "I'm going to eat better from now on, I swear" thing, so she is rocking a Cobb salad from Panera. "Shouldn't you just boycott Panda? And shouldn't you do that anyway, because it's Panda Express and that's barely food, and would your volleyball coach be even a little okay with you eating that crap?"

Pam's eyes go all wide and she runs her fingers across her cornrow Mohawk. "Oh I swear to God if you get all holy about food again."

Kayla winces and tosses her blond bangs to the side. "It's not again."

Now Pam rolls her eyes. "Post-Thanksgiving tofu fest. Check. Early January freak-out followed by a trip to Whole Foods with your mom, and then a million phone calls about how deprived you were and how gross radishes are. Check. Valentine's Day crash diet. Check. Earth Day's Day of Eating Earth, which is not happening again, by the way."

"Okay, okay," Kayla says, cutting a piece of lettuce into tinier and tinier pieces. "God. Self-righteous ever?"

We eat, unable to avoid the Sia video playing above our heads because mall officials have decreed it's a criminal offense to not be assaulted by at least six sources at any given second. Kayla intermittently texts Shaun, the Chess Club participant most likely to get a girl pregnant at MG.

"Bitch is resting-bitch-face-ing right at me," Pam says, still not over her made-up drama.

"I hate to disrupt this diatribe about a microaggression that may or may not have happened, or this world-changing conversation about Kayla's latest unnecessary diet, but I was wondering if for one second we could focus on me," I say. "I mean, what about me? What about my needs?"

"Drama queen," Kayla says, putting her phone down and forking lettuce into her mouth.

"Queer card," I reply, slapping an imaginary card on the counter. We all have cards we get to play, though I only get to play mine once a week because I lost a bet (Keanu Reeves is in fact Canadian, not dead). Pam, whose mom is black and whose dad is Mexican, gets to play her card daily, and Kayla, whose dad is Canadian and whose mom is Scandinavian, gets to play hers whenever the hell she wants. Because privilege.

The girls are looking at me, having decided to grant me center stage for a moment, and suddenly it's hard to figure out what to say. How I am supposed to feel in this situation. If, say, my mom quit the food truck and I was stuck with it and with an employee I barely know, but we weren't, say, about to be homeless. I can't figure it out, so I swallow, and I pivot.

"Can we just for a second focus on the fact that I will never, ever have a boyfriend because I am hideous, and because God forbid anything should ever go my way in this life, ever?"

Kayla rolls her eyes theatrically, looking a little like her saucy grandmother character from the spring production of *Pippin*, and Pam, perhaps sensing that this is not a groundbreaking conversation as we talk about my burgeoning spinsterhood every day, looks up at the video.

"Oh, look," she says. "Sia was once a victim, but not anymore."

"That hardly ever happens," I say, grateful the spotlight I asked for has been turned off.

The talk subsides, which is excellent because I am partaking in my favorite pastime, which is ignoring my pathetic life by fantasizing about having my first boyfriend.

I get pretty specific when I do this.

This time he is a redhead with a slightly bent nose and eyes so light blue they actually have a vague ocean scent. He plays trombone and he used to be friends with these kids who are now Alt-Right-ers and now that he's out they troll him online, and one day his dad, a construction worker, visits one of their fathers and says, "You make sure your Nazi son stays away from my boy." He likes to play Frisbee and makes viral videos of himself lip-synching to Beyoncé songs. We go to the same community college and get an apartment in downtown Mesa along the light-rail, and every night I make dinner—he loves pasta primavera—and we watch British costume dramas on TV. We get married after college and he gets an IT job and I get a job waiting tables while I write my first screenplay, and when I sell it to Hollywood and it becomes a movie, we move to Southern California and get a place overlooking the ocean for us and our two children, Aimee (after Aimee Mann, of course) and Dale (after Dale Bozzio of Missing Persons)—both girls, thank God—and they take his name because it's something with a little more kick than Edwards, like maybe Darlington. Yes! Dale Darlington. Totally.

"Oh my God," Kayla says, smirking at me.

I realize I'm smiling like a dork, so I adjust my expression. "What?"

"You're doing that thing again."

"I am not," I say, biting my lip and averting my eyes.

"You totally are. And shouldn't you have an actual date before you wind up with kids, living in Costa Rica?"

"You could not be more wrong," I say.

She puts her hands down on the table and crosses them, like she's waiting for proof.

"Laguna Beach. And he's Irish this time. Redhead."

She rolls her eyes. "You are such a ridiculous romantic. We need to get you your first boyfriend. This summer. Hey! We should do a makeover!"

"Um. No," I say.

"No. We totally should! Right today. Don't you trust us? Don't you trust me to make you so beautiful that no boy will ever be able to withstand your gorgeousness?"

"What would you do if I let you?" I ask her.

Pam, who I thought was not paying attention as she is still staring over at Panda in between bites of something orange chickenish, answers simultaneously with Kayla.

"Your hair," Pam says.

"Your clothes," Kayla says.

"I hate you both so much," I say. "Like truly, utterly hate you to my innermost self."

We wind up back at my place, after a stop at Forever 21, where Kayla bought me a pair of flimsy midnight-blue sweatpants with the word "Star" written all over them and a yellow hoodie with a photo of Jesus, with the zipper running right through the middle of his face. Mom is holed up in her bedroom with the door shut, which suits me fine because I can't with her right now. I put on the Thompson Twins on my turntable—I am obsessed with '80s synth-pop and their song "Lies" is everything—and Kayla makes me change into my new outfit. Once I'm dressed, I look at my reflection in the mirror.

"I look like a ten-year-old foreign exchange student," I say, and Pam bursts out laughing. She's taken the turquoise lava lamp off my desk and brought it over to my waterbed, where she's propped herself up on purple satin pillows and is tilting the lamp back and forth to watch the ocean-like lava ooze back and forth.

"Oh my God you do!" she says, and she rolls onto her back on my bed and just cackles. "We're gonna call you Ludwig, okay? You are from the Black Forest and your Evangelical hosts took you out on your first weekend in the country and picked out your outfit. Ludwig!"

Kayla is lying on my dark purple shag carpet, texting—Shaun probably—and I clear my throat a few times to get her attention. When she doesn't budge, I go over to where she's reclined and put my skinny, "Star"-studded butt in her face and wiggle it.

"Whoa, whoa," she says, looking up from the phone. "What's with the unwanted lap dance?"

"Your outfit is being besmirched," I say, and she looks up and I can tell her first impulse is to break out in laughter but she holds it back.

"Oh. Um. I think it's very—stylin'—" she says, and Pam throws one of my flip-flops at her. It hits Kayla in the side of the head. Kayla picks it up, dramatically rubs her forehead, and yells, "Hate crime!"

"Against a cisgender white girl with blond hair," Pam says. "Okay then."

I flop down on the carpet next to Kayla and enjoy this floor's-eye view of my '80s bordello-themed bedroom. A few years ago, I convinced Mom to take me to all the Goodwill stores in the area and we bought all the most depraved stuff—her word, once she got into it—which is why I have a disco ball with half the mirrored panels broken off above my bed, and one of my walls is covered in pink wallpaper with black velvet designs on it, and the others are adorned with album covers by Shaun Cassidy, Shalamar, and Duran Duran. It explains why the desk where I write my poems is replete with three lava lamps and vanilla candles. It's why my night table is a brassy cocktail waitress, with the glass table resting on her ample boobs.

"Let's play How Many Bodies! Teachers' Edition!" I say. It's this game we play where we try to decide how many bodies various people have hidden in their backyards. Because apparently everyone is a serial killer.

Pam laughs from the bed and puts a sequined pillow under her head. "I like how nothing ever gets done with us. We have literally done no things all day. We keep starting and stopping. We may be the least effective people ever."

"Speak for yourself. Mom and I did the food truck today for the first time," I say.

"Thank God!" Kayla says. "I was wondering if you were going through some teen boy phase where your pheromones smell like fried cheese."

I sniff my arm. I smell nothing. "Is it that bad?"

"Depends," Kayla says. "Are you looking to attract someone at a carnival?"

I curl my lip as if I'm upset. I never am with them.

"My mom freaked. She's done."

Pam cackles. Like literally cackles. "Oh my God I love Lydia. There should be a reality show about Lydia." She wraps herself in a pink feather boa that was hanging on my bedpost.

"Yes!" Kayla says. "*Vaguely Bipolar Housewives of Chandler.*"

I roll my eyes. "I didn't even give you the most random part of all this. Guy Smiley. He's taking my mom's place."

Kayla inhales dramatically. "What? From AP Comp? Back-row dude? That's not even random. That doesn't make sense. How the? Why? Is he like a chef or something? Is there like an Uber app for chefs, and did you pick him because he's hot?"

"He was just there. When Mom freaked."

Pam raises an eyebrow. "Super random. I give it a day. You and Guy Smiley? You know when you hear something and you know it isn't happening? This is one of those times."

Kayla nods and sits up. "Pam is right, for once. Anyway. We need to up the ante on this makeover, because if he doesn't get a date soon and I have to hear more whining, even ONE MORE TIME, I am going to spontaneously combust."

She jumps up and goes to my closet.

"Don't!" I yell, and Kayla looks over at me, amused. Pam jumps to her feet and puts her arms out like she's blocking me. She's joking, but I'm not. That's my private stuff. Mine. Whatever happened to asking permission?

"Please don't," I say, my face turning red. When Pam sees this, she lets me go, but Kayla has already opened my closet door. Pam goes over and they both look inside, and I hide my face.

They don't see it right away. "It" shall be described only as a marital aid here, because I do not think I can bear to go into specifics on this particular aid to my nonexistent marriage.

I didn't hide It, though, after the last time It was *maritally aiding* me. I did wash it, thank you very much, but then I just put it behind its shoebox home instead of in it, because Mom wouldn't step foot in my closet and I am so fucking stupid and lazy.

"Oh. Oh . . ." Pam says, stretching out the second "oh" into three syllables. Low-high-low.

"Oh . . ." says Kayla, elongating but staying on the same note at least.

"Please just close the door and let's not—"

They look at each other, and it's like they communicate something but I have no idea what.

"Who cares?" Kayla asks as she sits back down on the shag carpet. "Do you really think I don't have one? I got it at Castle Boutique. The saleslady hooked me up. Rabbit."

"Yeah, but—" My face has never been redder, and I feel particularly stupid in my current Ludwig outfit. It feels like steam could erupt from my ears.

"You have tons of butt shame," Kayla says, and Pam snickers until Kayla hits her in the arm. "You do, Jordan. It's not a big deal. Lots of people have butt sex. It's like, so what?"

I go over to the closet, pick up the It that is currently making it a possibility that I might literally die of embarrassment, and stuff It back in its shoebox home. I close the closet door and sit down against it, as if there's a monster in my closet and by sitting against the door, we're momentarily safe.

"I just . . . That's where poop comes from."

Pam laughs. "Are we really talking about this?"

Kayla isn't laughing, though. "Did you know that biologically speaking, the rectum is cleaner than the mouth?"

I roll my eyes. "What boy told you that, and what did you let him do to you?" I ask.

Pam cracks up and shakes her head. "It's true. My mom told me. Poop is like the great equalizer. There is not a person in the world who can say that they don't poop."

"It's just what makes you real," Kayla says. "Guys like real. Remember Dennis? One time I had to go and you know how the bathroom in our house is right next to my bedroom? And I know he heard everything. I wasn't, like, embarrassed, but I was a bit concerned because guys can be so stupid about stupid things. But I came back to the room and you know what he said to me? He said, 'I like that you're real. Real is sexy.'"

"Amen, sister," says Pam.

"I don't know. I think me and my friend"—I point behind me—"are going to be together for a long time. Because who the hell wants someone gross like me?"

Kayla gets up and sits next to me. She puts her arm around me, which is not a thing we do at all. "You're not . . . old."

I crack up and curl my lip at her like my feelings are hurt.

"I am. I'm gross because I'm a human being and that's the worst."

"If you're gross, I'm gross. And I know you're not calling me gross. You're totally normal like everyone else."

"Ugh," I say. "Normal is so boring."

Pam rolls her eyes. "What the fuck did Lydia do to you?" She comes over and sits down with us on my other side.

"I have no idea." I put my head in my hands.

CHAPTER FIVE

MAX

The street in front of Phoenicia smells like cumin and creosote even though the restaurant's been closed for hours. Because ASU is done for the summer, it's actually quiet beyond the bleating of cicadas and the occasional automobile heading down University, one block south. My heart is pounding because I'm walking next to Kevin, and I know what's coming. Or I think I do.

"Do you have protection?" I ask, not daring to look to my left but yearning to see his blue faux-hawk.

He laughs a little and says, "Relax. I've only been with like five guys."

Flash forward two hours and I'm in his dorm room. It's a night of firsts. First night after the end of junior year. My first college party. My first time in a dorm room. My first time turning off my phone and knowing that Rosa might freak if I don't get my brown ass back home soon. My first time, period. It's like I'm high, but I'm not. A couple beers. Things are getting real, fast. My heart is in my throat. My ears are stuffed up like when I fly to Colorado Springs to see my dad.

Kevin's shirt is off. Skinny-chested and narrow, with purplish nipples that stand out against his pale skin. He stands at the foot of his single bed, staring at me. I'm shirtless too. He shakes his head over and over, like I'm some beautiful thing, which is awesome and scares me shitless.

He says, "Are you my dark-skinned boy?"

A bubble of something slushy fills up my esophagus. I don't answer.

"Are you my Arabian prince?"

My jaw tenses. I want to make a joke about how fucking stupid that shit is, but I don't want to kill the moment. Too curious to see what's next. Too excited. Still, I gotta say something.

"My mom was born in Mexico City and my dad is from Indiana,"
I say.

He rolls his eyes. "Oh, come on. Don't be so sensitive. It's a fantasy, okay?"

Time goes sideways. My head fogs. Nope. Nope—

My eyes flash open. Even though it's hot in my bedroom, I shudder like I'm freezing, and I wince. I'm not trying to think about that.

I glance at my phone and press the button. 3:04 a.m. I sigh. Not a good hour to be up. Especially when you have your first day of work the next day. Food truck. With Jordan, who is—I dunno. His mom was a trip, but she won't be there. That's good at least.

I spent the night studying up on how to run a food truck. Lots of YouTube videos. I have no idea, so I watched a few. Jordan will have to fill me in on the rest, which I'm worried about. Based on our conversation earlier, he's not exactly the best communicator.

I lie in bed until I can't stare at the ceiling anymore, can't explore for another second the slat of light that runs diagonally across my ceiling from the moonlight. Will I be able to see it shift if I stare at it all night? When does it disappear, and how?

I get up, go into the kitchen, pour a glass of water, and chug it down. Then I wander outside and sit with my feet in the pool. It's not yet bath temperature; it will be in about a month.

I look up at the sliver of moon through the saguaros that flank our pool. Too bright for stars here, and I wish I could see them, wish I could ask them questions.

Like, what the fuck was that with Kevin?

It wasn't cool, the whole thing, to the point I can't really even—I don't know.

I need a do-over. I'm so stupid.

I slosh my feet through the still-cool water. The ripples undulate, and the reflections of the cacti shimmer. I stare and stare until the ripples subside, and once the saguaros are back in sight and steady, I shake my head.

Nope. I'm a warrior.

Mom and Dad don't agree on much, but they both have pretty much the same take on that; they just say it in different ways.

Mom always says all sorts of shit goes down in the world, and it's up to me to decide how to take it. The one way you're sure to be unhappy is to frown your way through life, she says, and she's right. Always look for the bright, vibrant color through the darkness. It's always there, but sometimes hard to see.

So I had my first time. Last night. I guess I'm a man now, right? Shit. Doesn't feel—shut up. Shut up shut up. You got some. You're being stupid. Dramatic. Dad says it's okay to be gay; just don't be a pussy. He's a comedian and makes gay jokes in his act down in Colorado Springs, but it's all in fun. He even has a joke about a guy licking his balls and how that's one of life's delicacies. That was sort of freaky when I heard him do it. I don't exactly get my dad on this stuff, but I know he loves me. But I also know if he heard these thoughts I'm having, he'd screw up his face and tell me to shut the fuck up with that pansy-ass shit. Warrior up. Warrior up, dude.

He's right. I smile. I breathe until my jaw unclenches. I have the power to change my thoughts. Like I did when we moved here.

I'm eight. We've just moved to Dobson Ranch, a suburban neighborhood in western Mesa near the canal. We had lived in central Phoenix. I'm tossing a Nerf football with my neighbor friend, Skeeter, and we're talking about going to the park and waiting for the ice-cream truck so we could get Drumsticks. These other kids I don't know so well come around, and they say, "'Sup, Skeeter."

"'Sup," he says.

I say, "'Sup," too.

"We're gonna hit the park so we catch Mister Softee."

"Cool," Skeeter says, and he tosses the football to me. I throw it over the side fence and say, "Cool," too.

"You're not coming, Maximo," this one kid says. He has a blond crew cut and he's short and round. He says "Maximo" like he's saying "dog shit." I didn't know he even knew my name.

"You need to stay here in case the migrant-worker truck comes and your whole family gets a job."

Everyone laughs. Skeeter too. He laughs.

A smile crawls over my face without my even trying. I laugh too. And then they all run off, leaving me there. I just stand there in the middle of the street until a pickup truck honks at me and I have to move. I go inside and play Grand Theft Auto. *I don't tell my mom. Next time I see Skeeter, we toss the ball again and we don't talk about it. And it's understood that when those kids come by, they're gonna go to the park, and I won't.*

I grimace for just a nanosecond 'til I catch myself. Then I smile until I feel better. I mean, there are terrible, racist-ass people out there. But also good people. Who am I gonna focus on?

Shit. I'm better than that. That's about those kids. I have the power to change my thoughts. Always did. I have the power to smile through all this.

No one gets the best of Super Max.

CHAPTER SIX

JORDAN

I'm sitting on the dirt in the front yard, watching the sun rise over the palm trees, waiting for Max. I look at my phone. 5:08. He's late.

As the hot morning breeze washes over me, I lean back on my elbows, and I wince as one of them hits a sharp pebble. My poetry journal is by my side. I'm bringing it because there's a part of me that hopes this isn't going to work, that we'll go out and no one will want our food and I'll be able to sit there and write poems, which is a weird thing to want since it would lead to our homelessness but there you have it. There's a part of me that hopes Max doesn't show up. A big part. He won't show, and I won't have a partner for the truck, and I won't have to go out and face people who are desiring good food and good service when I have zero experience with either. That's the worst. That not only will I be letting my dad down, my mom, myself. I'll be letting strangers down too.

A Dodge Durango pulls up and Max hops out of the driver's side. He runs his hands through his wavy black hair, and as he walks over to where I'm sitting, he gives that toothy Guy Smiley smile, raising his killer dimples. Some people are just blessed with good everything, and Max is definitely one of them. He's wearing a simple blank T-shirt and hideous tan cargo shorts that I would never in a million years be caught dead in, and yet somehow it just works on him.

"What up?" he says.

I stay seated. "What up," I say back.

He stuffs his hands into his shorts pockets. "So how does this work?"

I laugh. It just . . . works. There's a big fridge in the garage with supplies. We'll load the truck with them. We'll drive the truck to Ahwatukee, to the Sunday morning farmers' market. We'll ask someone where to park. We'll put up the whiteboard menu, we'll turn on the truck's power, and we'll take money and sell food.

"Okay, good talk," Max says. This is about my least favorite dude bro saying. Someday I'm going to mace a dude bro when he says that to me. For effect.

"Are you going to tell me anything?" he asks.

I have no idea what to tell, to be honest. Yesterday was our first day ever. I got nothing.

"Blind leading the blind," I say, and because I haven't stood up, he sits down next to me in the dirt.

"That's rough, dude."

I shrug. "Yup." I want to send him away. He seems reasonably harmless for a dude bro, but I want to send him back to whatever dude bro farm he was raised on.

"So . . ." he says, waiting for me to do something, I guess. I truly don't know what to do.

I trace a circle in the dirt with a tiny piece of stick. "You should probably go and find something better to do," I say. "Which would be almost anything. I mean. My mom pretty much cornered you, and it's not like two guys with no experience are going to exactly kill it. Have you ever even been on a food truck?"

He shakes his head.

"It's really hot, first of all. The AC doesn't work so we just have the ceiling vent, and the grill is on. It's nasty hot."

"I like heat."

I give him a dubious look, because we both know I don't just mean hot. I mean Phoenix summer hot. Yesterday it only got up to 104, and by the time I got home I'd lost five pounds of water weight. What's 115 going to feel like?

"No, really," he says. "I thrive on it."

"I've never cooked anything that's on the menu."

"I cook," he says. "And I like challenges."

I laugh and shake my head. "There's challenges and then there's . . . this. Have you ever cleaned out a fryer? Because I did yesterday for the first time, and it sucks ass. I still smell like grease."

"Do you want this to work?" Max asks.

"What? Yeah."

"Then stop trying to talk me out of it. I want this job. I want to make this happen. I like challenges. Okay?"

"You're crazy."

He scratches his neck. "Good pep talk, boss."

I roll my eyes and stand up, and he stands up too. "Jesus. Am I the boss?"

"You have the most experience."

I say, "By a day," and then I walk over to the truck, which is sitting in the driveway in front of our garage. "You know how to drive a truck? Because I don't. I don't even have a driver's license, and I am not getting behind the wheel of this thing. Nonnegotiable."

"Dude," Max says, shaking his head. "Dude."

Once we get everything loaded and secured—the counters have little lips so that the plastic trays holding raw chicken breasts don't fly across the rickety truck every time it takes a left turn—Max slams the passenger-side door closed, plops down in the driver's seat for the first time, and turns on the ignition. The truck buzzes to noisy life and it feels stuffy almost right away; no airflow, no AC. I remember it from yesterday, when Mom cursed the whole way to Gilbert. I sit near the front on a cooler that we've filled with bottled waters and canned sodas that we didn't sell yesterday.

"Dude. There's no speedometer," Max says. It's a truck my dad bought used about the time I was born, when he switched over from construction work to Coq Au Vinny, and at the time it was old. Now it's a relic from another era entirely, with dark wood paneling throughout. You could have a groovy '70s party in this thing for sure.

Max puts the thing in reverse and we slowly creep back out of the driveway. I can't see behind us, and Max is stretching his neck to the side like he's not seeing much behind him either. He stops the truck.

"Dude. The side window is all clouded up and I can't see the side-view mirror."

"How about the one on your side?"

He laughs. "What one on my side?"

I crane my neck. "Oh," I say. There is a mirror holder thingy, but no mirror in it. "Sorry."

"This thing is a death trap," he says, and he steps over to the passenger door and slides it open. The warm breeze comes in and actually it feels better than it did a second ago. "Now I can see," he says, and I think, *Sure, okay. We'll drive with the door open. What could possibly go wrong?*

He backs out of the driveway slowly, puts the car in drive, and we sit there, motionless.

"What the hell?" he asks.

He fiddles with the stick and we jolt into motion. He laughs.

"Actual drive is between neutral and drive," he says.

"Good to know."

"Also you don't have turn signals. I hit the signal and nothing happens. Death trap, dude. Death trap."

At this point, I'm thinking maybe death would be okay. Every time he says something about the truck, it punches me in the gut. Because this was my dad's pride and joy.

At the market, we set up between a smoothie truck and a burrito truck. I stand and carry out the whiteboard menu and put it where it was yesterday. I go around to where my mom turned on the generator yesterday, and I curse myself for not asking more questions before she sent me back out without her. I have no idea how to turn the power on, actually.

"Hey Max," I say, and he comes around to the side of the truck and stands next to me. He's a good-looking guy, no question. All bluster and confidence while I'm whatever the opposite of that is. Apologies and embarrassment. Awkwardness and sorrow. First dead in a zombie apocalypse.

"So how does this thing work?" he asks, and I laugh, because it's such a basic question. I should know. I don't.

He rolls his eyes. "Jordan," he says. "Really? You have no idea how to turn on the power?"

I shake my head.

"What the hell did you do last night?"

I shrug. "Hung out with friends?"

He sighs. "I actually watched some videos. You know. To prepare because I don't have a fucking clue how to run a food truck. Didn't occur to you to do anything, huh?"

It didn't, actually. I guess I'm not a details person. Until I was twelve, I thought that if you put chicken in a fryer, it just sprouted crust, like no need to add coating, just some magical process. Details. When I started jerking off, almost every time I'd get close to cumming I'd realize I hadn't locked the door, and my mom loves opening doors. Details. Thank God she never caught me, or I would have had to gouge my eyes out.

"Jordan," he says when I don't say anything.

I turn my head toward him. "What?"

"Are you on drugs? No offense, but it's fucking hot out here, and the truck needs power, and it's not gonna turn itself on. And you have to tell me what you know, and you're not telling me stuff. Or responding to stuff. I mean. It's cool if you are. Just tell me, dude. We have to communicate."

"I'm not on drugs," I say, gruff. "Jesus."

"Well then maybe tell me what you know? And like how much I'm gonna get paid? And do I need a license to be on a food truck? And how do we do this?"

I suddenly hate Max with a passion.

"I don't know anything," I say. "Okay? Nothing. And I don't know how much you're gonna get paid."

He screws his face up. "You are the single worst boss anyone in the world has ever had. You don't know what you're paying me? You don't know whether we need a food license? What the fuck, dude? Let's just get out of here. Damn."

He walks away from me, and all the blood leaves my face, because the reality hits me. Of course we're not going to make this work. You don't just make a food truck work without knowing stuff like how to turn on a food truck. I'm an idiot. I sit down in the grass on the side of the truck, and I pull out my phone. I look up how to start a generator on a food truck. I see some diagrams. A lot of them are for newer trucks that have buttons this one doesn't have. There was just this handle. I see one with a handle, and it tells me to flip a switch in the back and pull. I stand up, approach it like I'm approaching a horse I want to ride, and follow the directions.

It whirs to life.

I walk around to Max, who is sitting in the driver's seat, staring at me. "You figure it out?"

"I did," I say.

"What else can you figure out?"

I feel like I'm being yelled at by a teacher, and I hate it. But I take a deep breath and figure that I have two choices. One of them is far worse than the other.

"We'll make it work," I say. "C'mon. Help me out."

Thirty minutes later, against all odds, I have our credit card system up and ready and Max has set up the food we have, which is, admittedly, not much. All we have are chicken breasts, some shredded cheddar cheese, and some bins of chopped lettuce, tomato, and onion. And some rolls. Not fancy ones, either. Just like off-brand Wonder Bread. I go out, open up the ordering window, and I yell back, "Here goes nothing."

Max grunts at me. I'm like, *Fuck you, asshole. I'm doing the best I can, okay?*

No one comes. Part of that, I guess, is that it's 8:15 on a Sunday morning, and our menu consists of:

Chicken Parm Hero
Chicken Fingers with Marinara Sauce
Grilled Chicken Breast
Asian Chicken Teriyaki

This is my mom's doing. Back when Dad ran it, there were French and Italian dishes. Hence the Coq Au Vinny—he knew how to cook. Mom is more of a TV dinner gal, so she kind of went with what she felt she couldn't screw up.

It's not an inspiring menu, especially for breakfast.

We stand there awhile silently, and then we lean, me on the ordering window, my poetry journal keeping me company, and him next to the grill. I keep opening and closing the journal, wanting to write something, and at the same time knowing Max will think it's super weird. We watch the crowds bypass us for breakfast burritos and smoothies, and I wonder how I'm going to like a homeless shelter, because yeah. Here I come.

CHAPTER SEVEN

MAX

I love me some heat, but man. I must've lost ten pounds on the
truck today. When I get home, I'm not just drenched; it's like a
whole bunch of dudes sweated all over me. And not in a good way.

I jump in the shower and go full-on cold, which is lukewarm-
ish in the summer but still feels epic. I stand and let the cold
water attempt to wash away the oil from cleaning out the damn
fryer. It coats my arms completely, and the water can't touch it.
And it definitely can't get at the smell. I smell like McDonald's.

Today was a total disaster. Jordan might be seriously adorable,
but he's also clueless, and the least grateful person I've ever met.
I'm trying to help him, and he can't even . . . Dude doesn't even
know what he's paying me. At the end of the day he finally said,
"Ten an hour plus tips." I was like, fine. I'm not trying to break
the bank, and that's more than what I'd make doing fast food or
at State Farm, but it's all pretty messed up.

I throw on my blue swim trunks and head out to the pool,
the remnants of some sour feeling sticking to my ribs, even after
the shower. I slide open the patio door and the broiling summer
air punches me in the face.

Mom, who like me isn't bothered by the heat, is gardening in
the backyard, putting in some summer flowers on the little dirt
area where we used to have a brown statue of a grinning grizzly

bear. She's down on her knees with a yellow bandanna over her head. She turns her head when I slide open the patio door.

"How was it, mijo?" she asks.

I launch myself into the pool, and the water is just perfect. By August, it'll be like a hot tub out here. I come up, spit out some water, and rub my eyes.

"Not good, Ma."

"How so?"

I focus on the copper sun god that hangs on the side of the house and jump up and down to get my blood flowing. "The truck in general, Mom. It's not good."

She giggles a little. "Not a good truck? Flat tire?"

I laugh back. "Nah. Like the boss is my age, has no experience, and is irresponsible. Didn't know how to drive the truck. Wasn't sure how to turn it on. Definitely doesn't know how to cook. Didn't think to study up before his first day out without his mom."

"Ay," she says, and she puts down her gardening shears, kicks off her flip-flops, and sits at the edge of the pool, dangling her feet in. I pounce over and try to grab hold of the side right next to her. Too hot, so I splash some water to cool it down and some of it hits her. She grins and splashes me back.

"I think I gotta reconsider. No eggs, Ma. He has a breakfast truck with only fried and grilled chicken. I'm afraid I'm gonna be out of a job soon if I stay."

"Hmm," she says. "Sounds to me like you're bailing."

"This is different. This is just — bad, Ma."

She lifts herself up with just her triceps and slips into the water even though she's wearing gym shorts and a T-shirt. She pulls off her bandanna, throws it on the pool's edge, and submerges, coming up with a contented gasp. "You know that's what your dad always said. Always an excuse. 'This place was lame. This other place was too many jerks. They didn't get his genius,' quote unquote."

"Ma," I say.

She treads water with her legs and puts her hands up as if to say, "Sorry, sorry." She knows I don't like when she compares me to Dad, or trash-talks him. "You smell like french fries," she says.

"I know, right?"

"I remember working fast food. My first job." She grabs the side of the pool and pushes off with her legs, drifting backward as far as the kick will carry her.

Mom is a good one. She grew up in the Polanco neighborhood of Mexico City, which is pretty fancy. She came to Arizona State University for college, and she got her degrees there. Met my dad, which was good because it led to me being conceived, but in the end he was definitely not the right guy for her. Dad is cool as fuck, but comedians—especially nonheadliners—don't exactly have the most stable livelihoods. She's an actuary for State Farm, which means she's a whiz with numbers and figures out how many years people are expected to live, and how much the company is likely to pay out to them over a lifetime, so that, as she says, the powers that be can screw good people over.

She kicks her feet back and forth in the water. "You love to cook. Maybe help him fix it?"

"I've known him a day, Mom."

"I have faith in you. And you can always come work at State Farm."

I float, and I don't respond. And soon, I can feel Mom floating next to me. And we just hang like that for a bit. I'll figure this out somehow; I don't need her to do it for me.

He sits on my calves. I'm just. What? Dude, what are you doing?

I feel her hand on my shoulder and see that she's now standing in the water. "You okay, mijo?"

My feet find the bottom of the pool. "Yeah."

She raises one eyebrow. Her hair is starting to frizz. "When you're done out here, come inside. I'm worried about you, mijo. Something's not right."

I go back to floating without answering her. Sometimes she can be a bit nosey, my mom. A little controlling. I hear her exit the water, and then the patio door slides shut and I look up at the sky. No clouds. Just royal blue as far as the eye can see. I wish I felt as clear as the sky.

The air-conditioning feels great when I go back inside. My mom's reclined on the gray fabric couch, a glass of water in her hand, a towel under her. The TV is on that high definition station that's just a fireplace. Ever since she got our new 4K television, she's all up on this fireplace thing, even though you could currently cook a chicken on our deck if you let it sit long enough.

"Oh good, we can warm up," I say.

She laughs. "Damn right."

"Should I throw another log in?"

She cackles and pantomimes throwing a log at our TV. "Boom!" she says, exploding her hands.

She taps the end of the couch with her feet and I put my towel down and sit there, facing the TV. I can feel her eyes on my profile.

"All weekend. You're off your game, mijo."

I make a big show of leaning my head back like I'm exasperated. "You're hallucinating."

"Yeah, right," she says. "I've known you a little while."

I turn toward her and give her my best, most dazzling smile. "See?" I say. "All good."

She takes a sip from her water glass and raises her eyebrows at me. "That smile works with everyone else but me. C'mon. What's going on?"

"Mom. Stop."

"I know you like to say nothing, but something's up. I know it. I feel it in here." She points to her heart.

"I'm fine. It's nothing. It's stupid stuff." I flash her another smile.

She pulls an orange throw pillow onto her lap. "You know I'm not going to stop, so why not just get it over with and tell me? So I can stop worrying and go back to my fireplace."

I exhale. It's been a while since our last heart-to-heart. It was about a month after I told her I was gay, two years back. She was cool about it. Told me never to feel ashamed of who I am, and I was like, *Yeah. I know.* When she told Uncle Guillermo, our only relative in the States, he did the typical machismo thing for like a minute, until my mom reminded him that I play baseball and am bigger and stronger than him, and anyway to just cut that shit out. Which he did. She wanted to talk about sex and if I was dating, but I shut that down because, come on. She finally relented and said, "Just be careful, mijo. There's lots of users and abusers out there." And I nodded but I admit I was also like, *Yeah. Not that worried.* Nobody messes with me much. I don't take a lot of shit because of my size, probably.

I take a deep breath. If ever there was a mom a person could talk to about whatever the fuck that was Friday night, it would be Rosa Gutierrez. She's definitely cool. But something tells me not to.

"Just . . . boy stuff."

"Like, 'I lost my football' boy stuff, or 'I like a boy' boy stuff?"

"The latter," I say, omitting that I don't actually like a boy. If only.

"Tell me, mijo."

"Nah," I say, and I sit up. "Thanks, Mom. But I'm okay."

She raises one eyebrow at me. "You get this from your dad. He thinks talking is for girls too."

"I can . . . talk," I say.

She gives me that toothy mom smile. "You can, but you don't," she says.

And I can't argue with her there. And anyway, I feel a bit better after our talk, even if I only said a little.

_____

After dinner, I call my dad.

"Broseph!" he yells, picking up the phone. I don't know why he thinks calling his son Broseph is funny, but that's my dad for you. Oh well.

"Yo, what up," I say.

"Chillaxin'. How's school?"

"Over for the year."

"Right on," he says.

Dad's name is Ryan Morrison. He likes beer, fast cars, and TV shows where people get hit in the balls. Mentally he's about twelve. He's basically everything my mom isn't.

When I don't say anything else, he says, "You gotta see this new club. Destroying. They fuckin' love me. Those assholes at the Barn can eat my ass."

My dad, the poet. "Yeah?" I ask.

"Got this new bit about throwing up in your mouth."

"Sounds epic," I say. "Sounds like you're really making the world a better place."

He laughs. I laugh. "How'd you get to be such a smart-ass?"

"Gee, Dad, no idea."

He laughs some more.

When I get off the phone, I smile. I think about my mom and my dad, and wonder what in the world made them think they should be together. Did he change, or did she? Because once upon a time, they must have liked talking to each other. But now, I can hardly imagine that conversation. Not even a little bit.

CHAPTER EIGHT

JORDAN

Mom is in one of her good moods when I get home from the second day of just me and Max on the food truck on Monday afternoon.

"Taste test," she shouts from the couch in the TV room, and even though I'm covered in sweat and exhausted, I have to smile, because my mom's back. "I was gonna do it alone, but now that you're here . . ."

She's lined up five different rows of two jelly beans on the leather ottoman in front of the couch where we normally put our feet. I would probably not eat jelly beans off the ottoman Dorcas regularly sits her naked butthole on, but Mom is carefree that way and who am I to stop her fun? I drop my wallet and keys on the counter and join her.

She sits up straight and closes her eyes. "Put them in whatever order you want. I want to see if I can figure out the flavors without looking."

I shuffle them around a bit and hand her a light purple one. She looks like a little kid, holding her hand out for a treat. It's kind of adorable. She pops it in her mouth and her cheeks pucker as she makes a big show of trying to guess the flavor.

"Hmm," she says. "Chewing, chewing . . ."

"What do you think?"

"Nope. Withholding my guesses until I've had them all."

"You're a jelly bean connoisseur," I say.

She smiles, her eyes still squeezed shut, and then she shouts "Next!" in a funny falsetto, like she's the queen of England or something.

As I hand her the second, I don't notice Dorcas creeping around us. She jumps up on the ottoman, scattering the jelly beans, and hoovers down as many of them as she can before I can stop her.

Mom's eyes flash open. "Traitor!" she yells.

Dorcas leaps backward into the television. It begins to wobble and I run over and try to catch it before it tips over onto the floor. I get a sweaty hand on the edge of it, and it steadies a bit, but it continues to teeter and my second hand whiffs trying to get a hold of it. Luckily, Mom has jumped up from the couch and is able to get a firm grab on the other side before it thwacks the floor and shatters into a zillion pieces.

I look over at Mom holding the television up while I am standing there trying to balance the side of the TV like a stereotypical French waiter, and as Dorcas skulks away, we laugh and laugh, and I take back just about every negative thing I've been thinking about her all day as I was toiling away on the truck.

She sets the TV back up and gets a drinkable strawberry yogurt to wash down her jelly beans, and despite being disgustingly sweaty I flop down on the opposite end of the couch and start to tell her everything about the truck. Dorcas curls up by my mom's feet, still eating the last of the jelly beans she stole.

"So Max is . . ."

"Cute?" she says, raising an eyebrow.

"I was gonna say annoying," I say, grinning, and she raises her eyebrows a few times at me.

"Sure you were," she says, teasing.

"And what have you been doing today?" I ask, changing the subject.

She rolls her eyes. "Oh, you know. I get these ideas but then I don't, like, I don't know. My follow-through is subpar."

I smile at her. She smiles back, and then, it's so weird and so fast. The smile turns to a grimace, and it's like her face breaks and suddenly there are tears.

"Mom," I say, leaning forward.

"Oh God," she says. "Here we go again. It's all to shit."

I jump up and sit down next to her head. "Mom." I stroke her hair, which feels a little oily and unwashed.

"I almost went to Casino Arizona today," she says, and she sits up and puts her head on my shoulder and leans it into my neck.

"Oh." After Dad died, Mom went through a gambling stage. It wasn't a ton of money, but I guess it was enough to scare her, because she started going to meetings about it. She hasn't gambled since, and every year I go to her Gamblers Anonymous birthday, where people I have never met before hug me tight and tell me how great a support I am to Lydia E. I have never told Pam or Kayla. I definitely think they would not get it.

"I didn't, but. I definitely had the urge."

"Well you didn't, so that's something. Did you, like, call your sponsor?"

She nods her head gently into my neck and I reach up and stroke her hair. "Good," I say. "That's good."

"It's just the pressure," she says, and part of me thinks, *Yeah, I totally get that.* Another part is like, *What pressure? You sat on the couch all day.*

"Sure," I say. "Well you should be proud. Willpower and all."

"I guess."

"You're too hard on yourself. That's like a victory," I say, channeling the Gamblers Anonymous meetings I've been to. "You didn't gamble today. That's awesome."

She just keeps sniffling into my shoulder, and I keep on stroking her hair, and there's this part of me that wants to not be here, doing this. Being her strength or whatever.

I hate that part of me.

"I need more jelly beans," she says, and I laugh.

"Well c'mon then," I say, and I stand up.

"Where are we going?"

"Sweeties," I say, meaning the huge candy warehouse in Mesa. "Jelly beans for dinner," I say.

Her eyes light up. I don't think anything will ever make me quite as happy as when my mom's eyes light up.

"Yay," she says.

"And Pez for dessert."

"Ooh. Dispensers? Can we get Hello Kitty dispensers?"

I think of my dad, and how he probably did this in a more normal way. Cheer her up. But at least she's smiling and not crying. I do what I have to. After all, it's just me and Mom. We're all we've got. Mom had a brother who died as a teenager, and my grandparents on her side, Pops and Gammie, live in Ogden, Utah, and I get a card from them maybe every other birthday. My dad's parents died when I was a baby.

"Well obviously we have to," I say.

Sweeties with my mom is always like taking a kid to a candy store, because it is, in fact, a huge-ass candy store, and she is most definitely a kid when she gets in there. We walk quickly past the sugarless candies — I mean, come on — and she squeals with delight when we see the wall of Pez dispensers, and she goes off on how Princess Leia looks nothing like Princess Leia, and then she grabs two Hello Kitty dispensers as well as four Pez refill packages — one all sour Pez. Then she gives me a mini-dissertation on Hello Kitty and how the thing that is especially awesome about Hello Kitty is that everyone has a fake memory of her as being part of their childhood, but she really wasn't.

"Tell me one thing you know about Hello Kitty. Was she from a cartoon? No. A movie? No. She acts like she's Woody Woodpecker or Ricochet Rabbit, but really she's been superimposed upon all of our collective consciousness as if she was a thing. But she wasn't. She's a brand, not something to reminisce about."

We are pushing our little cart down the aisle where the Whoppers and various other malted chocolates live, and though I barely know Woody and have never heard of said rabbit, I nod. "You're actually right," I say, and she curtsies before throwing a red pack of something called Maltesers into our cart.

"Thank you very much. And of course none of that changes

the fact that we have to buy two Hello Kitty dispensers. Because Hello Kitty."

After, she sprints to the car, which is funny because she's not so much a sprinting type of mom anymore. When she gets to the car, she says, "If you get here in six seconds, you get an amazing, special treat."

I make a dramatic showing of running, and she smiles wide, and I do too.

In the car, she tells me to close my eyes, and I do. I enjoy the sensation of her making a few turns and not knowing where we're going, and I resist the urge to peek. When the car stops, I open my eyes. We're at Zia Record Exchange, which is about my favorite place in the world, and as much fun as it is to go there with Pam and Kayla, it's never better than when I go with my mom.

"Yay!" I say, and she says yay too.

We go inside and feed our vinyl addictions.

"Oh my God," she says as she sifts through the "A" partition of the rock 'n' roll section. She pulls out a rather dull cover with three '80s-looking guys posing in the bottom right corner. It reads *Alphaville* in a funny font on top, and underneath, in all lowercase, it reads *big in japan*.

She holds the record close to her chest, like she's hugging it. Her hazel eyes are so big and filled with joy.

"I heard this for the first time when Pops and Gammie sent me on this bike trip to France. I was seventeen. Oh my God. We have to buy this. We have to."

"Clearly," I say.

She nearly jumps up and down. "You're gonna love it. Love it. Oh my God." And then she's back to shuffling through the "B" section, and my heart feels like it could burst because seeing Mom like Mom again is everything.

We eat our jelly-bean dinner in my room. She grabs a pink boa from my bedpost and wraps it around her shoulders, and she sits down on the red beanbag chair in the corner, picking through the jelly beans carefully and throwing the licorice ones onto the shag carpet dismissively. Even Dorcas won't eat those.

The Alphaville album is all synthesizers and the singing is that Euro-emo style that would so not fly today. The "Big in Japan" song itself is just overflowing with cultural appropriation that would get the guys flogged in 2019 but apparently was all the rage thirty years ago. She listens, blissfully, with her hands behind her head.

"Oh my God," she says. "This so brings me back to biking these rural French roads, and the greasy guys at all the hostels. We hosteled for like thirty straight nights all through Brittany — *Breh-tahn-yuh*, they pronounced it, and the Euro guys were *so cheesy*. Those were the days."

I smile and recline too, trying to imagine my mom my age. I've seen pictures, but Mom is Mom, you know? She's not a teen-ager and she never was, no matter how much she tries to act like she still is.

Then, as the synth-pop assault continues on my phonograph, she sits up. "So what do you imagine?" she asks.

"Huh?"

"Like, imagine. For yourself. As an adult. Where do you live, what do you do, who are you with?"

I roll onto my side and hold up the side of my head with my

hand. We're having one of our sleepovers again. We haven't in a long while. I kind of love it. Where we just talk and talk and forget about the time. I miss these.

"I don't know," I say.

"Bullshit," she says, smiling. "You know. Tell me. Tell me!"

"Well he's a redhead," I say quickly, and she giggles.

"Knew it."

"Yeah, it changes. Like now, we live in maybe the mountains. Near a city because people are cooler in cities, but we're in a cabin in the mountains, and I write poems and I'm famous somehow, I don't know. Maybe I write books too. And he's in finance or something like that where he's on the computer all day making money, and we design the place so it looks, I don't know, kind of like this. Like a speakeasy, maybe, and we get our living room featured in some national magazine, and we throw these amazing parties."

"Oh Jordan," she says, and her smile is just blissful. "Do all that. Really. Do it. Don't let people tell you that you have to be anything other than what you are. You're really such an amazing person, you don't even know."

I choke up and have to look away, because am I? But Mom thinks I am, so that's cool.

CHAPTER NINE

MAX

You know that feeling you get when you have no idea what you're doing, like in calc, and then you see your teacher pause while trying to solve an equation on the blackboard, and you realize very quickly that she doesn't have a clue either?

This is how it feels when I arrive at Jordan's place at 5:00 a.m. on Thursday. It's allegedly our fifth day out. In our first four days, I'm guessing we have made two hundred dollars. Well, not made. Not including expenses. Just taken in. I'm the cook; I know how many orders we get. Whatever we've banked, it ain't great. And it's not including the money he is supposed to pay me, because to this point, I haven't been paid. On the way home yesterday, he said, "I know you're owed money. So far we haven't made as much as you're owed. I don't know what to do about that."

I didn't reply, and half of me thought, *I'm getting fleeced; get me the fuck out of here.* All this damn sweating, all this time spent in hell, and nothing to show for it. Cut your losses. And the other part, probably the part of me that Mom raised, has no quit in him. So I'm back here, a day later, hoping we finally take in some money so I can get mine.

Jordan starts loading the truck from the refrigerator and freezer in the garage, and I guess I'm supposed to just go ahead and help, as usual. But instead I just sit on the dirt of the front yard and watch. Watching Jordan move is just—he's graceful. The way those long, thin limbs break through the air, so effortless. What I wouldn't give to move like that, to not be so bulky.

For once, I don't get up and go, take over. I sit and watch. It's all I can do. This is just . . . Mom says insanity is doing the same thing over and over and expecting different results. If that's the definition, then we are being insane.

After a few minutes, he notices me. Jordan is not the most aware person of all time.

"What?" he asks, and he comes and stands in front of me, his hands on his skinny hips, his red T-shirt hanging off him like his upper body is a coat hanger. His lean chest pulls the shirt in.

"Naw, man," I say. "Naw."

He frowns. "So you're quitting? Is that what's happening here? Fine. I mean. Great."

"Naw," I say again, shaking my head. "Naw."

He kicks the dirt. "What the fuck does 'Naw' mean in this case? Don't just 'Naw' me."

I smile despite myself. It's not normal to be pissed, and at the exact same time think there's something freakin' adorable about this dude getting all angry. I don't know why. It just is. "You got any incense?" I ask.

"What? No. Why would I have incense?"

I hoist myself up. "Get me like a match, then. We're doing a food truck exorcism. We gotta get rid of whatever fucked-up demon is dooming this thing."

He stares at me. I smile a bit. He doesn't. He takes a deep breath. I watch him. He goes inside.

I sit there for a while, unsure if he'll ever come out. It's not like we have this killer connection, me and Cute Emo Dude. We've been on a food truck alone together for four days and our conversations have been entirely limited to food-related stuff and the fact that it is hot. That is about it. It's sucked so far, a lot. When he gets bored, he opens a journal and writes whatever in it. When I get bored, I crush candy or play Madden on my phone.

Then, after about two minutes, Jordan comes back out with the stump of a lit red candle in his right hand. He walks over to the truck and I follow him.

"Oh Gods of the food truck," he says. "Get the fuck out."

I crack up, and he does too. I say, "Get thee behind me, Food Truck Satan."

He waves the candle around and then runs up and down the aisle. "You have no business here," he says. "Git."

"Git," I repeat.

He pulls up a crate and sits on it. Then, as if he has a new idea, he pulls up a second crate, right next to the first one, and he taps it for me to sit down there. I do.

He says, "This food truck has impacted me in the following ways . . ."

I laugh at the unexpected shift. This guy is so . . . something, and I'm not used to it. "This is now a food truck intervention?" I ask.

He nods. "You have made me lose five pounds in pure water weight," he says. "These are pounds I cannot afford to lose."

I have to really push my brain to come up with something good. "Because of you, I have begun to think I might not be the great chef I thought I was," I say.

Him: "I have had to deal with the public, and the public sucks."

Me: "I have had to spend time with a guy who hates me."

Him: "I have had to spend time with a guy who thinks I'm a big loser."

We look at each other. He cracks a smile, so I do too.

Him: "Food truck, are you willing to accept the help we're offering you today?"

We sit for a while, as if waiting for the freakin' truck to say something.

"Did you hear that?" he asks. "I think he said yes."

Then I stand. "I think so too. And not just because I need this to get better, because you can't pay me the money I'm owed if we don't. Though that is a factor."

"Sorry," he says. "Really."

I shrug as if it doesn't matter, but it does. "Okay," I say. "Okay. You ready?"

"Ready for what?"

"You trust me?"

"Not sure. What's the plan?"

"You gotta trust me, dude," I say, and Jordan looks me up and down, up and down. Deep, dramatic breath.

"Fine. I trust you."

I blow out the candle and start carrying back the stuff Jordan took from the fridge, and he helps me. When we're done, I get in the driver's seat and he sits on his crate in the middle again, and with the door open, I drive us the mile north to my house.

CHAPTER TEN
JORDAN

Max opens his front door and the first thing I notice as we walk in is a blue spandex–clad ass, staring at me.

"Company," Max says, and the blue spandex–clad ass doesn't move.

"Well company is going to have to put up with my butt as a welcome because I'm in Downward-Facing Dog for another five breaths," the voice says, and I surmise that this is Max's mom. She has a slight Mexican accent, which Max doesn't have.

I want to say that Downward-Facing Dog should be called Upward-Facing Ass, but Max and his mom probably wouldn't find that half as funny as Kayla and Pam would.

As we walk in, the second thing I notice is that Max basically lives in my house, only reversed. Their sunken living room is to the right when we walk in instead of the left, there's a dining room straight ahead, and while our open family room and kitchen combination is straight ahead and to the right, theirs is to the left. The biggest difference is that where we have a dining table, his mom has a little yoga area, with one mat she is currently hovering over and several comfy-looking pillows next to her, two rolled-up mats against the wall. And whereas our kitchen is stuffed to the hilt with boxed treats—on every counter, stacked on the refrigerator—their counters are neat and clean.

"You should be at work, Maximo," his mom calls from the other room as Max opens the fridge. It is stacked. Vegetables, fruit. Dairy. I almost take a picture to send to my mom, so she can see what a real refrigerator looks like.

"That's my mom," he says to me, and then he yells out, "Raiding the fridge for the truck."

"The hell you are," his mom yells, and I hear her footsteps approaching. "Oh . . . hi."

Max's mom is wearing a red Diamondbacks T-shirt. She's short—like half Max's height—and her black hair hangs long down her neck, a bit frizzy. Sweat has beaded on her forehead and she wears a cream-colored clip on top of her head to keep the hair out of her eyes. She smiles, and I see where Guy Smiley got it from. Same exact smile, which almost cracks me up because on her, it looks gigantic.

"Is this your coworker?" she asks, and she sticks her hand out at me.

"Hi," I say, and I shake her hand. "Jordan."

"Ms. Gutierrez," she says. "Now what's this mistaken idea you have about you two raiding my refrigerator for food truck ingredients?"

Max points into the fridge. "We have no money and just about nothing to cook."

She winces. "No money and nothing to cook?" She looks me over like she's sizing me up and I cross my arms in front of my chest. Then she walks over to the couch, which faces the fireplace we never use in our house. Instead of a fireplace, they have an entertainment center, with a huge TV hanging in the middle of the wall. Ours is against the far wall instead. They have a love seat in that spot.

"Sit," she says. "Gotta get ready for work but first let's have a chat."

I tentatively sit on the love seat, and Max sits next to his mom. I'm not so sure I'm ready to be reprimanded by my coworker's mom.

"So talk to me," she says. "Sounds like your truck is not going so good."

I look down at my skinny knees. "No, ma'am. It was my dad's. He died a few years ago. My mom got the idea to take it out finally and we did on Saturday for the first time. My mom freaked, she hired Max to take her place, and we're just . . . doing our best, I guess. I honestly have no idea what I'm doing."

She studies me for a bit. Finally, she says, "Ah. And is this legal? You guys being out on a food truck together with no experience?"

I say, "Um. Well, the truck is legal."

"Do you need a food handler's permit?"

I study the Native American rug under my feet. It's turquoise and tan.

"Do you?" she asks again.

I shrug.

"Did your mother have one?"

I shrug again.

Ms. Gutierrez frowns. It's a powerful frown too. Like it makes me want to get up, walk out of this house, and never turn around again.

"Jesus," she says. "This is illegal, Maximo. I won't let you do this. I can't."

"Mom," he says. "Stop."

"Stop what? I know I told you to stick with it, but from what I hear, you're not legally working on that truck. You could get fined or arrested. This isn't right."

"Mom!" Max stands and walks into the yoga area, and he motions for her to come. "Please."

She follows him, looking back at me like I'm a piece of dirt, which is basically what I feel like. I sit there wondering what the hell I'm going to do when she forbids Max from working with me. I can't blame her; it's what I'd do if I were a mom. But the truth is I don't have any Plan B at all. This icy feeling spreads down my arms and legs. Doomed. Not good.

They finally come back. Ms. Gutierrez's face has changed a bit. She looks like she just saw a sad movie.

They both sit down and face me again. I lower my eyes to the rug again and study the patterned design. Lots of triangles inside triangles.

"Okay," Ms. Gutierrez says. "First off, the truck is off duty today. And I'm not fixing this; you are. But I will help. And if you want me to take the day off work to help, you just tell me."

I blush. I hate this feeling. Like I'm a waste case. Which I'm so not. It just seems that way from the data, and I get that. I'm the boss on a rogue, illegal food truck, and that's all she knows about me. I wonder what changed her mind. I'm afraid to know what Max said about me and my mom to make this change happen.

"Okay?" she says again, waiting for me. I look up, and her

eyes are searching for mine. I hold her look as long as I can. It's a kind look, I must say. Strong but kind.

"Yes," I say. "Thank you."

"First up, you need to get online and figure out how to make this legal. You must need some sort of license. And you're sure you have a permit for the truck?"

"Yes," I say. "I've seen that. I know my mom got it in the mail. Renewed it. The rest of it, I don't know."

"Well let's get going," she says, "Second up —"

"I got it, Mom," Max says. "I can do this. We can."

She looks over at him. "You sure?"

"I'm sure. We're gonna make this food truck our bitch."

She laughs. "Okay," she says. "And you call me before you do something that gets you thrown in the slammer, hear?"

Max says, "I'm pretty sure they aren't throwing food truck people in the slammer."

"Don't be too sure. Just be smart, okay?"

"Okay, Mom," he says.

"And you," she says, looking over at me. "I'm sorry for what's going on in your house. That sounds not too good. Are you okay?"

"Sure," I say, thinking, *I have no idea.*

She regards me for an uncomfortable five or so seconds. "Okay," she says. "Okay. Now I'm off to work. Good luck, you two."

CHAPTER ELEVEN

MAX

The much-needed food truck intervention that Jordan started hits a snag when Mom starts asking questions, and suddenly, instead of getting ready to go out, we're studying an online manual about food safety.

Who knew all these rules? I feel bad for all the people I served the last few days, because while I always wash my hands, and I know that raw chicken is probably contaminated with salmonella, I had basically no idea about a lot of other stuff.

Like, did you know that bacteria grows on many foods when they are kept between 41 and 135 degrees? I did not, actually.

Did you know that you're supposed to discard gloves before touching ready-to-eat food? I did not.

Did you know that Coq Au Vinny almost definitely gave somebody the shits on its first few days out and about, because I, the cook, was unaware of at least ten rules? I know that now.

Oops.

"How long until a bunch of former customers come after us with pitchforks?" I say.

Jordan laughs. "Pitchforks that should probably be sterilized, but we haven't been sterilizing," he says. I glance over and he has this goofy, adorable smile on his face. In the light of my living room, his eyes have a little bit of emerald in them. And yeah, he has acne, but in this light, I can see underneath the slight redness around his nose and on his cheeks. Kid has beautiful skin under there, waiting to come out. I can tell. I have to look away, because he's the kind of adorable that doesn't know it's adorable. That's the best kind.

"Word, dude. Word."

"Well, going forward we will kill no people," he says, and I laugh.

I say, "It's funny because my mom would shit if she knew this shit."

"It's funny because we are dangerously stupid."

"Sorry, people we may have harmed," I say.

"Yup," says Jordan. "Sorry."

While I read up on things I should have known five days ago, I think about what my mom said when I told her about Jordan's mom and the meltdown, and how he and his mom are gonna be out on the street if this doesn't work.

"Dios mío," she says, and I have to agree. *Dios mío.*

It turns out we aren't completely scofflaws; we have thirty days from when we start working in the food service industry to get a card. Jordan is in violation, though, because someone on the truck needs to be able to show they know this information, and he hasn't known it. Well, now we do. And we both pass the online test, print out cards, and suddenly we are permitted.

"So let me ask you," I say. "What would you want to buy on a food truck if you were out today?"

Jordan reclines on my couch. "Cold stuff."

I nod. "But like what?"

"Could we do like a frozen lemonade?"

"Hmm," I say. "But is there lots of money in that?" I pull up YouTube on my laptop and we start watching videos. I search food trucks, and we watch whatever clips we find, and soon we are down the YouTube rabbit hole. I show him the video the Amigos love of the dog chasing the bear, and he shows me this video about all the things we don't say when we text. It's funny because it's true, and also it's the kind of humor that makes you think. Before Jordan, I didn't know I liked that kind of humor, but I guess I do. Then he shows me this Randy Rainbow guy. It's the gayest thing I've ever seen and it's kinda hilarious in a very non-Amigos way.

I guess the truth is I assumed Jordan was gay, but since he never seemed to notice my existence, he was off my radar. I figured he probably had some adorable, lanky boyfriend somewhere and would have no time for an unrefined guy who plays Madden with his buds on Friday nights. And then, when we started to get to know each other last week, we had a task, and I was focused on the whole terrible boss angle. But now, for the first time, we're kinda getting along, and it's okay. I rack my brain for some sort of video I can show him that will nonchalantly show him that I'm gay too, because I don't know if he knows. Or cares.

I settle on this clip of rugby players in Australia, where guys keep getting pantsed and don't stop running down the field.

"Whoa," he says.

"I know, right?"

"Do you play sports?"

"Baseball," I say.

"Does a lot of naked stuff happen on the baseball field?"

I laugh. "Baseball diamond," I say.

"That sounds kinda gay."

"I guess."

"So are you?"

"Yep."

"Oh. Okay. Didn't know that."

I have to look away, because something about the cutest of skinny white boys acknowledging my gayness for the first time is . . . a lot.

I stare at the floor, swallow, and say, "Well, now you do."

And we sit there and kinda soak that in. That we are two gay dudes who before this didn't know that about each other or like each other much, and suddenly Jordan isn't totally the worst in my book, even if he's nothing like me and my buddies. And I wonder if I'm okay to him.

I hope so.

CHAPTER TWELVE
JORDAN

Dorcas's tongue has range and accuracy.

She's the kind of dog who makes Q-tips totally unnecessary. If I just lie there in my waterbed and let her put her head on my chest, once in a while she'll lift up her face, zone in on her target, and zap my ear with her sandpaper tongue. I'd say she's gotten a good two inches up into my ear canal, which I'm sure is totally sanitary given the fact that her favorite hobby is sniffing other dog's buttholes, but oh well.

We are luxuriating and undulating in my (water)bed on a Friday afternoon. We're here because Max and I took another day off from the truck and made an awesome, amazing, epic plan, starting tomorrow, to achieve food truck world domination. I am not 100 percent sure it will work—not even 30 percent, really—but we definitely have a better shot than we did a couple days ago, when we were plan-free.

Dorcas laps my nose with her seemingly endless tongue. It's amazing that she can rest her chin on my stomach and still reach my face.

I'm thinking about Max. Who is, apparently, gay. This is new information. I had him stereotyped as a basic dude bro. He is a dude bro, I think, but not a basic one. Nope. He showed me a very nonbasic dude bro video of football players losing their shorts, and I was like, *Oh. Okay. Wow.*

The tragic thing about this is that it was easier when I had nothing in common with him. Now that we did a truck exorcism together and I figured out he's actually kinda cool, and now that I know he's also gay, I have to contend with the mean practical joke of the universe. Which is to say: Now I have if not a gay friend at least a gay acquaintance. There are LGBTQ kids at school, but I am not exactly the most social person. So now I have a gay . . . something, and he is so far out of my league that we may as well live on different planets.

Yep. I'm pretty sure that's worse. I focus on the Andy Gibb poster on my wall and ask: *Andy, is this worse?*

Yes, he says. *Clearly worse, darling.*

Dorcas turns her snout until she is facing me head-on, and she gets a little too up into my nostrils. I push her snout away, prop my head up on a satin pillow, and text Pam and Kayla.

Me: Whatcha up to

Kayla: Pretty Little Liars

Me: There are other shows out there. U should try watching one sometime

Pam: Nope

Me: Are u together?

Kayla: Yup

Me: Without me. Nice

Pam: Figured you were working?

Me: Not today long story. Dorcas wants to see you. Come over?

Kayla: Only if Lydia is there

Me: Nah no idea where shes been all day

Kayla: Fine well come anyway

Me: Yay

Thank God for Pam and Kayla. My life was so boring before them. We became friends spring semester of freshman year, when we were in the musical *Birds of Paradise* together. I played Homer, the talented, nerdy actor hopelessly in love with Julia, played by Kayla. Pam played Hope, who was in love with Homer. The love triangle was awkward as fuck for a while. I thought they were mean girls who hated me. Then they came over one day, ostensibly to practice lines, and they did a gay intervention.

"You're gay, you know," Kayla said. She was standing in our living room, her arms crossed, Pam right at her side.

I don't know what they expected. Tears? Me to be like, *Oh my God! You're right! How did I not realize this?*

"Duh," I said.

Pam and Kayla locked eyes.

"Oh," Pam said. "So you know that already."

I repeated, "Duh."

"We thought you were a hopeless closet case. We were, like, going to help you come out."

"I'm hopeless. Just not a closet case."

This made them laugh, and we all loosened up, and suddenly the play got way better. Or I should say, the play was still awful because I am not a great singer, and Pam is also not a great singer, but we had a total blast and I was let into the club. We've been inseparable ever since. Kayla is still all about theater. Pam and I have never done another show. Pam moved on to volleyball and I moved on to lying in my waterbed with Dorcas, doing nothing.

I jump off the bed and Dorcas leaps off too, wagging her tail at me. Poor thing. Summers suck for Dorcas. Any time after about nine in the morning, the sidewalk is too hot for her. So is the tile next to the pool. She can go out the doggie door to do her business on the shaded side of the house, but that's about all the fun she has. I normally take her for a morning walk, but now that I'm working starting at five, she's not getting that either. I know my mom isn't picking up the slack, so she's getting basically no exercise. Poor girl.

I get an idea I love.

I pat the side of my leg, which means follow me. Dorcas walks at my side to my mom's bedroom, which is at DEFCON 3. Her treadmill-hamper is covered with clothing from the past two weeks, I'm guessing, and there are empty soda cans and four half-full glasses with various rotting liquids on her night table. I roll my eyes. I don't feel like cleaning up right now, but I go to her treadmill and carry her dirty clothes to the actual hamper in the corner. Dorcas follows me every step, which is part of why I need to teach her how to exercise inside. Mom used to at least hang with her all day, but I think Mom's forgotten about Dorcas, pretty much.

We got Dorcas a year after my dad died. Mom was in this short-lived religious phase — hence the biblical name.

We went to the pet shop at Arizona Mills. It was called Puppies

'N Love, which is a little too cute a name, and the place smelled like sweet aerosol spray, which was clearly just covering up the odor of dog crap. I saw this bichon frise. She was so sweet, with black eyes like tiny marbles and the softest white fur. Even though Mom wanted a bigger dog, she allowed me to sit in the tiny, glass-enclosed visiting room with the dog.

Oh my God, did I love that bichon. She just sat on my lap like she belonged there, and I stroked the top of her bed and she stuck her tongue out in that contented way that says, *Keep doing that forever, please.*

I was set. I had already named her Snowball. But Mom had questions.

"So are you a chain?" she asked the flummoxed, barely adult salesgirl who was working with us.

"We have another store up at Paradise Valley," she said.

My mom raised an eyebrow. "Oh! At the mall there? That's so expensive!"

"We're like the discount center I guess," the girl said.

"So, what?" my mom said, crossing her arms over her chest. "Are the dogs cheaper here?"

The girl said, "We sort of get the ones that don't sell right away."

My mom's eyes opened real wide. "You mean these are OUTLET DOGS?"

The girl didn't know what to do with my mom. Few people ever do. She just shrugged, and my mom said to me, "Say good-bye to the dog."

"No!" I said.

But she insisted, and she grabbed my elbow and hauled me out of there, and there I was, sobbing in a mall, while my mom told me there are more fish in the sea, or dogs in the yard, or whatever.

"You don't buy the first dog you see. You comparison shop," she said.

She didn't understand me. She didn't get it. That of course if it were up to me, I'd get the first dog I fell in love with. Because I loved it. And what more is there than that? How do you comparison shop love?

And then she sweetened up, and she promised me an even better dog, as well as an ice-cream sandwich from Slickables, and I was pretty much over Snowball.

We wound up going to the pound when my mom decided that it was a waste of money to spend $1,800 on an animal. Dorcas was a gray-black goldendoodle. She had only been at the pound a day. When she saw us, she wagged her tail so hard that her whole butt wagged, and that made us laugh. The guy there was like, "You don't find a dog like this at the pound too often," and I wasn't so sure he wasn't being like a used car salesman, but my mom was charmed. And I had to admit I was too. The way Dorcas stared directly at me with her mouth open in seeming wonder made me feel like someone liked me. And I know that's pathetic but it's true.

I look at Dorcas now as she stands at the foot of the treadmill.

"You need exercise," I say, and she just looks at me like, *Bitch, you are aware I don't speak English, right?*

I step on the treadmill and search for the "On" button. The

moving pad comes to life with a quiet whir and I start slowly walking in place.

"See what I'm doing?" I say to Dorcas, who clearly does not understand language beyond the most basic of commands. "I'm walking. Exercising. You want to try?" I pantomime walking, while walking, which is unnecessary.

Dorcas opens her mouth in what looks like a smile but turns out to be a big yawn.

The doorbell rings. Dorcas leaps in the other direction and gallops off to the door, barking like a madwoman. I keep the treadmill on and follow.

When Pam and Kayla walk in, Dorcas jumps up on each of them, Pam first. Pam gives her a big welcome, kneeling down to her level and letting Dorcas lick her face. Kayla does her usual "I know where that tongue has been" thing, creeping backward and patting Dorcas on the head with her arms extended.

"I was teaching her to walk on the treadmill," I say.

The girls share a look. "Oh sweetie," Kayla says. "That's so bleak."

"Come on. Help me," I say, but Pam is busy ignoring me, walking to the kitchen and grabbing a soda from the refrigerator. She gets two and throws a Pepsi to Kayla. They sit down on the couch and Pam flips on my television.

I sigh, audibly. "No," I whine. "No more TV. That's all my mom does. I can't take it. Please? Can we please do a non-TV activity? Anything. I would literally do anything."

Pam surfs Hulu and Kayla turns to me and says, "We did the mall for lunch. I think we're in for the day, sweetie."

I flop down on the chair. "We can stay in. Just, let's, do

something? Make a YouTube video? Or help me get Dorcas on the treadmill? I left it on, even. Come on."

Pam does not stop flipping channels. "That is so not boyfriend-getting behavior. No one's ever put 'I enjoy teaching my dog to walk on the treadmill' on Tinder."

"Oh!" I shout. "I have news. I have gossip! So good!"

This gets their attention and Pam puts down the remote. They wait for me to expound.

I shake my head. "Nope. Not unless you turn off the TV and do something with me. I'm so bored."

Kayla raises one eyebrow. "I'm worried this gossip is going to be not worth it."

"No. Totally worth it. Swear on my life."

"But no treadmill thing. That's so not going to happen," Kayla says.

"Fine," I say. "Something else."

"Dog makeover!" Pam shouts, jumping up from the couch.

Kayla jumps up too. "Yes!"

I shake my head. "Guys . . . come on. You're—objectifying my dog. Not cool."

"She'll love it," Kayla says, and she's already walking toward my room, so I guess we're doing it.

Twenty minutes later, they're dressing up my dog in my clothing when I say, "So Max is gay."

Kayla struggles to get a neon-pink tank top on Dorcas, who looks unamused. She looks like a chagrined dog wearing a poorly sized tank top. "Who the hell is Max?"

"Do you even listen when I talk? He's the guy helping me with the food truck?"

"What food truck?" she asks.

I sit up from my waterbed, where I've been lying, and I pantomime slapping her across the face and she dramatically flips her head to the side.

"So he's gay?" she asks.

"I was a little surprised. I mean. Total dude bro. Not that a dude bro can't be gay, I guess, but the percentage of gay dude bros has to be on the low side."

Kayla goes to my dresser and grabs a pair of black ankle socks. "Do you think he's like a 'I'll let you give me a blowie but I won't kiss you' guy?"

I giggle. "I'll ask him."

She gives the socks to Pam, who begins to put them over Dorcas's front paws. Dorcas tries to free her paws and growls a bit. Pam succeeds and goes searching for more socks for her back feet. "Well if he's Mexican, maybe," she says. "My gay cousin on my dad's side is one of those closet guys. Machismo is like huge in our culture."

"Ugh," I say, wondering if that's how Max really is. "So tired."

Pam sits on the shag carpet down by Dorcas's rear legs and starts to put socks on them. "Max is really cute, right? I remember from AP," she says.

I shrug. Fact is he's mega cute.

Kayla says, "He is. You should date him. Two boys on a food truck. It's like a great trashy male-male erotica novel. 'Pump me full of diesel fuel, Max.'"

"You read those? Ew."

"Do not," Kayla says, rolling her eyes in a way that confirms that yes, she most certainly does. "Boys and boys together? Hot."

"So you objectify my dog and you fetishize my people," I deadpan.

Pam and Kayla stand and admire their work. Dorcas stands there, tongue out, panting, in two pairs of black ankle socks and a pink tank top. It's not a great look.

"She needs underwear," Kayla says.

I jump up. "And now you're fetishizing my dog. You are not putting my underwear on Dorcas," I say.

Kayla smirks like, *Yeah. You have any say whatsoever in this decision.* She goes to my dresser and starts opening drawers.

"Can you not?" I say, but no one is listening to me. "Seriously."

"Overruled," Pam says. Kayla has handed her a pair of light blue bikini briefs she's found in my underwear drawer. She holds them out in front of her like she's admiring them.

"Please stop," I say, and I know it's stupid, but my chest is actually getting tight. It's like, *I said no.* What part of no do they not hear?

Pam says to Kayla, "You hold her steady." Kayla holds Dorcas's midsection, and while Dorcas struggles to free herself, Pam starts to lift Dorcas's legs and slide the underwear on her.

I have this urge to scream. It's so weird. It's just my wives being silly. But the treadmill is still running, and anyway, I said no. They do not have my permission. It's like they just came in and took over, and suddenly I want them gone. That's never happened before.

But I can't say that. So I sit down on my bed and say, "So how do I play this thing with Max? Us both being gay and all?"

Pam succeeds in getting my underwear on Dorcas, who looks both ridiculous and pissed. My stomach turns. I was kidding earlier, when I said they were objectifying her. But now I sort of feel that way. I want to protect her from being dressed against her will. I can't. I lie back and stare at the ceiling.

"Just forget he's gay," Kayla says. "Not just because he's a dude blow. Ha! Dude blow! Classic! You just—you don't shit where you eat. And you eat on that food truck."

"I don't eat there," I say.

"Um, hello, Captain Oblivious. I meant it as a metaphor. You need the food truck to work in order to eat. So don't, like, shit there."

"Ew," I whisper. "Stop."

Pam says, "Or maybe eat just a little. Like, no strings attached. Because he's hot so it's okay. God do I wish I were a gay guy. You have all the fun."

I don't even respond to Pam's messed-up-ness with a look. Instead I can't help but think about the point-counterpoint they've given me. First off, they're jumping the gun. But yeah, Max is kinda hot. And we'll be spending all this time together, and now the barrier is gone because we both know the other is gay, and I wonder: What would he think of me? If I had to guess, he wouldn't. Think of me. I'd be like this annoying skinny dude with acne that he has to spend time with. But it isn't like he's been dismissing me, exactly. A couple times, I've actually wondered why a guy like him would listen to a guy like me as boss, because I'm so—I don't know. Not boss-like, and I don't know what the hell I'm doing, and everything he does is so—masterful. Like he belongs in the world, whereas I belong on some heretofore uninhabitable planet that dude bros have been taught to avoid like the plague.

"Careful," Pam says, elbowing me in the ribs. "Your brain just exploded. You've just married Max, haven't you? Where are you two living?"

"Have not," I say, but I suppress a smile because, yeah. I could imagine that fantasy, at least.

CHAPTER THIRTEEN

MAX

"Who the hell buys a Choco Taco?" Zay-Rod asks as we scan the ice-cream freezer at my local Circle K. It's late Friday afternoon, the day before the new and improved Coq Au Vinny gets reintroduced to the world at the Gilbert Farmers' Market, and I'm trying to make sure to enjoy every second of my free time.

"I thought that was a Mexican thing," Betts says, and Zay-Rod and I share a look.

"It's a Mexican thing like Taco Bell is Mexican food," Zay-Rod says.

"Oh come on. Doritos Locos? That shit's the bomb!" Betts says as he grabs a Klondike.

We don't even need to comment on that one. I grab a Twix, because caramel. Zay-Rod, an ice-cream purist, picks himself a Drumstick.

After we pay the lady with the scratchy cigarette voice, we unwrap our treats and start the walk back to my place. We're pooling. My mom is the favorite mom; she grills the best hot dogs and makes the best tamales, so it's usually our pool where we hang, and we usually wait until she *just happens* to be home from work. There's that sizzling summer noise that's actually cicadas but sounds like the sidewalk is blazing, and I can feel the sun attacking the skin on the back of my neck as we walk up Noche de Paz toward my street. My Twix ice-cream bar is immediately softer than it should be due to the heat, so I snarf it down in two bites. Olives that have fallen off trees and have been ground into the sidewalk dot the asphalt, and we have to step over an occasional gray and dying palm frond.

"So here's my imitation of Zay-Rod doing a slam poem," Betts says, handing me his Klondike. He keeps walking and he clasps his hands in front of his chest, which is actually what Zay-Rod always does for some reason whenever he does his slam poetry in front of the church in downtown Phoenix on Third Fridays. It's a monthly street party where we hang out and eat food off trucks and sneak sips of beer out of paper bags.

"A frog comes out of its shell. The sun beats down, hot, hot hot, and the frog, seeking shelter, finds a . . . tree . . . and"—at this point he does this thing where he unclasps his hands and raises his arms like he's exalting the heavens. It's a pretty spot-on imitation straight from the Zay-Rod canon—"the powers that BE stomp the little frog." He stomps. "Stomp. Stomp. Stomp." I can't help but crack up because it's not a terrible impression, and Zay-Rod punches my shoulder.

Betts continues. "The frog needs to go back to his shell. I am that frog! I am that frog!" Betts pulls his hands back down, clasps them again, and then does a big, exaggerated bow, and I pump my fist like crazy.

"What's your damage, dude?" Zay-Rod asks. "First off, frogs don't have shells, dumb ass. Second off, you suck at poetry. Third, try doing something other than sitting on your fat ass. See how that goes."

"Good comeback," Betts says.

Zay-Rod grabs the Klondike out of my hand and Betts says, "Hey!" and reaches for it. Zay-Rod opens the wrapper and takes a huge bite, and a piece of loose chocolate falls onto his white T-shirt. He swats it off but it leaves a skid mark.

"Serves you right, ass," Betts says, grabbing his Klondike back. Zay-Rod lets him take it and pulls off his soiled shirt.

He says to Betts, "You're the kind of dude who peaks in high school. By twenty-five you're gonna be bald as fuck, with a big gut like your dad."

I laugh at that one too, because yeah, I can totally see that.

"And you," Zay-Rod says, pointing his index finger at me. "You should have my back but of course you don't because you're so stupid. I think your mom and dad were brother and sister."

I roll my eyes. "At least they aren't father and daughter, like yours," I say, and Betts tries to high-five me. I pull away, and when he stumbles forward, I push him onto the concrete.

"Ouch!" he says. "You crazy? The sidewalk is eight thousand degrees."

He stands and we walk on in silence, enjoying our snacks. Betts brings up the idea of hitting the batting cages over in Kiwanis Park. Coach warned us we better stay in shape over the summer and hit once in a while. So far we haven't done either. Zay-Rod vetoes that idea.

"So the kid, Jordan. He's gay," I say.

"You thought he was," says Betts.

"Well now I know for sure."

"You gonna bone him?" Zay-Rod says. "Or you did already."

I punch him in the shoulder. I hate that shit. When I don't answer, Betts jumps ahead of us and does this imitation of me that isn't even close.

"I'm Maximo. I'm a Romeo. I make the boys all . . ."

I give him the finger. "You need a rhyming dictionary?"

"I was gonna go with 'grow-me-o.'"

"Glad you didn't," I say.

"Do you like him?" Zay-Rod asks.

I laugh, but the guys don't laugh back. "No. I don't know. Not really," I say.

The truth is he's got a lot of shit going on. I'm not like in the market for drama. And at the same time, he's so damn cute. I say, "I hope my mom is doing tamales."

"Maximo always changes the subject when he likes a dude," Betts says.

"Betts always talks about me in the third person because he can't conjugate a verb," I say back.

Zay-Rod is still stuck on Betts's imitation. "Frogs in shells. Why in Jesus do I continue to hang out with you? You're too stupid to live."

As we go in through the open side fence to my backyard, Zay-Rod turns his trash-talking assault on me. "You're the least Mexican Mexican, dude. You think you so fly because you dark and shit, but you a big old Klondike. Brown on the outside, white as shit inside."

"Go write a poem about frogs," I say. My mom is in the back-yard, starting up the propane grill. I hear the two clicks and then the roar of the flame as she hits the lever.

"You want hot dogs?" Mom asks.

"What? No tamales?" I say back, and she frowns at me.

"Ungrateful," she says, and she starts scraping off the grill.

"Zay-Rod says you and Dad are brother and sister," I tell her.

She laughs. "Xavier. You were always my favorite but now I don't know."

Zay-Rod laughs. "Sorry, Ms. Gutierrez." She smiles at him to show she's kidding.

I strip off my shirt and jump into the pool. The water is still cool enough that it's somewhat refreshing. When I go under, my head spins crazy. I like to think the heat doesn't bug me, but it's like 114 out and we just walked a mile. It gets to me some.

As I find my equilibrium and come up for air, Betts jumps in just about right on top of me, knocking me back underwater. My head spins again and for a second I feel like I'm going to drown.

I thrash my arms, and my brain goes somewhere weird.

"I'm gonna jet," I say. Kevin's dorm room.

He smirks, and he sits on my legs. "Nah," he says. He's smaller than me, but something about this move is so brash that I don't even counter it. He sits on my calves and pushes down, and I am stuck. I have to laugh. What else can you do but laugh?

And suddenly I'm at the bottom of the pool and I cannot move. Time slows. I open my eyes. I feel like nothing can touch me. Like if I screamed, no one would hear. And they wouldn't. For some reason, this terrifies me, and I don't know why.

Then I feel a pull on the bottom of my red swim shorts. That unfreezes me. I struggle to the surface, swat Betts in the neck, and grab my shorts away from him before he can get them off.

"Why do you want me naked so bad?" I ask, trying to catch my breath.

Zay-Rod jumps just about right in between us, and this time, while we are under, Zay-Rod succeeds in pulling down my suit.

"What the hell, dude?" I say when my face once again emerges from the salt water. "When in the world has there ever been two gayer straight dudes than you two? You can't keep your hands off me." I bend over and pull up my shorts. I can hear my mom laughing at the grill.

"You do have a nice butt," Betts says, kicking his legs up and floating on his back for a second. "For a dude," he says to the sky.

I wince and think about how straight dudes are all caught up in gay sex stuff. Like when I came out to my dad down in Colorado Springs over spring break. *It's okay to be gay, but real men don't take things into their bodies. That's what girls and women do; it's what separates us.* So when Betts does his whole "You got a nice butt" thing, I kinda want to strangle him a little. It's straight supremacy.

Instead I grab a yellow noodle, submerge it in water, put my mouth on one end, and blow. Water soaks Betts, who interrupts his float, grabs the noodle from me, and beats me over the head with it.

"So when do we get to meet this new boyfriend of yours? You never introduce us to your boyfriends," Betts says.

"You blame me?"

Zay-Rod laughs. "Truth."

My mom approaches the pool. "First I've heard of this. New boyfriend?"

"The kid from the food truck," Betts says.

My mother nods, like, *That's some information.* I want to tell her no, like, *Don't worry, Ma. We aren't dating. Guys like Jordan don't date guys who hang with guys like Betts and Zay-Rod.* This other part of me wants her—and them—to butt the hell out.

"Are the hot dogs ready?" I ask, and my mother rolls her eyes.

"You need to teach this boy how to communicate," she says to my friends.

"Yeah, ask these guys for help. Good thinking," I say.

CHAPTER FOURTEEN
JORDAN

The worst thing about Coq Au Vinny's re-boot is the truck's design. It would be so much better if we could just change the name so that people know what we are. As it stands, it's Saturday morning at the Gilbert Farmers' Market, and I'm concerned that no one in the world is going to come close enough to see our whiteboard, which contradicts the angry bird logo on the side of the truck.

How are they going to know about the frozen drinks and cloud eggs?

Cloud eggs are this thing we saw on Instagram, where you create like a baked meringue circle, put the egg yolk in the middle, and then bake it. I haven't tasted one, but I'm intrigued. Someone online said it tasted like egg-flavored marshmallow. I can't really imagine that.

"So here goes nothing," Max says, cracking the first egg. He separates the whites from the yolks, putting the yolks in a small bowl. Then he starts whisking the whites to within an inch of their lives, and I stare at the whites as they slowly stiffen and form peaks.

"You're amazing," I say, and he snorts.

"That's me. Max the Amazing Egg Whisker."

"I couldn't do it."

"That's something you should probably deal with. Who can't whisk an egg?"

I ignore his dig and start in on my contribution. We convinced Max's mom to part with her Vitamix, and I'm going to have two frozen drink offerings: frozen mango lemonade and frozen cherry lemonade. I have enough lemonade concentrate and frozen fruit to make a hundred lemonades. At five bucks a pop, that's five hundred dollars net if we sell out, and it cost me just under a hundred bucks for the ingredients at Safeway. Not bad for a day's work, and I figure if we sell out, maybe we can streamline the process and sell even more on days in the future.

I place my notebook down by the sink, aware that for the first time, I'm not likely to get much writing done today. I actually wrote some funny stuff and some poems last week. Then I start with the first can of concentrate, combining it with water to create sixty-four ounces of lemonade. I shake and shake and shake, and then pour myself a little bit. Real tart, real sweet. Not too bad. Then I pour eight ounces into the Vitamix, tear open a package of frozen mangos, and pour a quarter of it into the blender. I hit the button and watch the machine whir to life. I didn't actually try it at home; it seemed simple enough, but as I watch the ingredients combine, I realize maybe I should have experimented. My lemonade looks frothy but watery.

"Hmm," I say, stopping the blender for a moment.

Max walks over. "How did it work at home?"

I press the button again as an answer. He presses it off.

"Jordan. Tell me you tried this at home. I was doing cloud eggs all night last night."

"Sounds like a real party," I say, and I press the button again.

"Dude," he says, shaking his head and moving away. "Dude."

We're falling into this routine, where Max is awesome and I'm a screwup. I can't say I love it. I purse my lips and try to put it out of my mind.

I find that if I do half the packet of mango instead of a quarter and some ice—yes, I didn't even think of ice, I'm that dense—my drink thickens up in about a minute on high blend. I wait until it looks sufficiently thick, stop the blender, and pour myself a cup. It's bright orange-yellow, a color that would definitely catch my eye if I were walking by and thirsty.

The taste is, well, it's pretty good. Mango-y. Sweet. Refreshing. Super cold. Max watches as I drink and I make an exaggerated show of enjoying it.

"Ahh," I say dramatically. "Perfection. Imagine: I was able to blend lemonade and fruit all by myself, without testing it out at home!"

He gives me a dirty look, and I assuage him by offering him a sip from my cup. He pauses for a moment, and I realize that there is a sort of intimacy to sharing a cup. But finally he takes it, and I have to admit my arms tingle as I watch his Adam's apple go up and down while he tastes it.

"That is some sweet shit, dude. How much sugar is in that lemonade?"

I shrug. "Frozen."

"You know, we could have actually done real lemonade."

I swallow, tighten my jaw, and—remembering how much I need Max—I try to keep things light. "We could do lots of things. At this point I'm just looking to make some money."

I set things up so that we have a blender full of mango

lemonade, ready to go. A real food truck would probably have two Vitamixes, one for each fruit. As it stands, I realize I'm going to have to hope people want the same one over and over, or else there's gonna be lots of Vitamix washing.

Once I'm set up, I watch him tenderly place the egg yolks in the center of the white clouds, which look like marshmallow fluff circles. I have to admit that I'd totally order one of those. Max is a talented guy. Too bad he's stuck with a slack ass.

"I told my friends that my truck mate is gay," I say, after Max puts the tray of twelve cloud eggs into the oven.

He looks over his shoulder as he shuts the oven door. "How did that go?"

"They started to play matchmaker," I say.

He laughs. "That's so funny. Same as my friends. It's like, what if every time two straight people met, we went around saying, 'You guys are both straight! You should date!'"

I laugh too, even though I realize that this argument isn't exactly fair. Straight people meet all the time. By the numbers, it's rarer for two gay people to meet. Also I guess I kind of was asking Pam and Kayla, so it's not like they overstepped. Still, I say, "Exactly. Of course, one of my friends was all 'Don't shit where you eat,' which is a disgusting image."

"True," he says. "As if we're a bunch of sex-starved pervs just looking for a willing hole."

I laugh and blush at his use of "hole." And also because, well, I am sort of a sex-starved perv looking for a willing whatever. But Max doesn't need to know that.

When the eggs are ready, we put up our awning and open for business.

"Cloud eggs. Frozen lemonade!" Max calls, and even though being loud is way out of my comfort zone, I recognize that this is basically it. That my family's future depends on the success of this food truck re-boot. So I start yelling too, and then I start coming up with clever slogans.

"Got frozen lemons? Learn to make frozen lemonade!" I yell, and Max snorts.

"Cheesy," he says.

I shrug.

"Mango lemonade. Round the corner cloud eggs are made," I yell, and this one just makes him say, "Stop. Please. Stop."

"Hey, at least I'm trying," I say.

We're quiet for a while, and then Max surprises me.

"Our cloud eggs will make your dreams come true," he says. "Come on and give a cloud egg a try, and tell me it didn't change your life. It doesn't change your life, it's on the house."

It's not catchy, exactly, but onlookers stop and approach.

"Cloud egg? Okay. I'll bite," a woman says. "How much?"

"Seven," Max says. "Get it with a frozen mango lemonade for ten instead of twelve."

She raises an eyebrow and reaches for her pocketbook. "Sold."

Max smiles that golden grin of his. "You won't be sorry. One cloud egg coming up!"

I take the woman's credit card, charge her ten, and then go back to the blender and prepare her a drink. The sugar smell of the concentrate is so strong that I momentarily worry. It was one thing when I was imagining feeding someone my creation; actually giving the woman a frozen mango lemonade brings out all sorts of butterflies in my chest and stomach.

Max hands her a small, red-and-white checked paper dish with the cloud egg regally sitting in the exact center, a fork lying at its side. I hurry up and hand her a see-through-plastic sixteen-ounce cup of mango lemonade.

"Lovely," she says, and we stand at the window and watch for her reaction. She forks in some of the egg white, and her eyes go wide. "Oh my! The consistency is more marshmallow than meringue," she says. "I wasn't sure. And is that Parmesan I'm tasting in there?"

"Yes, ma'am," Max says.

"I kind of love it!"

A line begins to form, and my heart soars. We have a hit! This is happening.

She takes a sip of the lemonade, and her expression changes in a different way.

"Is this . . . lemonade mix?"

"Um," I say, my heart crashing into my shoe.

She shakes her head. "Now that is not quite so special," she says, and she takes off the lid and pours the contents of the drink on the ground. A poodle pulls on its leash and comes to lick it up, much to the chagrin of its owner.

"Warren!" the owner yells, yanking the dog away.

"I'm sorry," I say, and the woman half smiles.

"Fifty percent," she says. "I'll come by next week, and I fully expect a free fresh-squeezed frozen lemonade."

"And you'll get it," Max says, and I feel about two inches tall.

We spend the next two hours serving up mostly cloud eggs and the occasional frozen lemonade. The cherry is a big hit with kids, who don't seem to have much of a sense of the difference between store-bought mix and fresh lemonade, thank God.

A few times we have to make people wait five minutes as Max makes another tray of cloud eggs, but mostly we get into a pretty good rhythm of me taking orders and him serving, and soon we're even able to talk a bit between us, which is kinda nice, actually.

Until he goes back to our topic from before.

"My buddy Betts is on my jock to meet a boyfriend of mine. I don't know why he cares so much."

"Have you ever introduced anyone?"

He shakes his head. "None of his business. They're too up in my stuff all the time."

"I hear you," I say, not really knowing what it would be like to want to hide boyfriend stuff from Pam and Kayla.

"And anyway, it's not like anyone's even been that close to being my boyfriend. It's like, *When someone interesting shows up, I'll let you know, okay?* Leave me alone, right?"

Max hands me a cloud egg, and I take it and look away, feeling like barely a person. Of course he's not interested in zit boy, the skinny kid who can't even make lemonade. What was I even thinking?

"Right," I say. "As if we're all attracted to each other. As if we see some gross gay dude and we're like, *I want that. I must have that.*"

He laughs, I laugh, and I wonder about what it would take to get a full body and personality transplant.

CHAPTER FIFTEEN

MAX

We take in nine hundred dollars our first day with cloud eggs, thank you very much, and you better believe I feel like a freakin' superhero.

In a world in which some deign to simply scramble their eggs, Chef Max saves an area family with his delectable cloud eggs! Story at eleven!

And that nine hundred bucks was without much in terms of drink sales, as Jordan decided that frozen lemonade concentrate would get the job done. Really, dude? Your life is on the line, and you went with Minute Maid? I don't know, man.

He's quiet as he hands me my ten bucks per hour plus half the tips, which turns out to be a hundred and five dollars. Then he hands me an extra two hundred for my work last week.

"Thanks," I say, and Jordan mumbles, "Don't mention it." He's back to being spacey, and it's driving me crazy.

I go over in my mind what I could have said that would make him act that way. We were talking about our friends, and how they are all up in our business about who we're dating, or in my case, not dating. I said I hated that. He agreed. I said I'd let them know if and when I found someone even close to my type.

My throat tightens. Shit. Why am I such an ass? I told Jordan, who is gay and available, that I hadn't met anyone even close to my type? Why would I say that? I mean, he was all "Don't shit where you eat," and I guess I was just being defensive? I thought that took me out of the equation. I don't know.

How can Jordan not know he's adorable? I mean, this thing where he doesn't like himself is kinda written all over him. And I guess I want to fix him, make him understand he's better than he thinks, and maybe I have from the start. But I didn't really think it would be that hard, because, I mean, his lines. Delicate and perfect. His limbs, moving like a dance. His fine features, like they could be on a doll. Minus the zits, yeah, but that doesn't really bug me. I can see underneath. His thin, almost slight nose and lips. Those light green eyes filled with mystery. I don't look at rugged guys like me. It's just not my thing, which is why it's so funny when Betts is all flirty. He'd be like my last choice. Jordan? A bad idea, because all we do is fight. But yeah, cute as all hell. And thoughtful. The stuff he says makes me think. I like that. I want more of that in my life.

"You were great today," I say, and he laughs, almost like a snort.

"Yeah, I'm a real food truck mogul."

"No, really. You and I? We're a great team. I'm glad I took this job. I like working with you, Jordan. I like you."

He looks at the floor and doesn't respond.

I want to say something else, but I know I'm already way too much. Out on the edge of a cliff. Like the precipice, where you teeter before falling off and breaking your neck.

We go silent as we clean up, and I begin to feel like I have fallen. I said those sappy "I like you" things, and he left me hanging.

And that fucking sucks. Maybe I need to cut my losses. We'll work together. We don't actually have to be friends, and it's not like he makes friendship even possible. I can't say anything without him taking it personally. It's exhausting. Too much drama.

He wants to go home right away after, but I insist that we should take the time to prep for tomorrow, which means buying more eggs and also actual ingredients for lemonade. And when he rolls his eyes, it takes everything I have not to yell at him. I mean, I'm saving his freakin' family. You'd think he'd be a little nicer about stuff. Jesus.

"I gotta tinkle," he says, and he jumps out the back of the truck.

"I'll miss you very much," I say under my breath. "You're a real pleasure."

I take a tray over to the sink to clean it, and Jordan's notebook is there.

I can't help it. Call me curious. What was he writing last week when the truck was so dead?

At the top of the first page, it reads, Combined Movies.

Under are three entries:

The Fault in Our Star Wars: A sci-fi geek points out all the plot inconsistencies in the original Star Wars trilogy, and promptly gets cancer.

Eat, Pray, Love, Actually: A deeply unhappy woman travels the world, only to wind up in London, before Christmas, where she kills herself after hearing the song "Love Is All Around" one too many times.

Orange Is the New Black Swan: There's a new black swan in town, and her name is, ironically, Orange! All the other black swans hate her, she kills one, and winds up in jail, where she becomes a devout lesbian.

The last one cracks me up. Jordan doesn't always show it, but he's funny. When I first met him, he said something like "We do Italian things with chicken," which isn't funny ha ha, but funny like a unique way of speaking. I wonder if he's holding back? Like not comfortable being himself with me?

I turn the page, and the next page says, FOOD TRUCK FROM HELL.

Under is a poem.

Fuck my life
S.O.S.
I am stuck
On a food truck
With a guy
Guy Smiley
Who drives me nuts
Who thinks his life is so perfect
S.O.S.
My mom
A herstrionic time bomb
The truck our savior
Will surely stall on the highway
Any day now
Fuck my life

I stare at the poem, focusing in on the line about Guy Smiley, and my stomach twists.

I think about me, at eight, with Skeeter and those guys. How they left me all alone, and I smiled.

I think about me, last year, when Marquez from the baseball team made a fag joke when we were in the dugout at San Marcos, and I smiled.

And after, when Betts lingered by my locker, and he put his arm on my shoulder and he asked, "You okay, dude?" And I smiled. Of course I was.

I always am.

The morning after with Kevin. "You enjoy yourself?" His face looks seedy, like slimy almost, a film of grease around his lips like he's just eaten hash browns from McDonald's.

I smile. "Yeah," I say.

Jordan hops back up on the truck and I turn to him, the notebook still in my hand.

"Hey," he says, forceful, angrier than I've ever seen him. "Did I say you could read that? You have no right—" He comes and grabs it out of my hand. It is still open to the poem. He looks and he reads, and a look of something else comes over his face, which turns white.

"Max," he says. "Sorry. I mean. Sorry you read that, and sorry I wrote that. You should ask before—" he exhales. "You shouldn't have read my private stuff. But also I wrote that last week and I didn't mean it even then, and definitely not now."

I smile. I don't know what else to do.

"Dude," I say. "It's all good, dude. Sorry I snooped. Not cool. I won't do that again."

We finish cleaning up and head off to the market and the energy between us is all messed up. Jordan is suddenly very talkative, like overly, like he's trying to make up for writing the shitty thing he wrote about me in his journal, and I'm over smiley, I guess, and over laugh-y, guffawing at every little thing he says as if I'm a freakin' idiot. I can't help it. I don't know what else to do.

CHAPTER SIXTEEN

JORDAN

On Sunday we go to the Ahwatukee Farmers' Market, the scene of our awful first day, when we sold twenty-eight dollars' worth of food.

But that was a week ago, when we were Coq Au Vinny and clueless. Now we are either Coq Au Vinny, if you look at the truck, or Savory and Sweet — Max's name — if you look at our whiteboard.

That was also a week ago, when Max and I hated each other. Now we — I don't know. I really don't. I think maybe Max thinks I hate him, because of this poem I wrote that he read when I was off the truck yesterday at Gilbert. And yeah, that was a total invasion of my privacy, but it's hard to be mad at him when I know he thinks I hate him. My clumsy attempts at making him understand that are not exactly a rousing success.

"We're gonna break a thousand today," I say as Max is prepping his cloud eggs and I am chopping lemons. We went to Safeway yesterday and I bought fifty pounds of lemons for seventy-five dollars, and forty pounds of sugar for twenty-four bucks. Add ice to that, and I basically put out a hundred and twenty bucks for ingredients. I don't know how long it will take, but we have enough supplies for two hundred frozen lemonades. At five bucks a pop, we'd make a thousand dollars out of our hundred-and-twenty-dollar investment.

In other words, we're a bunch of geniuses. If people buy it.

"That would be awesome," he says, and I wish I could figure out whether we're good or not. It's so hard knowing, and it sucks not to know.

I am psyched as I write *Homemade Frozen Lemonade* under *Cloud Eggs* and Max's new item, *Breakfast Grilled Cheese*, on the whiteboard in blue Magic Marker. I stand back and regard it, and then, feeling ballsy, I erase it and write: *Jordan's World-Famous Homemade Frozen Lemonade*.

After I write it, I beckon Max out to see it. He comes out and stands next to me and crosses his arms.

"It's . . . long," he says.

"There's room."

"It's . . . not necessarily, um, true."

"Since when do advertisements need to be true?"

"True 'nuff. I like it."

We open for business, and fairly quickly I find the fly in the ointment of my lemonade boast.

"What's so special about the lemonade?" a burly guy with curly black hair and a mole on his chin asks.

"Homemade," I say.

"Yeah, but you say world-famous. What's in it that's so special for five bucks?"

Dang it. I hadn't thought about that.

"Well, it's . . . organic."

"Cool," he says. "Organic lemons and sugar, both?"

"Yep," I say, swallowing.

"Okay."

I nod. This is not exactly true, but there's really no way he'll find that out unless he comes on the truck and roots through our trash.

"Is that it?"

"Um. Well, there is usually a special . . . ingredient," I say.

"Sure. I know Bruce's truck down the way has pomegranate and that stuff is great."

"Ours is prickly pear," I say without thinking.

"Hmm," he says. "Okay. I'd try that."

"Well, it's not quite ready," I say, backing up and smacking into Max, who is standing at the grill.

"Did you forget the prickly pear again?" he asks.

I say, "Dang it."

The guy says, "When do you think you'll have it? Would love to try. Frozen prickly pear lemonade sounds off the hook."

"An hour," I say, and he smiles, salutes, and walks away.

So that's how I wind up in an Uber, heading to the closest grocery store, Bashas'. It's only half a mile away, but in this heat? I don't think so.

I ask the Uber to hang when we get there. He takes that as an opportunity to drive away when I close the door, and I think, *Well, there goes your five-star rating.* Bashas' doesn't have prickly pear in any form, of course, so I make an executive decision that probably won't win me a place in heaven but should get us through today.

Max is busy doing two jobs when I get back, and there's an actual line. Impressively, I see he's actually sold some frozen lemonades, and I remind myself to keep trying to get back into his good graces. The dude is a machine, and a nice one, to boot. I decide if we do make a ton of money today, I'm gonna give him a percentage on top of his salary. He'll like that.

"What'd you get?" he asks when he sees that the bag I've brought back could not hold even a single prickly pear.

I beckon him over, hiding from the view of those in line. I show him what I have. He laughs.

"Seriously, dude?"

"Hey. It'll be like a psychology experiment."

He shakes his head, but at least he has a smile on his face, and I feel like maybe we're back, past the trouble from yesterday. And I haven't even unveiled my secret weapon yet. I might not either. Depends how I feel, I guess.

I cross out my menu item and write it again. It's even longer now: *Jordan and Max's World-Famous Organic Homemade Prickly Pear Frozen Lemonade.*

I turn the sign toward Max, and he squints as he reads it. He grins, and when I get back on the truck, he whispers, "Leave me out of this, dude."

I mumble, "Too late. You're in. If I go down, you're going down with me."

Something about the sentence sounds vaguely sexual to me, and when Max's eyes don't leave mine, I feel this jolt of energy climb up my spine and look away. It's super weird.

I find that a drop of the red food coloring does a nice job of turning the lemonade a pleasing, light shade of electric pink. My heart is pulsing as I pour our first lemonade for our first victim, a girl maybe in her twenties who barely looks up from her cell phone while ordering, waiting, or receiving her drink. I watch as she takes a sip.

"Mmm," she mumbles, licking her lips, and as she walks away, I turn to Max. He's watching too.

"One down," he says.

The next one goes to a hipster guy, who scares the shit out of me when he starts talking about prickly pear, and how it's one of his favorite flavors.

"I've never had it in lemonade, let alone frozen," he says. "I'm actually a little excited about this."

I've already taken his money, and I kind of want to give it back to him, because surely someone with great prickly pear knowledge will be able to tell that his favorite flavor is absent from our drink. But instead I make change for him and walk the figurative plank, back to the Vitamix in the back of the truck. My heart pulses as the blender buzzes, and when I hand him the light pink frozen concoction, I keep my eyes averted from his.

He isn't going away, however. He inserts the straw, sucks in a worthy sip, and gives us his report.

"Mmm," he says. "Taste that prickly pear tang. Wow. It's actually even better than I thought it would be."

I smile, and Max comes up to the window. "That's why we call it 'Jordan and Max's World-Famous Organic Homemade Prickly Pear Frozen Lemonade.'"

"Amen, amigo," he says, and I wonder how often Max gets spoken to in Spanish, and whether it bugs him. I've never heard him speak in Spanish, not even once.

My success leads Max to get a little more brash too, and when we have a lull in service, he goes out to the whiteboard, erases something, and writes more. He turns the sign to show me.

Coq Au Vinny uses all organic and locally sourced ingredients, he has written. I laugh.

"We are so going to hell, aren't we?" I say.

"Probably," he says. "But we'll go there a lot richer. Just watch."

Max wasn't lying. The lines grow and grow, and suddenly we're this incredible moneymaking machine. At one point, our line is more than ten people long, and what I notice is that when people stand in line, others tend to take notice and come investigate. From about ten until twelve fifteen, when we close up, we are swamped, and I barely notice that the oven and grill have heated the truck to a level that makes it just about impossible to breathe. My body begins to feel chilly, with sweat soaking through my red T-shirt and white shorts, and Max, who is even closer to the flame, is even more drenched. He also looks radiant. Like he was meant to do this. And the amazing thing is this pang of something that goes through me as I watch him in action, speeding around the grill, spritzing water next to the grilled cheese sandwiches to make the grill sizzle, going through plastic glove after plastic glove, lifting tray after tray of cloud eggs out of the oven and spatula-ing them into red-and-white checked paper dishes with the grace of a pro.

He's magnificent. Max the Magnificent.

He's a food truck deity. I feel my heart pulse as I watch his broad shoulder muscles glisten sweat, and I have to look away because parts of me are beginning to tingle, and those things should not happen on a busy food truck.

By the time we close up, we are swimming in sweat, cash, and credit card receipts. I have no idea how much we made, but a ton, and I can't wait to count. But first I make sure to spend the very last bit of energy I have on cleanup, because I want Max to notice my effort. I really do. I want him to see that I can work hard too, that I'm not a total waste case.

He doesn't say anything, but I see something in his eyes as we clean up that tells me he appreciates my hard work. He turns off the grill and oven, and an ever-so-slight breeze blows through the truck when I open the back door. It's not cool, but anything is cooler than what we've just worked through, and we catch each other's eyes, dramatically wipe the sweat from our brows, and smile.

I melt inside. If only I could make Max feel half of what I feel right now, which is more alive than alive. More real than I've ever felt. Like I want to dance and jump in a pool and sing and giggle simultaneously, even though I'm not really one to do any one of those things singularly.

When we're done, I decide I have to do it. Share what had felt like a secret weapon, like maybe I was trying to manipulate him a bit into liking me again, but after today, now that we have bonded as brothers-in-arms on this food truck, it feels like something I just want to share. It's out there, but somehow it feels right.

He's leaning against the grill, which is no longer exuding waves of heat, looking at his phone. I walk over, my journal in front of me. He looks up. I hand it to him.

"What's this?" he asks.

"Duh," I say. "You know what it is."

"I don't need to—why are you handing it to me?"

I look away as momentarily this new confidence in me wavers. I breathe through it.

"I'm a writer," I say. "I wrote something last night. I want to share it with you, because. Well, because you're becoming a friend, and I know it's weird, but I wanted you to know that the shit you saw yesterday is not, um. About you, I guess. It's more about this. This is who I really am."

He stares at me, not harshly, and I can't believe I am about to share my innermost thoughts with a dude bro. But I feel drunk with closeness. Maybe it's a kind of heatstroke? I don't know. I just . . . I want Max to know who I am.

It feels dangerous. Like he could laugh after reading it, and I would melt into a humiliated puddle.

He opens it, and I help him flip to the poem I wrote last night. I swallow deeply, a mixture of dread and something foreign — pride? Realness? — mixing in my throat.

Loneliness
By Jordan Edwards

Loneliness
Dresses in black
Combs the side streets for weeds to pluck
Invents dramas involving imaginary lovers
Sits in a scalding bathtub 'til the water goes cold

Loneliness
Pretends to be noble

But wouldn't know nobility
If it sat on its face

Loneliness
Lies so far underneath the loam
That it would take a steel shovel
To dig up
And oxygen is running out
Fast

I swallow again as his eyes stop moving and I realize he's gotten to the end. The oxygen has been sucked out of the truck, it feels like. He stares down at the page, motionless.

"Well? Please say something. I know it's not that great." His next words hold far too much power, and I hate the feeling and also I love it.

"Wow," he says. He closes the book and looks up at me, his dark eyes soft and warm. I am utterly covered in sweat, tired, cold, and needing more.

"I don't know anything about lyrics or poems or whatever, but I think it's cool. Really cool. I like that he needs a steel shovel underground to dig up."

"Thanks," I mumble, my eyes mostly averted, every few seconds sneaking back to look at his. His are focused on the poem still. It's unbearable, how much I need. Unbearable and stupid.

He hoists himself up on the grill, goes "Ow!" and hops back down. He says, "I feel bad that the oxygen is running out. That kinda sucks."

I swallow and keep my eyes trained on the floor beneath me. More. I need more. Anything please. Just more.

He reaches over and hands me back the poem. "You're an amazing writer," he says. "I admire that."

"Thanks," I repeat, and I chance looking back into his eyes. He's smiling at me. They're smiling at me, and I'm petrified, and grateful, and hooked. On Max. Which is such a deeply bad idea. But I can't help it.

CHAPTER SEVENTEEN

MAX

He showed me his poem.

No one has ever entrusted me with something that delicate before.

It's weird and I don't want to get all corny, but it's like I saw Jordan today for the first time. Like with the funny movies he wrote I saw his humor, and I saw his snark with the rude poem about the food truck from hell. But this was different. This was real.

I don't have people in my life who write poetry. Zay-Rod writes slam poetry, but it's political stuff, and that's fine. It's just not—personal. Like it flies off into anger without ever revealing the soul.

It made me wonder: Could a guy like Jordan, a guy that graceful, a guy whose walk looks like a dance, could he like someone as thick and clunky as me?

Could he look past my rough exterior to see that I have a heart too?

When you're like me, when you're a dude who plays baseball and hangs with his bros, you aren't supposed to have a heart.

But here's the secret: I like tender. Maybe more than I should.

I wish I could show him my heart. That's dangerous, though. You show it and people laugh. Nothing is worse than people laughing at your open heart, which is why I think guys don't do that so much. Which is why I can't believe Jordan trusted me enough to show me that.

I want to be worth that.

So when I get home, I close my door and make sure it's locked. I don't know why. I just don't want Mom walking in and seeing this. Not that she'd mind, but this feels . . . private.

I sit down at my desk, and I close my eyes and think about Jordan's lonely poem.

A shovel, digging upward. Wow. And the oxygen is running out. Wow. I close my eyes and I picture Jordan digging up, and suddenly I'm hoping someone is digging down to meet him.

I pull out my supplies from the bottom drawer. I haven't done this since ninth grade, when Mr. Zimmer saw my saguaro tree and used it as an example of what not to do. "Maybe you're more of an athlete, Morrison," he said, and I smiled as everyone laughed.

It's a black, zipped container with about fifty pencils in various colors and various textures, from hard to soft, and a kneaded eraser that's good not just for blotting out mistakes, but also pulling apart. I used to have a nervous habit of doing that, like I couldn't go two seconds without rolling a ball of gray eraser around in my fingers and then pulling it apart and stuffing it back together.

I open my old notebook and flip through the pages. Sure enough, the last page is the saguaro tree. It looks pretty good to me, with about six arms of varying height, all with that prickly texture of the one in our front yard. The shade of green looks just right. I don't know what Mr. Zimmer saw; maybe he was just trying to be funny. But yeah, it definitely stopped me from drawing. I dropped the class, even. But right now, I don't care.

I look at the page and I see a pit, like one someone might dig. Then I imagine it from different angles. Am I at a side view? I find myself scrunching and pulling at the kneaded eraser as I think. I see a guy tangled in tree roots underground.

I settle into a side view. I take a small piece of charcoal and rub it across the page, creating a place for Jordan's loneliness to be. I don't know what's above and below the ground; I just need to get rid of the blank paper. I remember that from when I used to draw all the time. It was like, getting rid of the blankness gave me permission to get started.

I rough out the side of Jordan's face. He's underground, confined. He's partially digging, and partially pushing against the surface. Suddenly he has a hand clawing at the surface, his thumb on the outside, which means his arm is tucked at his side. I lose my breath seeing the outline of that skinny arm, confined. Then I add his left arm, pushing up at the surface. I create the sinews in his clawing right arm, the dirt falling on his face as he tries desperately to remove the earth.

I want the edge of his face to show, just his jawline, as if he's turned away, avoiding the falling dirt. It's all charcoal still, sketched on the page, erasable, which is good because so far it sucks.

A hack. I'm a hack. I have no idea how to —

I shut my brain off and trace some gnarly roots that run down into the ground, like from a tree above. The roots entwine his wrists like handcuffs, and again, I'm finding it hard to breathe, staring at this thing I'm creating.

I smear some charcoal along the roots to create a shadow quickly.

No. His body should be under the roots, under the tree.

I deepen his hands, the claw feature. Then I go into the claw hand with the eraser as it's getting lost in there. And what's going on above the earth? This is the hard part. Seeing what isn't there.

I like the shovel in the poem, but in this picture I see a person above there, crouching down in the dirt, just as dirty, just as invested in the scene as Jordan.

Is it me? Am I above the ground, digging down?

I turn the page sideways and charcoal sketch a boy's face staring down, right against the ground. His hair falls forward in the face.

Shit. The damn paper's too small.

Too damn bad. I continue.

But first I look at what I have and my heart jumps. Two boys staring at each other but unable to see, the ground separating them. It's intense, like very.

I sketch the boy on top's hand against the dirt. His palm is inches from the other boy's claw.

Damn. I am the boy on top. And I'm as close to the ground as I can be. And hopeless to help, which sucks the worst. I want to help, but I can't. I'm waiting for Jordan to dig himself out.

I turn my attention back to Jordan's face. It's not what I intend. Jordan looks like Jordan but not like Jordan at all, and there's no way to make him more Jordan. There's no space for all that Jordan-ness to be added.

I add a knee to my aboveground boy, who doesn't look like

me but I am definitely him. The first knee I sketch with charcoal is too high, so I lower and shadow it, and then I give my character strong eyebrows and I see for a second the real me crouching there on the ground, and it's scary.

Damn. Betts and Zay-Rod would not get this at all. I would never show them this.

I sharpen a dark black pencil, its shavings twirling out like a little mushroom head.

I place a piece of white paper below my right forearm and lean in to focus on the eye. I want a very specific emotion there, like, I'm not sure what but something. It could be panicked, but it's almost like the person on the top knows more than the person on the bottom.

Like he's been there before, underground.

I use white pencil to pop the top guy's eye out a bit more.

Man. I didn't know so much about this drawing would be the guy on top. I thought it was going to be a shovel but the shovel didn't want to be there.

I turn the page upward so I can check the perspective. It looks about right. Sometimes when you draw flat, you can't see how things will look right-side up.

The upper character has dirt under his nails that I create with more black pencil, and sweat on his face, which I don't want to be perfect drops of dew but more just like black lines that add to the movement of the piece.

I add some white smudges to make him more three-dimensional.

Hmm. The boy has no clothes. No clothing line. Maybe shorts? I don't know yet.

I stand up and move over to my bed. Sometimes I need to get away so I don't lose perspective. When I come back, what I see is a mess that might turn into something.

I focus in on the tree. Maybe it's an avoidance so I don't have to deal with Jordan's face yet. I switch to a different pencil to give the tree its own texture, different from the rest.

I realize I'm drawing a tree again and I smile, thinking about Mr. Zimmer's comment. Well, maybe I am a jock. Maybe I can't do this. But I like it, you know? I like trying.

I can't find the guy on the bottom. I smear some color together, and focus in on the outline, and suddenly it's like, *There you are.* He shows up and what's so funny is the guy on the bottom is darker than the guy on top, which is opposite. But somehow it just works. I strengthen the jawline with more charcoal.

I wonder if Jordan would let me draw him. This isn't him even if it stands in for him. It would help me get beyond skin texture and eye color. Man, I need to ask him. I wonder what he would say if I asked?

I sketch in his top eye. I won't know the emotion for sure until the eye comes through. Then I'll know if it's right or not.

I flare his nostril more to make him more panicky.

I erase his ear. I do not like what happened there at all.

There's a knock on my door and I respond with a fevered "What?" as if I'm jerking off.

"Never mind," my mom says, and I hear the smirk in her voice. She thinks she's caught me in the act.

"I'll be right out," I say, trying to sound more normal and less jerk-off-y. Of course that just makes me sound more guilty. Oh well.

Damn. Jordan looks a little like a fetus. That's not great.

I use white pencil to show more of his eye, to invoke that sense of panic.

There's not the right terror in Jordan's face.

To fix the face, I fill in the blank space next to it because there's no light down there. I look at it. It looks a little more right that way. I take the black pencil and re-sketch an ear. Then I look at what I have again.

The boy on bottom looks like he's given up. Like he's sort of clawing, expressionless. And I have this crazy, crazy thought:

Am I actually the boy on the bottom? Am I digging up and out of oxygen? Is Jordan digging down to save me?

CHAPTER EIGHTEEN

JORDAN

On Monday, we try the food truck area on the north side of the Arizona State University campus. It's a lunchtime gig, so suddenly we need to do something other than breakfast grilled cheese and cloud eggs.

We meet at my place at eight, which gives us three hours to shop, prep, arrive, and open. Not as much time as you might think. The sun is already fully up, which is what happens here in the summer because Arizona doesn't do Daylight Savings Time. Because it's so hot, we wind up on Pacific Standard Time in the summer and Mountain Standard Time in the winter.

"What about chicken and waffles?" I ask. We're sitting in the living room.

Max winces. "I don't know, dude. The heat from the fryer? That could get intense. Plus cleaning it."

I nod. He's right. "I keep going to chicken. But we had all that boring chicken stuff before and it didn't sell. On the plus side, Coq Au Vinny would actually make sense if we did chicken."

Max pulls out his phone and goes to YouTube, our trusty source for stealing good food truck ideas. He surfs around and finally motions me over.

"How about this?" He plays me one of those videos where the cooking is done in fast motion and what normally takes an hour plays in about a minute. I see lemon and sriracha, and I admit it makes me salivate. I like spicy and citrusy. A lot.

"Well we already have a lot of lemons," I say.

"Exactly. Plus basically what we want to do is marinade chicken, grill it, and sauce it. Let's come up with two or three combos and just do it."

We decide on lemon-sriracha, mango-cayenne, and habanero-peach. I've never had any of them, and I tell Max that. He smiles.

"Me neither."

"Well what could possibly go wrong?" I say, and then, because I see a slight bit of hurt register on his face, I say, "I trust you. Completely. If anyone can do this first time out, it's you."

He nods and his eyebrows relax.

We go to Safeway to get our ingredients. It's awesome because we can afford it. When I told Mom how much we made Saturday and Sunday, she looked so proud and grateful, and she hugged me tight, which was great. And then she teared up again, and she started in about what a success I've become, and I don't know. It was like I was receiving a lifetime achievement award and she was talking to an imaginary audience. It was . . . odd, and it made me all fidgety.

Then we go to Food City because they sell prickly pear fruit. I was on board to continue with the red food coloring, but Max said sooner or later someone would figure it out. I pick up ten with the green skin for four bucks. The fine folks at Food City have removed the thorns, and they look like a cross between a pear and a melon — pear-shaped and colored, but with hard melon skin. As we stand in line, I feel a bit like I'm in Mexico; I'm the only white person here.

"Mucho Latinx," I say, and Max looks at me and says, "What?"

I repeat it, and he says, "Whatever the hell PC shit that is, is just—grammatically wrong, for one thing. If you mean there are lots of Latino people, you'd say, 'Muchos Latinos.' If you mean it's very Latino, you'd say, 'Muy Latino.' As for the Latinx thing? I have never met any Mexican person who has ever said that, as far as I know."

My face turns red. "Oh, okay," I say, glancing around me to see if anyone else heard my stupidity. "Sorry. Microaggression."

He rolls his eyes.

I say, "What?"

"I just—I'm not down with that. Microaggressions and shit. You didn't know the right grammar, and the Latinx thing is new and some people use it, but not me. Who cares? People say shit and some of it is wrong and some of it is racist and it's like, whatever. You can focus there, or you can live your life. IMO."

I nod, even though I don't really know if I agree with the last part of what he said. I mean, with friends is one thing, but I'd be horrified if in school some jock kid came up to me and was like, *So what do gay people think about . . . ?* I'd totally not be okay with that. Even if I didn't say anything, which I probably wouldn't, Kayla, Pam, and I would dissect that micro-aggression for days.

"Yeah, sure," I say, and we unload our prickly pears on the conveyor belt. "Sorry."

He stops and looks at me. "Are you actually apologizing for apologizing for a microaggression?"

"Sorry," I say again, and he grins.

We arrive in this big parking lot where four food trucks—one grilled cheese, one Vietnamese, one burrito, and one hamburger—are already setting up. We take the far end and Max starts working on his marinades, which I guess is a lot of guesswork about proportions of heat to sweet. I get to work on my frozen lemonade. This time I start by cutting up the prickly pear. The first one I just about eviscerate, unaware of what I'm doing. But then I watch a YouTube video and find that if I cut just so, it comes out looking like a cucumber.

I take a taste of the fruit. It's like an earthy watermelon, with hard seeds in it. I pull the seeds out of my mouth and wince. It does not taste very much like red food coloring at all, and I worry that it's not exactly going to augment our world-famous frozen drink.

But when I blend some up with ice, lemon juice, and sugar, it tastes totally refreshing and delicious. I hand Max my cup, he takes a sip, and nods affirmatively.

"Serious business, dude. Nice."

"Thanks, man," I say, and I feel like I'm being a different person and I don't entirely know what's happening to me. Part of me is like, *Bitch, please. When's the last time you called someone "man"? Never. That's when.* Part of me likes it, even if I can't imagine Max or any other "dude" ever hanging out in my bordello bedroom.

When Max has his chicken breasts marinated and ready for the grill and his sauces ready for slathering, and when I have my Vitamix ready for action, we turn to each other and smile.

"Ready?" I ask. It's already so intensely hot in the truck that I cannot imagine how I'm going to withstand four hours of this. And yet I'm ready to try.

"Oh," he says. "One sec."

He goes over to his backpack in the back of the truck, fishes around in it, and takes out a notebook. He brings it over to me.

"So last night. I—you know how you showed me that poem?"

"Yeah," I say, and I look away. My pulse quickens.

"Right. Well, I couldn't stop thinking about it. And you don't know this but I used to draw? So. Um. I drew something."

"Oh," I say, and my whole body goes numb. Of all the things he could have just said to me, this is perhaps the most surprising. Unless he had said, "At nighttime, I turn into a superhero and save the Phoenix suburbs from dragons," his words could not be more unforeseen. And even that, in some ways, would have been less shocking.

His hand shakes as he turns the pages, and I am amazed that he's actually nervous. Why? What in the world would make Max nervous? He has the whole world figured out.

"Here," he says.

The black-and-white drawing, in charcoal and pencil, is of a boy underground. There's a tree and roots heading down and the roots wrap around him, and he has his hands clawed like he's trying to dig up. My chest buzzes and my jaw goes numb. It's beautiful. On top of the earth, another boy lies, looking down, and what's amazing is that the boys are basically lying on each other, with only the thin earth between them.

No. Nothing in the world has ever, ever been more surprising than this. I am lost for words. Just looking at Max's drawing, my whole body goes erect. My eyes, my hair, my nipples, my cock, my toes.

"Oh," I say, adjusting my stance. "Cool."

He pulls the drawing slightly away, like it's a living thing and it is offended by something I've said. What I want to do is cry, actually, but I cannot cry, because that's not what a boy does when Superhero Max shows them a drawing. They say, "That's good," I guess, and not much else, because saying more would be the scariest, most out-there feeling possible, and I don't know if I can do it.

"No," I say, breathing into the deep part of my chest that is twisting and trying to make sure my erect soul does not overstep. "I mean, it's really great, Max. I—I love it."

"Oh," he says, no expression on his face. "Oh. Okay."

"Yeah."

We don't say anything more. I can't breathe. I don't know what he's thinking. I truly, utterly have no idea and couldn't possibly guess. Relief? Why would he care what I think, anyway? That's the biggest mystery of all.

"You're a really talented artist. How can you be talented at so many things?"

"Nah," he says, but his face reddens slightly, and I recognize that actually he does care what I think. Which is crazy with a capital "C."

I am so relieved when he puts the drawing away, because I feel as though I will lose consciousness if I stare at it any longer, if these foreign feelings course through my brain and body for even one second more.

My hand shakes as I write up our menu. Then we open the

awning, and even though it's summer, immediately all the trucks have long lines. Our lemon-sriracha chicken is quickly our biggest seller, and we do a brisk frozen lemonade business too.

"Where's your local source for lemons?" a brash, red-haired woman in a sunflower dress asks. She looks graduate-school age. She's chewing her first bite of lemon-sriracha chicken and she holds her lemonade in her left hand.

I swallow. "I have to protect our sources," I say, a bit jittery.

She screws up her face at me. "It's lemonade. Not journalism," she says, and once she's gone, I glance back at Max and lower my voice.

"Do lemons grow in the summer here?" I whisper back to him.

He shrugs. "I think of all citrus as winter, early spring, maybe?"

"This locally sourced thing is—what do they call it—problematic?"

"Maybe everything but the lemons are locally sourced?"

I turn back to our line and smile. "What can I get you?" I ask a very hippy-dippy-looking older guy in gray sandals and a faded orange tank top.

"Where do you get your chicken?" he asks.

I make sure not to move my eyes from his. Good liars are able to hold eye contact while fibbing. I am able to do it, which may mean that I am a bad person. I'm not sure.

"Kennewick Farms," I say, using the first word that comes to my mind.

"Oh," he says, smiling. "Where is that?"

"Kennewick."

"I'm not familiar with that. Is it near Winkelman? I know Double Tree Ranch pretty well."

"About an hour southeast of there," I say, and then, realizing that an hour southeast of an unknown location could be in New Mexico, I add, "Maybe just a half hour as the crow flies?"

"Huh," he says, and I can't tell if his bullshit meter has just been activated. Possibly. "I'll just try a prickly pear lemonade, I think."

"Sure," I say, and because I am wanting to prove that I am a basically honest person on a basically honest food truck, I come back holding a piece of prickly pear. "You'll love it."

He just stares at me, and I realize what I've just done is that thing where you've just cheated on a quiz, and out of a guilty conscience, you make sure you say something to your teacher as you leave the classroom. Something like, *Man, that Julius Caesar sure was assassinated in 44 BC*, and your teacher nods at you, and you realize you might as well have just said, *Hey, I cheated on the quiz. Here is the one fact I know that is supposed to throw you off scent.*

The next time I have a chance to say something sotto voce to Max, I mumble to him as I brush past. "We're gonna have to go on the lam in a hurry. I'm setting off bullshit meters left and right."

He laughs and puts his mouth close to my ear. "We'll take it as a good sign that you're a shitty liar, I guess."

My ear feels on fire. "Am I?"

"The worst," he says, and I can't help but smile.

The next guy, college age with a blue faux-hawk, wants a habanero-peach chicken breast, without a bun. We don't actually offer buns (it says nothing about bread on the menu), so I nod. It's an easy order to grant.

"Habanero all day," I say, and Max says, "Roger that." We've picked up some good food prep slang from our video watching.

I take the guy's money and try to sell him on a lemonade, but he's not buying. Max says, "Habanero up," turns around, and hands me the paper dish. He stops moving. Freezes up.

"Oh, hey," the guy says, smiling.

Max just stares. "Hey."

"Didn't know you worked a food truck."

Max looks suddenly stoned, which is weird. I've never seen him at a loss for words. "Yep."

"We should hang out again," the guy says. "Kevin, in case you forgot."

"Sure," Max says. "Okay."

I pry the paper dish from Max's clenched hands. I am all agog. Like, what just happened? Former hookup? I realize I don't know almost anything about Max in terms of that.

"Text me," the guy says, Max nods, and the guy walks off, and I'm like, *Huh?* It's a little funny, actually. How could a waif of a skinny dude like that make Max speechless? And then I realize: That guy is about my build. Maybe Max actually likes 'em skinny?

Nah. No way.

A few minutes later, Max glances over to see how big the line is. It is slowing down.

"I need to take a break," he says.

"Can you wait? I don't know how to do the chicken."

He shakes his head. "Break," he says, not looking at me, and I'm like, *What the fuck?*

He jumps off the back of the truck and disappears, and I turn and look at the grill, feeling lost. I've watched him enough that I basically get how long it needs to cook, and how to squirt the water to make the grill sizzle, and how to cover the chicken with the round, silver thing so it cooks in the juice, and how to squirt the sauce on top after and serve the chicken with a slice of tomato and two pickle spears, like a sandwich minus the bread.

As I take orders, grill chicken, blend lemonade, and plate dishes all by myself, for what is probably five minutes but feels much longer, my mind is on Max. Is he going off to find Kevin? Is he making a date? Was he trying to be polite and not do that in front of me? This ugly feeling wraps around my throat and chest. Like I'm the butt of a joke. Like, make sure you don't do it in front of Jordan, because he's a wuss and it'll hurt his feelings and he can't take it.

As I throw away a burned chicken breast, I start to feel furious. Working my ass off while Max works on his secret dating life, which puts him so far ahead of me, so far out of my league, that it isn't even funny.

He comes back wordless, not even a sorry.

"Don't worry," I say. "I held down the fort while you did whatever."

"Thanks," he says, not taking the bait, and once again I'm totally unsure of everything in my life. Who is this guy, Max? What are we? Why did he bother to draw that picture and show it to me, if he doesn't even give a shit about me?

CHAPTER NINETEEN

MAX

I'm handing Jordan a particularly awesome-looking habanero-peach chicken breast when I lose control of my hands and my stomach heaves. Luckily, I'm close enough to the handoff that no one notices. I put my hands behind my back and feel them shake as Kevin recognizes me.

He's all, "We should get together again." What do you say to that? Not if you were the last dude on earth, bro? So I said, "Yeah, sure."

And truthfully I don't really get what the big deal is, or why my stomach heaves, or why I'm being such a pussy, as Dad would say. So my first time sucked ass. Big deal. But my stomach jumps and my body starts its shaking at the hands and I can't wait for Kevin to get the hell out of there. I excuse myself from the truck and Jordan is all helpless and I try to be nice about it but sometimes a dude just needs to warrior up. So I leave, hoping Jordan can figure shit out without me for a few minutes.

I barely make it to the garbage can behind the burrito truck. That's where I hurl. I close my eyes, not wanting to see the contents of my stomach as they are sprayed into the trash. I throw up once, open my eyes, spy a chunk of something green and square that I cannot recognize, and spew again, and once I'm emptied, my head spins and I lean back against a big, shady tree while I catch my breath. Then I cup my hands around my mouth and inhale, and it's nasty. How the hell am I gonna go back to work like nothing just happened?

How the hell can I not? Jordan isn't gonna be able to do everything by himself for too long.

So I walk back, trying to slow my heartbeat. Wondering why the hell I just threw up like some weak-ass dork, not like Super Max at all. I have to be able to control my body. What kind of dude can't even do that?

I climb onto the back of the truck and quickly grab and swig a cold bottle of water before Jordan even notices I'm there. I breathe into my T-shirt and sniff surreptitiously. A little better at least.

"Don't worry," he says. "I held down the fort while you did whatever."

Is there a little attitude in his words? Jesus. I ask Jordan to do one thing ever, and he gives me shade. I decide to pretend I don't hear it, because if I think too much about it, I'm gonna go off on him.

"Thanks," I say, and I pop a piece of Trident gum into my mouth, wash my hands carefully, and get back to grilling chicken. And soon I'm feeling more like myself, and Jordan and I are back to being a team.

I get this idea. At first I'm like, no way. Because like a minute ago I was barfing. But sometimes you just want to get back to normalcy as quickly as possible. So as we start our cleanup, I ask.

"What are you up to later?"

"Why?" Jordan asks, and I laugh. He can be so weird. It's like he never had lessons in social cues. He showed me his poem. I drew him a picture. We have moved past the *We're just coworkers* phase, and truthfully? I like him, okay? I like him.

"I was just thinking. We should go get some fresh prickly pear."

"Huh?"

"We say locally sourced. It's all working. Let's actually pick some prickly pear and use it in the lemonade."

He sighs dramatically. "Can't we just continue to lie?"

"I guess," I say, crossing my arms. "But. Um."

He stops cleaning out the blender and looks at me. "What?"

"Are you really going to make me say it?"

"Say what?"

And I realize: He actually doesn't get social cues. Like, at all. We were getting along so well, and all day I was thinking how it would be fun to actually do something, like not on the truck. And he has no idea. Wow.

"I like hanging with you," I say. "Okay?"

He drops the sponge he's been holding in his left hand. "Oh."

"Do you want to do something? Like prickly pear hunting?"

"Oh. Um. Yeah. Sure." He swallows a smile, and then, on the way down, he finds he can't hold it in. I feel myself blushing because Jordan is so. Damn. Sexy. And totally oblivious about that fact.

He drops me off at home so I can shower, and around four I pick him up in my Durango. He climbs in smelling of soap and sweat, and he juts his face in front of the air-conditioning vents, which are on full blast. My dashboard thermometer says 121 degrees.

"Jesus," he says, and I accelerate down Curry.

"Too hot for ya?" I ask, and he snorts.

"I refuse to have conversations about heat or humidity," he says.

"So we just ignore weather from here on in?"

"Let's just say, 'That's a lot of pasta.' That will be our stand-in for any and all weather-related discussions."

"You're weird."

"You're just figuring that out?" He points out the window. "Slow down."

I slow a bit. "Why?"

He points again. "Prickly pears, silly."

I keep driving slowly, trying to figure out what it is that Jordan is thinking. That we'll go in people's yards and pick fruit? First off, not many houses have them. We pass many lots with tall saguaro plants towering over ranch houses, some at precarious angles, like a strong wind could blow it crashing onto the roof. Fewer yards seem to have the small cacti that we're looking for. Second, that's just. No.

"Stop!" Jordan says, and I tentatively pull over next to a pink tract house with a dirt yard filled with various cacti.

I stop the car and look over at Jordan. "You are aware that you're not supposed to, um, trespass, right? Like going onto someone's property is not allowed?"

He shrugs. "Do you think they're really going to miss a few green bulbs?"

I stare at him for a bit and finally shake my head and put the car in drive.

"What? Why?"

"Jordan. Dude. You ever have someone pull a gun on you for trespassing?"

"No. Have you?" He crosses his arms in front of his chest and pouts a bit.

"No, but also I don't want to. Folks are crazy. You never know who has a gun and who is all, 'Get off my lawn or I'll blow your head off.'"

"Fine," Jordan says. "But just know that you're being ridiculous. It's cactus. We would be relieving them of little green bulb-y fruits from cactus plants. We're not stealing hubcaps. Jesus."

I don't respond. Unspoken in this argument is the fact that when your skin is brown and you live in the suburbs of Arizona, you don't stroll onto some stranger's property to pick prickly pears. Maybe if you have white skin you can. But I don't want to discuss that. Instead, I turn up the radio. Daft Punk comes on. Jordan sighs dramatically and turns the tuner knob.

"Are you really messing with my radio?"

"Are you really defending Daft Punk? They don't even have faces, Max. They are faceless musicians. Unacceptable."

I don't know how to argue with that sort of twisted logic, so I let it go. I turn west on Elliot and head toward South Mountain. I think about Betts and Zay-Rod. Right now I could be relaxing with them in Betts's living room, sipping a Pepsi and eating some Poore Brothers jalapeño potato chips. Instead I have this enigma of a new friend whose very presence makes me both inexplicably excited and nervous, who doesn't approve of faceless musicians. Who puts on some weird '80s shit, that '70s, '80s, and '90s channel that old people listen to like my mom.

"So who was that Kevin guy?" Jordan asks, and my stomach drops. I don't respond.

"No answer," he says.

"It's private," I say.

"He your boyfriend?"

"I don't have a boyfriend."

"Someone you hooked up with?"

I punch the steering wheel, and the horn wheezes slightly from the impact. "Jesus. None of your business. Stop asking."

"Okay then," Jordan says. "Sorry."

We get quiet again, and again I'm thinking it was a mistake to make this plan. It's like I only like part of Jordan. The fun part. The part that doesn't ask a million personal questions like we're on some talk show. I don't want to talk about that. How is that not clear to him?

We don't say a word to each other until we park on Desert Willow Drive in Ahwatukee. There's an opening in the fence that leads to a path through the desert that, if you take it all the way, leads to South Mountain. I turn off the ignition and we hop out into the unforgiving heat of the hottest part of the afternoon.

"Sweet gay Jesus," he says. "What was I thinking?"

I laugh. "I like it."

"You like a hundred and twenty with no shade?"

I shrug. Anything over 114 and it's a bit like your skin sizzles. To me, it makes me feel alive, like the Arizona sun feeds my bloodstream and makes me invincible. It's not that it doesn't sap me; it's just that if I can take this, nothing can stop me.

"Think of it as a challenge," I say as the relentless heat chills my body.

"Huh," Jordan says as we pass through the fence and step onto the desert sand. "What do you mean, a challenge?"

The air actually sears your lungs when it's like this. It's

thrilling. "Before refrigeration most people just didn't settle here. The white men back in the pioneer days? They didn't stop. Went right on to California as if this was uninhabitable. So if I can thrive in it? Then nothing can stop me. Makes me feel powerful."

"Huh," he says again, and suddenly as we walk he flexes his biceps. I glance over, unsure if he's serious or not. He's not laughing, and I'm like, *All right. There ya go.*

"I can do this," he says.

I pull off my shirt and flex. "Yes you can. We can totally do this."

He stops walking and turns toward me. He takes off his shirt, and suddenly we are both bare-chested. There's something kinda hot, kinda primal about his coat hanger shoulders and flat chest. I can't explain it; I just like it. I avert my eyes but smile, so he knows I'm with him. He smiles back. He takes a few deep breaths and I breathe with him, like we are in the midst of a workout, almost.

"All right," he says, spotting a patch of cacti about twenty feet ahead. "Prickly pear ho!"

I laugh. The air scalds the inside of my nose. "Prickly pear ho," I say. "Sounds like a really unpopular prostitute."

He giggles. "You're actually funny," he says.

"Thanks, I think?"

It turns out we need the T-shirts for our hands, because we didn't bring gloves and the green prickly pear plums grow right on the cacti, often right next to needles. I jab myself trying to grab a piece of fruit, and a dot of blood pearls on my left forefinger.

"Ouch," I say.

Jordan uses his shirt-covered hand to steady a cactus leaf, and I slowly, carefully grab a green plum and crack it off.

"One," Jordan says, and he bends over, already winded. Even though it's a dry heat, my eyelids start to feel wet. "Shit. That's a lot of pasta."

I lead us to a cactus plant that has multiple bulbs on it, and now our biggest issue is that we have nowhere to put the prickly pears. Jordan makes a bowl out of his shirt, and I start to pile them in there. Soon we have ten, and we're walking farther from the car in silence, the desert totally abandoned. We're like two ancient foragers; I kinda love it.

We strip another cactus of fruit, and I'm loading up his shirt bucket, and I'm watching as Jordan's face gets red. Then redder. I laugh a bit, because it's all a bit extreme and dramatic. I mean, yes, it is seriously hot out here; I can't take the convection-like heat too deep into my lungs. But we've only been out for about ten minutes, and we've been walking slowly. But as I head toward a big brush of green cactus covered in green and purple bulbs, Jordan stops walking and bends over, putting his hands on his knees.

"I can't . . ." he says.

"Okay," I say. "We can go back."

"No," he says, and his breathing is rapid, like way too much for the situation. "I can't. Get back to the car. I can't do it. I can't. I can't."

He squeezes his eyes shut and sweat pours down his forehead, and I mutter "Shit" under my breath.

"I'm so stupid. I shouldn't. I'm not like you. I can't . . ."

"Okay," I say. "Okay." I put my arm around him and let

him lean on me. We are maybe five minutes from the car, and I realize that I should have been more thoughtful. I could do this all day, but Jordan is obviously different. It didn't really occur to me. With Betts and Zay-Rod, we're competitive with each other. Even if they got tired, which they wouldn't this quick, they'd never show it because it would be seen as weakness. But Jordan is leaning hard, and his legs feel like they're trembling, and suddenly I'm not sure what I'm supposed to do.

"Let me sit," he says, and he's definitely hyperventilating, which is making this worse. If he'd stop taking in so much oxygen, I'm pretty sure he'd be fine.

"Where?" I ask. Below us the ground is pebbly and covered in cactus detritus. Doesn't look like a place you'd want to sit. He starts to sit and I grab his midsection. "Come on," I say.

He looks at me. I give him the most empathetic look I can, given that my inner thighs feel like they're burning from the heat. First I grab his shirt basket. He doesn't resist. Then I turn from him and lean over. "Jump on," I say.

"What? No," he says. I'm too tired to argue, so I just stay in position, and he takes a deep breath, slings his skinny arms over my shoulders, jumps up, and wraps his feet around my calves.

I laugh a little as I adjust to the weight. "Didn't take much to convince you, I noticed."

His breathing has slowed and I feel like I can hear the smile in his voice. "Desperate times," he says. I can feel his breath on the top of my head, and it's a weird sensation because it's actually way cooler than the temperature.

My soaked quads start to quiver when we're about a hundred feet from the car. I step through the opening in the fence, and I decide that I'd rather really work for twenty seconds than labor just a bit for a minute. So I take off.

"Whoa!" he says as I sprint toward the car. "Careful. I break easily."

I keep running, half enjoying the burn and half wishing Jordan weren't such a wimp.

We get to the car, I unload him, open the car door, set the prickly pears in the back, start up the motor, and put the AC on full blast. The seats scald our legs, and even touching the black rubber steering wheel makes me pull my hand back.

"You know, some people have those window shades for their cars, so that it doesn't feel like sitting on the surface of the sun when you get in."

I give him my deadliest look, which he catches right away. "Jeez," he says. "Sorry. Man. That's a fuckin' lot of pasta."

We drive in silence for a bit. I'm thinking about how Jordan sounded when he was hyperventilating. That whole "I can't I can't" thing.

You know who he sounded like?

His mom. That first day.

And that's something I'd never say to him. Ever.

CHAPTER TWENTY

JORDAN

It's awkward in the car after Max saves my life.

There's no water, and I need water. But what super sucks is that getting water means stopping at a Circle K or something, and honestly I'm not getting out of the car again. I hate to ask him, but I kind of want him to get out and get me a drink. Or better yet, I want him to like pull into a garage, pick me up, and deposit me on a couch and turn up the AC until we're freezing.

Which is a lot to ask of someone who just saved your life.

Seriously. I'm pretty sure he did, because there's a reason the population was much smaller here before air-conditioning, as he explained. The land is uninhabitable, and today is particularly awful — 124, Max's dashboard temperature reads now — and there's simply no shade in the desert. Also it's still just about the hottest time of the day. No wonder we were all alone out there. Terrible, terrible idea, Max had. I'm a little pissed at him for bringing me out there. Next time he asks if I want to hang out, I'm going to insist on an indoor, chilled, and well-ventilated activity for sure.

The silence has a tone to it. Is he mad at me? Embarrassed for me that he had to carry me? Well join the club. And then I realize that I didn't even thank him for carrying me, and my throat catches. I don't know. Sometimes I wonder about me.

"Thanks, by the way."

He doesn't answer right away, and my brain does what my brain always does — makes up a story about what he's thinking.

Jordan is a pussy boy. I can't believe I even wanted to hang with him in the first place. Get him and his useless ass out of my truck.

"Don't mention it," he says, and I recline and close my eyes. My throat is totally parched, like sandpaper.

"No really, thanks. I'm aware I'm the worst."

"Seriously, dude?"

"What?"

He sighs. "Never mind."

I crease my forehead. I hate when people do that. Edit themselves because they think I can't handle something. "No. Tell me."

He shrugs. "You sound just like your mom sometimes. She says she's the worst too."

I laugh and fold my arms over my chest. How come I always forget? When someone says never mind, you should always believe them. I'm so stupid.

"Well there ya go. I'm not perfect. I get that you are, but I'm an actual flawed human being. Thanks for the important life lesson."

"Dude," he says.

I turn toward the window and take in the mostly empty strip malls. "You can just drop me off at home," I say. "Thanks for everything, but I think I'm gonna chill in the relative comfort of my bedroom, with the air on blast."

He doesn't respond. He's heading east on Elliot, and he doesn't say anything, so I assume that's what's happening. Aborted hang-out on account of pussy boy. I can hardly blame him. I'm fucked up, and on top of that, I'm overly dramatic. I suck.

The truck passes I-10 and then Priest, and then he gets in the median lane and pulls into a Sonic Drive-In. I used to love Sonic. Worst hamburgers ever, but where else can you get a blue coconut slush with candy bits mixed in? Nerds, they use. How ingenious is that? I wonder if we should add that to our menu, or if we'd get sued if we did.

"Drinks on me," I say, my throat scratchy.

"Okay," Max says, and I wonder two things: One is if this is how real boys make up after a little argument. If it is, I'm truly okay with it. Two is if this is his way of letting me make it up to him. The whole life-saving episode. Fine with me.

"Whataya like?" I ask.

"We're doing a lemonade flight."

"A wha?"

"You never had a bacon flight?"

"A what?"

"Dude," he says. "My mom took me to this awesome place called the Oink Café. South Tempe. They do this bacon flight where you sample, like, all eight kinds of bacon. Jalapeño. Apple cider, maple."

"Do they include a defibrillator?"

He rolls his eyes and smiles a little. "God. Could you be any more like a cranky eighty-year-old? Here. Repeat after me: 'Get off my lawn.'"

I laugh and my shoulders loosen up a bit. I imitate the grandfather from *The Simpsons*. "Get off my lawn."

Max smiles. "Perfect. So are you in? Frozen lemonade flight? We'll go from Sonic to Sonic, trying out all their lemonade concoctions to see if any of them are as good as ours."

I can't help but smile back. Yes. This is totally something I would do with Kayla and Pam.

"Sure," I say.

He presses the red button and almost immediately, a girl's voice asks us how she can help us.

We peruse the lengthy drink menu. They have lemonades and limeades, frozen and not, and there's a list of about twenty flavors you can mix in to them. Some of them make sense, like peach or strawberry. My mind immediately goes to the ones that don't make sense. As thirsty as I am, I can't resist.

"Large frozen banana lemonade," I say.

Max gives me a horrified look. "Okay," he says.

"Oh come on. There has to be a part of you that wants to find the weirdest mix."

"Nope," he says. "Atomic lemon lemonade, large, frozen," he says into the microphone.

"Boring."

"Smart," he responds.

The cost appears on the screen, and I mock groan. Then I put on my best Grandpa Simpson voice again. "Six fifty? When I was a kid, two lemonades cost five fifty."

This cracks Max up. "Oh my God," he says. "You're like the world's most boring old dude."

I say, "I'm Stan, the Somewhat Uninteresting Curmudgeon."

This earns me an actual cackle from Max, which surprises

me. I always worry that the weird shit I think will be too much for him, but sometimes it really isn't.

He says, "You kids, get off my lawn! You can stand there later, when it's dry."

I counter with, "When I was a kid, I walked three blocks to school, in reasonably comfortable shoes."

Our drinks arrive, and I immediately find out that there's a reason people don't do banana lemonade. I happen to love banana flavor, especially in Laffy Taffy. But it goes with lemon sort of like cantaloupe goes with chocolate. Yep, tried that one before. Never again. The sweet of the banana hits the sour of the lemon and it sort of trips over it, muddles it, makes it nearly undrinkable. Still, I am so thirsty I'd drink a banana lemonade. So I do. But not without making an exaggerated face while I do.

Max laughs. "Delicious, huh?"

"The best," I say, taking another slurp.

Max takes a huge, loud sip and then returns to his Grandpa Simpson impersonation. "You kids don't know the value of a hard day's work. The value can be determined by calculating the salary, plus benefits. Ow! Jesus! Brain freeze!"

He hides his head under his arms, as if the brain freeze won't be able to find him down there.

"Press your tongue to the top of your mouth, hard," I say.

"That's an old wives'—oh! Wow. Okay. Life hack by Jordan."

"Stick with me, kid. I am a Somewhat Uninteresting Curmudgeon in training."

Max smiles at me and takes another sip through his straw. I

meet his eye contact and take a similar sip, and then cringe when the banana syrup hits my taste buds. "God does that suck."

I decide to abort the banana lemonade halfway through, and Max pulls the car out of the spot we're in, and then directly into the next spot. I laugh, surprised. I like silly Max.

I order a frozen cherry limeade, which Max at first says does not count on our lemonade flight. But I explain that limeade is lemonade's weird, ugly kid cousin, and we laugh about what it's like when limeade comes over and wants to play *Kabuki Warriors* on Xbox, which I surmise from the way Max says it was an old, shitty game. I pretend I have any idea about these things, and suddenly we are off to the next Sonic, the one a mile from me on Dobson, for more drinks.

I've never really believed in the whole jacked-up-on-sugar thing. Until drinks four and five. We order some cheese sticks to soak up some of the extra sugar, and as the sun sets, we are literally buzzing and coming up with the worst possible food truck ideas.

"Fruit salad," Max says.

"Ew. Yes. Something about cutting up fruit on a hot truck. Agreed. What about a fondue truck?"

He laughs. "So we just give 'em like a big vat of cheese?"

"And a bucket of cauliflower to dip in it. That wouldn't be cumbersome at all."

"Cumbersome," he says. "You are the anti-Betts."

"I don't know what that means."

He takes a huge slurp of his grape limeade. "Betts. Him and Zay-Rod. They're my boys."

"Do they know you're gay?"

He nods.

"You said you play baseball, right?"

He nods again.

"How does that work?"

He rolls his eyes. "Well, there's this ball, and you pitch it . . ."

"Fuck you. I know how baseball works. That's the one with the basket?"

He laughs. "Yes. That's exactly right."

"I mean how does it work, being gay on the baseball team?"

He shrugs. "I haven't told them, other than my boys. I just think, I don't know. It's none of their business."

I laugh. "It's interesting how that works. When it's someone who won't take it well, suddenly it's none of their business."

Max doesn't say anything and I realize I just said an asshole-ish thing. So I say, "I just mean. No, I get it. There are definitely people I don't talk about it in front of. Most people, really. Pam and Kayla are basically my world. Or they were. Until."

Max smirks, and I redden. It's a little much to put on him, given that we're basically hanging out not on a food truck for the first time. But the truth is this is the first time I've ever hung out with a guy alone. Sometimes Kayla would bring this guy Matt Story with her to the mall, but this is way, way different. And that's something Max does not need to know.

"I'd like to meet them," he says, and the worst ever idea comes to me. And before I can allow myself to get all scared, which would basically be a normal reaction in this situation, I pull out my phone and text Kayla.

Me: You wanna meet Max?

Kayla: Who?

Me: The dude bro. From the food truck?

Kayla: Um. Ok?

Me: Yay. Pam there?

Kayla: Yep

"Drive," I say, and Max looks at me like, what?

I laugh. I am literally high from sugar. "Sorry. Poor communication. Want to meet Pam and Kayla, like right now? They can't wait to meet you."

He shrugs, clearly more comfortable meeting people than I am. Because if he suddenly decided I had to meet these Betts and Zay-Rod bros, I would be like, *Oh, I'm busy that day.*

"You're kinda awesome, aren't you?" I ask.

"Fuck you," he says, as if I'm insulting him. And in some ways I am. It's like I'm commenting on the obvious: That he's special and he knows it. But also I'm serious. Because he carried me to his car when I got overheated. And he ignored it when I got all dramatic when he said I was like my mom, and that was the perfect thing to do. And he pulled into Sonic and suggested a lemonade flight, which is pretty much the best idea ever.

And now he pulls out and we head to Kayla's, and I put aside every fear I have about the oncoming train wreck.

CHAPTER TWENTY-ONE

MAX

It's the kind of night where time is suspended. We must have spent six days in my truck, drinking more frozen lemonade than any two people have ever drunk in one sitting. And I don't mean like time moved slowly, like I was bored and couldn't wait to get the hell out of there, like one of those epic dinners at Uncle Guillermo's. It was more like time ceased to exist, and the jokes kept coming, the laughter, and I kept thinking, *I have to remember that one*, and then I'd be three jokes later and thinking, *What was that thing we were laughing about like an hour ago?*

I have to think that's special. When time stops, or you forget about the next thing, and when Jordan suggested introducing me to his girlfriends, I said, "Yeah. Sure."

Kayla's place is in one of those county island subdivisions down south of Elliot where lots of people have horses. Mom told me once that the huge properties down there are that way because of a law made years ago that prohibited the properties from being subdivided smaller than one acre or something like that. As we pull up, I can see that she has one of those backyards that could hold a football field, and I immediately imagine playing touch football back there with a whole bunch of people. That would be sweet.

But anyway. Kayla's folks must have big bucks.

As it turns out, I recognize Kayla and Pam for sure. Kayla is white and blond and kinda cheerleader-y, wearing tight orange shorts and a white tank top as she invites us in with a "What up bitch?" Pam is slightly darker than me, with huge boobs and a smile that would stop traffic. Betts and Zay-Rod would definitely approve, and I wonder what it would be like to do a group hang, all six of us.

Really weird, I figure out very quickly.

"So what are your intentions with our husband," Kayla says, and Jordan socks her in the shoulder, hard. She retaliates, harder, right into his chest, and he just about falls to the ground. He rubs his chest as if she might have actually broken a rib, which clearly she hasn't.

I laugh. "Intentions?"

"Yeah," Pam says. "He's gay. You're gay. We all know you guys can't keep it in your pants. I mean, Jordan can, I guess, because he's still a virgin. He almost kissed this one boy—"

This time Jordan smacks Pam, and when she steps to him, I intercede, because I am actually a little concerned about what a wallop from Pam could do to Stick Boy, if Kayla's love tap nearly knocked him over. Pam has her some biceps.

"What's with the violence, dude?" I ask.

"We are a violent people," Kayla says. "In case your intentions are bad. Just know that."

"The more you know," I say.

Pam glances over at Kayla, and the two share a look. She looks back at me, smiles, and comes over and hugs me. "I like Max. I approve."

They start saying stuff about '80s bands that I don't understand because I don't know who the Thompson Twins are, or Missing Persons, and when I say as much, Kayla gives me this incredulous look.

"Dale Bozzio? Like the original Lady Gaga?"

I shrug. Not ringing a bell.

"What do you listen to?"

I shrug again. "Whatever's on. Machine Gun Kelly. Train. Imagine Dragons."

Jordan puts his head in his hands and shakes it vociferously. "No, no, no," he says. "No self-respecting gay guy listens to that shit. That's like dude bro shit."

Pam says, "No self-respecting Mexican has ever listened to Imagine Dragons. Ever."

"Um, okay," I say, unimpressed with their logic or their classifications. I listen to what I like. Whatever the hell I want.

"What has killed more people? Trains or Train?" Jordan says, and Pam and Kayla laugh, and then Jordan puts his hand on my shoulder and says, "We're just funnin'."

I raise an eyebrow. "Yeah. I've met you. I get it. The kids and their sarcasm and all that."

Jordan gets mock stern and points at me. "You kids and your sarcasm. When I was your age, we were sarcastic sometimes, and other times we were serious."

I laugh. "When I was a child, we walked three blocks to school," I say.

"We used that one already," Jordan says, and he turns to Kayla and Pam and says, "We're working on a character. Stan the Somewhat Uninteresting Codger."

"Curmudgeon," I correct.

I glance over, curious to see Pam and Kayla's reaction. It's a mutual eye roll. Which makes me feel a little more at home. Betts and Zay-Rod? They wouldn't even know how to react to that shit.

"So what are we gonna do?" Pam says. "So bored. Summer sucks so hard."

Kayla's eyes light up and she shouts, "Dream throwing!"

This apparently means something to them, because Jordan shrieks, "Yes!" He runs upstairs like he actually lives there, sort of like I'd do at Betts's place. Pam and Kayla sprint up after him, so I follow along.

When I get to Kayla's extremely girly-girl room upstairs, Jordan is already sprawled out on her pink-sheeted bed like it's his own, and the girls are on the floor, tearing pieces of loose-leaf paper in half. Kayla grabs a coffee mug that reads *You're the Lorelai to my Rory* from her desk and pulls out four colorful pens. She tosses one to Jordan, and then, when she sees me at the door, hurls a green one at me. It comes straight for my eyes, and I catch it.

"Wooh!" she says. "Athlete?"

"Yup," I say back.

Pam gives me a side-eye. "Gay, hot, athletic. What's the catch?" she says to Jordan.

"Dude bro," he says, and they laugh.

"Hey," I say. "I'm right here."

"Broseph," Pam says, mocking, and just like that I decide they are basically Betts and Zay-Rod but female. We trash-talk and don't mean it. If Jordan likes them, they gotta be okay. And if they're making fun of me, that has to mean they like me.

"Wassup, bro," I say. "So I was kickin' it with this ho and she straight up shot me down, yo. She was all, 'Enough with the brobalization. I seen enough of you people, yo.'"

Pam laughs. "Serious, yo. That shit is sick!"

I say, "Straight up. What's the haps?"

"What up, dog?" Kayla says.

"Oh my God," Jordan says. "Is that really how you talk to your friends?"

"Naw. We just stick the word 'bro' in every sentence, and say 'gnarly' and 'no way, dude' and 'for serious though' and 'bam.' Like every other word. Bam."

"And you wear a hat backward, right, like always?" Kayla asks.

"Dude," I say. "We are total stereotypes, dude."

Jordan says, "You don't gots to be Sherlock Bromes to figure that shit out."

"Jordan in the hay-ouse!" Pam says. "Bam!"

I laugh despite myself. "I think this is on the verge of being offensive."

"No way, dude," Pam says. "For real though. I want in on your bromance. I about had it with these two. Too much estrogen, bro."

I laugh. "You're in. We're like dude bros with a heart of gold. Are we done making fun of me now? Can we move on to Jordan, who definitely deserves this more than I do?"

He gives me a mock shocked look and then sticks his tongue out at me, and I admit I get kinda flushed in the face.

"Can a dude bro even be gay?" Kayla asks. "I kinda think of dude bros as macking on the ladies."

"Um," I say. "Apparently. 'Cause I'm all about the dudes, bro."

"And your friends are cool?" Pam asks. "With you being a bromosexual and all?"

I shrug. "They're my boys. We cuddle. They're not too worried about it."

"I think I love them. Who are they? Do I know them?"

"You know Xavier Rodriguez?"

She shrugs. "What's he look like?"

"Shaved head. Tall. Kinda light-skinned. Does slam poetry?"

She shakes her head. "Cute?"

"He's my boy. So, no. But yeah, I guess. The ladies dig him."

Kayla sticks her finger down her throat. "Yeah. Not seeking a dude bro. A straight one, anyway."

Jordan says, "Well I'm kinda dude bro hooked now. This one carried me out of the desert when I was basically dying of heat prostration today. True story."

Pam crosses her arms across her chest and looks at me. "Was our boy getting all dramatic again? He does that."

Jordan gives her the finger.

"Maybe a little," I say. "I don't think he was actually dying, but yeah. Carried him."

"Oh my God," Kayla says. "I'm embarrassed for you, sweetie."

Now she is the recipient of a middle finger from Jordan.

I look at the pen Kayla hurled at me. "So what do we need the pens for?" I ask.

"We're going to throw dreams. We put our dreams on the paper, and we put them in balloons, and we send them out the window to wherever they are needed," Kayla says.

I cannot imagine any situation in which Betts would be a

party to throwing dreams. Even Zay-Rod, slam poet that he is, seems like a poor candidate for dream throwing. But I don't want to not be a part of it, so I hide my fear and discomfort and say, "Sure."

I look at Pam. I can't help it. I don't know her, but I subconsciously look at her for backup, because even though I hate it when people label stuff in this way, it truly does sound like some white shit.

Pam doesn't seem to share this opinion. She is looking up and down my body. "You are so not about this."

I shrug.

"It's okay," she says. "We just. You don't have to, is all I'm saying."

"No. I want to," I say, and she gives me a hardcover book called *Don't Let Me Go*, hands me some scraps of paper she's torn up, and throws another ballpoint pen — this one pink — at my chest. I catch it.

"It can be anything," Kayla continues. "You can write a dream you have for the world, or a love poem. Something that will make the world a better place."

I tentatively sit on the floor near the door and stare at a blank piece of paper that Pam has put in front of me. A love poem? What the fuck do I know about love? Jordan writes poetry. I draw, I guess. So I start to draw. With two pens — one green, one pink — I don't have much, so I start drawing a landscape. A sun setting over the ocean. I create waves, peaceful, and a palm tree forms, and I make a story in my head in case they ask what my dream is. A perfect day with a loved one. A boyfriend. Cracking jokes and having adventures and chilling out. And a lump grows in my throat because maybe he's not a boyfriend, but today. Today was like my dream day. And I realize: It is a dream. I have created a dream to throw.

"This has to be so weird for you," Jordan says, looking over at me from the bed.

"No," I say. "It's cool." And it is cool. I mean, it's just not what I'm used to. I smile at Jordan and his look over at me lingers a second, like he's trying to figure out if I'm really okay with this or not.

"I hope I still have balloons," Kayla says, standing up and going to her closet.

"Otherwise you can use condoms," Pam says. "God knows you have enough unused ones."

"Wait. Are you prude-shaming me?" Kayla says, and Pam cracks up. "We actually are going to have to use condoms, because, yeah. I didn't replenish my balloon supply since last time." She riffles through her bedside table drawer, and then she throws condoms at all of us. One lands right next to my knee. It says *Project Hard Hat* and the foil packet is yellow.

Jordan tears into his blue packet and pulls out a blue condom. Watching his delicate fingers unroll it is about the sexiest thing I've ever seen and I can't look away. Then he starts to blow into it like a balloon. It inflates a little, and he holds the air in for a moment before allowing it to pour out like a fart.

"Throwing dreams in a condom seems a little on the nose to me," Jordan says. "Since me getting laid is a dream that will never come true."

My face gets all hot. I don't even look up to see if anyone's looking at me. I can't.

"I've missed this so much," Pam deadpans. "You talking about how hopeless you are."

She jumps up and gets on the bed with Jordan. She turns him toward the wall and spoons him, and this nice warmth passes through my chest, watching someone give Jordan affection.

"You are not hopeless," Pam says softly to him. "You dress horribly and you need a makeover and maybe a new hairstyle, and your personality is . . . not ideal . . . but, I mean, you're hygienic, I guess. So you have that going for you."

That makes me laugh, and Kayla comes and sits next to me. "I think I like you," she says.

I'm imagining spooning Jordan. Feeling the warmth of his thin legs against mine. My stomach against his lower back. I'm dizzy thinking about it.

"Um. I think I like you too," I say to Kayla, and she leans her head against my shoulder and I keep my eyes trained on the bed, imagining changing places with Pam.

CHAPTER TWENTY-TWO

JORDAN

"You take me to all the best places," I say, trying to shout over the thump-y music at Lo-Lo's Chicken and Waffles in Scottsdale.

Max doesn't even look up. He just keeps wolfing down his fried chicken thigh. He has crumbs all over his face. "They have damn good chicken," he says, still chewing. It sounds like, *Thev am gud icken.*

"Apparently. Though I might have preferred Gloria's Salmon and Donuts. Or maybe Fi-Fi's Steak and Biscuits."

He groans and pulls a chunk of meat off the side of the thigh and stuffs it in his mouth. "Some of your jokes are cheesy as fuck," he says.

Other than a quick shower at home, I have now been with Max for fifteen straight hours. I'm not even tired, to tell the truth. It feels a little like the world has stopped. Like our housing problem doesn't exist. Like tomorrow doesn't matter. I kinda love it. Especially right now, as I watch him massacre a piece of fried chicken like the dude he is. Especially after I introduced him to my wives, and we threw dreams in a condom out the window.

Especially after the text I just got.

Kayla: OMG he likes you! Totes adorbs

Pam: Totally. You need to jump on that now.

Kayla: If you don't, I will transition and jump on that. That boy is yummy!

Pam: He's out of your league, K

Kayla: Fuck you bitch

Finally I interject.

Me: Wives. You are interrupting my date

Me: OMG OMG am I on a date?!?!?!?

Me: I am drunk on Max

Me: He could NOT like me. Right?

Me: Right?

Kayla: He's yours, baby. Just stop making weird jokes about codgers or whatever. I think he's pretending cause that shit is so not funny at all

I respond with a meme of this angry-looking woman giving the viewer the finger, and I put away my phone and turn off the volume. Max is forking up some sweet corn that is drowning in butter. "How come I think that's about me?"

I roll my eyes. "Oh my God you are so full of yourself."

He gives me a charity Guy Smiley smile, and then he speaks while chewing. "You gonna touch your food?"

The truth is I'm afraid to. I'm afraid I'll look like, well, him. Which is funny because I totally don't care that he looks like a chicken predator, like some sort of feral wolf who has just made a kill. I just don't think it would be such a good look on me.

"Eat something. You'll blow away," he says, taking a sip of his purple Kool-Aid. I have a blue one. This must be about the fifth sugary drink we've had today. I freakin' adore today. I take a sip and imagine how stupid my tongue and lips must look. Purple looks good on Max.

"I prefer to drink my meals," I say.

He cracks up. "We're definitely on a sugar binge. Sugar is our crack."

I pretend to be high off my ass, swaying incoherently back and forth. My elbow knocks into my blue Kool-Aid and almost spills it. Max cracks up again.

"You're like, getting high to forget your pains."

"Hell yeah I am," I say.

"What ails you?"

"Well, I guess the whole I'm-about-to-be-homeless thing, maybe?"

He nods his head. "That makes sense. Though we're doing pretty good, aren't we?"

"I guess so," I say. "What ails you?"

He shrugs. "Nothing. I just like sugar. And fried."

I laugh, and he puts an entire fried chicken leg into his mouth. It comes back out a mere bone, stripped of crust and meat. I look down at my plate. There's a breast, a wing, and a waffle underneath. I tried to order a chicken tenders basket, but Max immediately looked at the waitress, shook his head, and said, "Sheeda's Special." I was like, *Huh?* But he sent the waitress off and promised me.

"Chicken on the bone," he said. "It's more tender. More delicious."

I've actually never eaten chicken on the bone. I like the tenders, because I can pretend that the meat comes from a lab or something. The bones are a little primeval for my taste.

I stare down at what used to be the wing and breast of an actual bird, take a deep breath, and pick up my knife and fork. Max literally reaches across the table and knocks the knife out of my hand.

"Whoa," I say. "That could have fallen on my leg and chopped it in half."

"It's a butter knife, dude," he says. "Pick it up with your hands."

I screw up my face at him. This feels wrong. I just want to slice off a piece. "Can't I—"

"Pick it up with your hands," he repeats. "Trust me."

I've done a lot of new things today. Introduce a boy to my wives, go out into the desert when it's a hundred and twenty to hunt prickly pears, operate a grill by myself. All in all, it's been the best day of my life. I take a deep breath. I pick up the breast, bring it to eye level, and smell it. Man, does it smell good. The crust is golden brown, flaky. I bite down. My teeth break through the crust and into the flesh, which is hot and juicy, and immediately the juice sprays my upper gums and then down onto my tongue.

"Oh my God," I say, even though my mouth is full.

Max beams at me. "Right?"

As I chew, the warm liquid—is it frying oil? Is it chicken juice? Why don't I care?—fills my entire mouth. "Food of the gods!" I exclaim, chewing.

"Yes."

I pause to enjoy the experience, and once I swallow, I say, "How did I not know about this? That chicken fingers are, like, starter chicken. Is it a different animal?"

He cracks up. "Better on the bone," he repeats, and some-thing about the way he says it is so freakin' sexy, and first I avert my eyes. And then I sneak a peek back at him, and his eyes are staring right into mine. My heart pulses and my cheeks heat up. I hold his gaze. It is the visual equivalent of a mouth full of perfect, fried, on-the-bone chicken.

"So now we do something you want to do," Max says, and I laugh, because, like, what do I like to do? This, obviously. But before Max, all I tended to do was stuff with my wives, and a lot of that was mall-related. Plus it's eleven at night, and I should be home by now. If I had a mother who noticed things, I should have been home hours ago.

Fuck it. I don't want the best day ever to end, so I rack my mind for any semblance of a fun idea. It makes me think of hoo-ligan do-gooders. Which, when I tried to explain it to Pam the first time, she said, and I quote, "Flat-out no."

Can I convince Max? Is it possible if I tell him this will be the thing that puts him over the edge and makes him vow never to hang out with me again?

That sort of thinking has not been useful today, on this best of all days. So I just tell him.

"I've always wanted to be a hooligan do-gooder."

"A wha?"

I swallow. "Hooligan do-gooder. We combine the chaotic energy of hooligan culture with do-goodery — acts of kindness. We see what is wrong with the world and we aim to make it better. Through hooliganism."

Max is smiling that wide smile again, and he's shaking his head.

"Okay then," he says as the waitress comes over and asks if

we want yet more sugar water. We definitely do, so she takes our glasses.

"You're going to leave me here," I say.

He laughs, and there's something about his laugh that makes me laugh too.

"If I left you here, who the hell would translate into normal and understandable what the hell a hooligan whatever is?"

I take another bite of chicken and try to formulate this somewhat amorphous idea from last year and put it into understandable words.

"Hooligan do-gooder," I say. "So what if, instead of stealing pets from people, which would be actual hooliganism, we stole lonely people and gave them to pets? Maybe not steal, but like if we found a lonely person, we could do a home invasion, kidnap them, and drive them to the local shelter? They'd be afraid for their lives, sure, but then we'd take off the blindfold and they'd be around all these adorable dogs. We'd say, 'Adopt one of these, or we'll kill you.'"

He pours a whole river of syrup on his waffles, which are covered in chicken crumbs. "That would be, um, creepy."

"Well, yeah. And they'd be super disoriented, but in the end, they'd realize we'd given them a reason to wake up in the morning. Through hooliganism."

Max takes a bite of waffle, licks his lips, and rolls his eyes. "You are so weird."

"True," I say, starting in on my wing, which is harder to eat as there is far less meat on it.

"So like is there a real-world, eleven p.m. example of hooligan do-gooderism? 'Cause I'm not down for kidnapping."

"Do-goodery," I correct, taking a bite of crust that is so salty and perfect that I almost ask him if we can skip the hooligan do-goodery, which will never come close to topping this moment, but the waitress comes by with our drinks in to-go cups—hint hint—and tells us they're closing up for the night. "And yeah. I have an idea."

I blot my mouth with a napkin and try to come up with something actually doable on the fly that would be fun. I have nothing immediately, and then I get a vision. I giggle. It's random, for sure, but so am I. I'm not sure exactly how we'd do it. But we could do it.

"Do you trust me?" I ask.

He grins. "At this moment? About this?"

I nod. Max studies my face. I wipe it with the back of my hand, fearful it's crummy.

"What the hell, dude. Sure. I'm down for whatever."

"Famous last words," I say.

CHAPTER TWENTY-THREE

MAX

I'm not a real *mystery activity* sort of dude. But it's nearly Tuesday morning, Jordan and I are having weird fun, and I'm not ready to go home. Some of that may be about how damn sweet Jordan looks when he's holding a chicken wing in his skinny hands, how his light green eyes get big like he's doing a science experiment, like he's never eaten a piece of actual fried chicken before, which of course he hasn't. Also I never know what the guy is going to say next.

"Next stop, Walmart," he says.

See what I mean?

I turn on the ignition and the AC whirs to life outside Lo-Lo's.

"Walmart, eh?" I ask, and he nods. "And can you promise me there's nothing illegal that's about to happen? I'm not down with Tent City."

"Tent City doesn't exist anymore," Jordan says. Yeah, duh. This is not the encouragement I was looking for. I glance sideways, waiting for a little more information. "I don't think so, but no promises. If it's illegal, it's more *You kids go on home now* illegal than *We're hauling you into jail* illegal."

My chest tightens, like after he suggested we trespass into people's yards to pick prickly pears. But I don't say anything. I don't want to ruin the mood.

"Okay," I say, becoming concerned that maybe we should have quit after fried chicken. "Are we, like, doing good hooligans at Walmart?"

He laughs. "Hooligan do-goodery. And no. We need supplies."

"Then supplies we shall have," I say, trying to sound a bit like Jordan, but the voices in my head are doing cartwheels and I'm having second, third, and even fourth thoughts.

The artificially cheerful fluorescent lights greet us and momentarily disorient me. The store is nearly empty, except for a woman wearing what appears to be a flower pillowcase as shorts, and a creepy-looking guy with perv sunglasses, the kind that are too big for his face.

"We need as many stuffed animals as we can carry," Jordan says as he leads us down the aisle to the right.

"Okay," I say, and I slow my pace as my brain tries to come up with an excuse in case I need to abort this mission. Because the stuffed animals thing? Sounds a little weird to me. What the hell are we gonna do with "as many stuffed animals as we can carry" at just after midnight on a Tuesday morning?

"Also we'll need a ladder."

"Of course we will," I say, and I take a deep breath and flash him an encouraging smile, which is as much meant for me as it is for him, and Jordan smiles back in a way that makes me feel at least a little more at peace with this weirdness.

We find stuffed animals in the toy section. The cheapest animals are a buck fifty each. There are ducks, chickens, teddy bears, tigers, birds, cows, zebras, squirrels, monkeys. He starts grabbing pairs of each and cradles them to his chest. He looks like the big winner at the state fair's water gun balloon race booth.

"These are all good choices," he says, looking down at the monkeys, zebras, and tigers in his arms. He unloads them into the cart.

"Yes. Um. Monkeys, zebras, and tigers are . . . good," I say, deadpan, and Jordan nods. I grab some birds and teddy bears and chuck them into the cart, but when I pick up some cows, he bats them to the floor.

"No!" he says, deranged-like. "No cows."

"Um," I say, and I pick them up and place them back on the shelf. When Jordan leads us away from this aisle—I guess we have enough appropriate animals, I don't know—I jump up onto the cart and surf it like a skateboard, coasting down the aisle.

"Stop! Ladder time," he says, and I get that he's doing some corny old-school Hammer shit, but I ignore it because it's late and I just can't.

We settle on a folding step stool for sixteen dollars. After he pays—thank God we netted eight hundred this afternoon, because it's been an expensive day—he asks me to drive us south on Scottsdale Road toward Tempe, and then we do so, in silence.

"Do you hate me?" he finally asks.

I can't help but exhale dramatically. "What?"

"I know. We've been hanging out all day. But I kind of think you just feel bad for me, because of my mom or something. Like you're babysitting me."

I open my mouth and no words come out. I truly don't know how to respond to this. There's insecure, and then there's whatever this is. And I wonder if this is like a sign. That even though he's adorable and we're getting closer and I like it, I should run away, fast. Because maybe watching him walk makes me shiver and he's fun to hang with and a good poet and says interesting shit that makes me laugh, but how can I ignore that the dude I've just spent an entire day with asked me if I hate him?

"You're not saying no, which is a bad sign," he says.

"Oh my God," I say. "Shut up. Like seriously. Shut up."

"Shut up?"

"Shut up," I repeat. "At a certain point, you have to man up, and not be asking pitiful-ass questions like that. It's after midnight. We're in my car together. We're going to hooligan do-good or whatever. No, Jordan. I'm not your babysitter. That is some fucked-up shit, dude."

The car goes quiet again, and I pass the various cabarets that dot Scottsdale Road in south Scottsdale.

"Do you want to just head home?" he asks. "Maybe that's enough for one day?"

I slow the car down, which is fine since the streets are pretty much deserted. I turn and glance at him. He turns toward me. I pull off the road into a small strip mall where all the shops are closed for the night. I park again, this time in front of a tattoo parlor.

"You're better than this," I say.

"I am?"

"Yeah. You're better than asking me if I hate you after I spent all day with your ass. I like you, Jordan. You're different. You make me more spontaneous, and I like that. I don't hang with people unless I wanna hang with them. So if you're gonna be all mopey and shit and act like you're not worthy, I'll take you home. Otherwise, shut the fuck up. Okay?"

He looks down at his lap. His profile, in the moonlight, is so beautiful, so delicate. Like I could break him. I don't want to break him; I just want him to have a harder shell.

Finally he glances at me for a quick moment before looking out the window, away from me.

"Okay," he says.

"Okay?"

He meekly smiles, not turning my way again. "Okay I'll stop with the stupid questions. You know Papago Park?"

"Yes. And good," I say, and I shake his shoulder and muss his hair a bit, which makes him fix it self-consciously. And I pull back onto the road.

"In all of this, I didn't even text my mom," he says, as I enter Papago Park from the north. He tells me to keep going straight.

"Maybe you should," I say. "I did. I kinda got in some trouble the night before I met you. Didn't text her and stayed out all night."

"You stayed out all night? What were you doing?"

"Still straight?" I ask.

It takes him a moment to realize I've changed the subject. "Yeah. We're going to the zoo."

"It's closed," I say.

"Duh. And you didn't answer my question."

I don't, and when I see the sign, I turn right and pull into the empty parking lot. I turn off the ignition and the truck moans to a halt.

"Text your mom," I say.

"Geez. Man of mystery," he says. He pulls out his phone, looks at it, and puts it away. "Who am I kidding? If she were in one of her moods where she cares, she'd be texting me. She's passed out. She doesn't hear anything at night."

"If you say so," I say, and we open the doors. The streetlights shine above us. Despite the fact that it's 12:27 a.m., heat radiates off the asphalt. It feels like we've just walked into a sauna.

I pull out my cell phone, turn on a flashlight app, and we walk up to the entrance. I hold the step stool and Jordan has the bag of small stuffed animals. I admit it's kinda awesome to be the only people here.

"I guess you must be wondering what we're doing here with stuffed animals?" he whispers, even though we are clearly alone.

I nod. He places the flashlight under his face so that he looks demonic. I laugh.

"Ancient tradition states—" he says, and then he breaks into laughter. "Sorry. Got nothing. We are here because while the zoo is an awesome place to look at monkeys while drinking an over-priced grape slush, it is also like a jail to those very same monkeys, and all the other animals. Our act of hooligan do-goodery is an artistic one."

We stroll toward the entrance. It's a large arch you walk through, and illuminated on top of it is a big globe. We walk in, keep walking, and finally we get to a shuttered main entrance with ticket booths.

"Shoot," he says.

"What?"

He sighs. "I was hoping for a tall wall."

"Okay."

"Hmm," he says. "Plan B. Stay here."

He jogs off to the wooded area to the side of the zoo, and I hear him doing something with the bag. He comes back and shows me the contents of the bag with his flashlight. Gravel.

"We'll use this to mark the pathway."

I don't even ask. He kneels down at the shuttered doors and starts to create a one-foot-wide mini-pathway through the asphalt with the gravel, and though I don't really know what he's doing, I sit down on the hot asphalt and join him. The parts he does are curvy, so I mimic them.

Once we have a path that's about twenty feet long leading from the entrance toward the parking lot, Jordan empties the bag of stuffed animals, and he begins to place them, two by two, in a line as if they're walking up the path.

I laugh. "Ah," I say, and my worry about going to jail goes away.

"I saw this in my sleep," he says. "They'll get the message, don't you think?"

"I think so, dude." I grab a couple zebras and put them at the end of the path.

"And zebras shall lead them," he says.

I say, "Where is not clear."

"True."

We step back and look at our project. A procession of stuffed animals appears to be taking flight from the zoo.

It looks—weird.

I start laughing. I glance over at Jordan and he looks similarly amused, and then he starts laughing and our laughter reverberates through the quiet night.

Then I see lights in the distance.

"Shit," I whisper. "Mission aborted."

I grab his arms and pull him toward the parking lot, but it's too late. There's a car pulling in next to ours. My heartbeat soars. I pull him back into the zoo area and scan for a good hiding spot. There are bushes right at the edge of the woods to our right, so I pull him in that direction and I feel him nearly fall. He rights himself and we sprint toward the woods, then I jump behind a shrub and Jordan carefully follows me, trying to avoid the branches that I didn't worry too much about.

We watch, breathless, as the car stops, the guy gets out, looks at our car, looks around, and, possibly because he's underpaid or perhaps because he doesn't give a shit, drives off. We stay there for a few extra minutes, in silence, as he drives away.

I find myself feeling kind of incredible there, at almost one in the morning, behind a bush at the Phoenix Zoo with a beautiful guy who doesn't know he's beautiful. I feel invincible. Superhero-ish.

I turn toward Jordan. He turns toward me. Our eyes meet and in his I see so much all at once. Fear. Humor. A question. And hidden behind it, I see something I wasn't sure was there. It's in the arch of his eyebrow, and the unflinching way he holds my stare.

I curl my lips into a smile as a kind of question. His lips curl too. That's all I need. I lean forward and jut my neck out at him. His face is frozen.

I put my lips on his. When they touch, my heart lurches, time stops, and he gasps.

His mouth tastes like light syrup, sweet and vaguely maple. I open my lips just a little and he does the same, mirroring mine. Our lips stay connected, and then I slightly breathe into his mouth, and his whole body shakes. Mine too.

His mouth is so tentative, and I wonder: Has he ever been kissed before? I want my lips to heal him, to protect him from everything. From his crazy mom. From the people who have hurt him, because no one is as tentative as Jordan without having gone through some shit.

I pull back slowly. I search his face. He averts his eyes for a moment and I give him some time to look back at me. Which he finally does. His light green eyes focus on mine again, and his face reddens just a bit, and he smiles.

"Well," he says.

"Well."

We exit the bushes, which is a good idea because no, I'm not gonna have our first time be in the bushes at the zoo. And I can't help but think about kissing Kevin and how it was just—not this. I didn't want to. Maybe that's why the whole thing was so weird. I don't know. Just thinking about it, and just thinking about seeing him earlier today—well, yesterday by now—makes my chest shiver.

"You okay?" Jordan asks, and I almost laugh, because he's the one who needs to be asked "Are you okay" in this situation. Not me. I'm pretty sure this kiss is newer to him than it is to me. But instead I just say, "Yeah."

We grab the step stool and the empty bag and leave our hooligan whatever thing—our artwork, I guess—for the world to see in the morning. We get into the car in silence and it's nice not to have to talk. To chill and drive through Tempe in the deep night, two dudes who happen to work together, and happen to, I don't know.

I turn off the lights of my truck and pull up in front of his house. We come to a stop and sit there for a bit, unsure of what to say, I guess.

"I gotta," he says, and I look at him and smile and he does a Jordan smile approximation, which makes me smile wider, because. He's so damn Jordan.

"Yeah," I say, and he nods and throws open the door and sprints toward the front door.

And I drive off, thinking that I've just had about the most exciting day of my life, and wondering how it's gonna play tomorrow in the truck.

CHAPTER TWENTY-FOUR

JORDAN

I prop myself up on a satin pillow and wrap a celebratory boa around my legs, which feels like the thing to do when you kiss a boy for the first time. Then I have a 2:00 a.m. texting session with Pam and Kayla:

Me: You awake

Kayla: No

Me: That was a trick question, because asleep people can't text

Kayla: This better be worth it or I will beat your ass

Me: Worth it

Kayla: Worth it how???

Me: We kissed

Me: !!!!!!!!!!!!!!!!!!!!!

Me: !!!!!!!!!!!!!!!!!!!!!

Me: I kissed a boy and I liked it

Kayla: That's awesome sweetie. Was he a good kisser? I'm guessing yes

Me: How the hell would I know

Kayla: True. Oh no. Were you a bad kisser? You probably were really bad. Did he drop you off at home and drive away? Cause that's what people do with bad kissers.

Me: (After sending a meme with a teenage girl giving dramatic side-eye) Fuck you bitch

Pam: You know that thing where you're asleep and your phone keeps vibrating? That shit needs to stop

Kayla: He kissed a boy and he liked it!

Me: I kissed a boy and I liked it

Pam: Okay okay fine but can you shut the fuck up about it until after 9 a.m.?

Me: Sorry

Me: I

Me: Am

Me: Sorry

Kayla: Also me too

Kayla: Sorry

Kayla: So sorry

Pam: K you are both on ignore congrats tho on the kiss he is good for you

Me: Thanks Pam love you like crazy

Pam: K me too hitting ignore now

Me: You still there Kayla

Kayla: Of course because I'm your actual best friend and I care about your feelings

Kayla: She is going to slap me when she reads that in the morning

Kayla: Do you think this is like a thing now? You and Max

Me: I have no idea?!?! How will I know?

Kayla: Guys, esp dude bros are notoriously assholish about hooking up. But Max is better than that. I think?

Kayla: You'll look in his eyes and just know

Me: Oh my god I have a bf! Maybe?!?! A bf!?!?

Kayla: Love you sweetie. More than Pam obvs

Pam: (After sending a meme with Chucky giving the middle finger) Fuck you bitch

CHAPTER TWENTY-FIVE

MAX

The night of the zoo kiss, I find myself unable to sleep. I am thinking about Jordan's lips against mine, and how he actually whimpered when they touched, and how real it felt.

It's amazing. The simple act of kissing with someone I really like can just send me. Like a drug, maybe.

And then there are the times it doesn't feel like that. At all.

Nausea fills my throat. I'm like, *Do I need to vomit?* I laugh. I liked the kiss. Jordan made me want to do the opposite of vomit.

So why would I even focus on that?

I'm alone in my bedroom. Lying down in bed. After a first kiss with a dude I like. So what's this heavy syrup filling up my sinuses? Expanding upward.

I shut my eyes tighter, ignoring the weird feeling behind my eyes.

It stays, and then it gets worse, and I even think maybe I should call 9-1-1. Suddenly my face is numb with this syrupy feeling. It's in my nose, in my head, sloshing down into my chest. And I'm like, *Am I going crazy? Focus on the positive. Focus on the good stuff.*

Kevin, the name, appears in big, bright lights, and I thrash it out of my brain. My head hits the headboard slightly and that makes me dizzy, but it does nothing to stop the slush. *Oh no.* I think to myself, *Oh no.*

I make a deal with God. *Please, God. Let me just feel the good thing, not this other—*

God says no.

I pinch my eyes closed. There's a milky, full feeling gathering around my heart. A sludge. Slush. My body goes heavy all the way through, and suddenly I'm underwater again, like when Betts jumped on me, and waves of it fill my sinuses, the veins in my arms, my inner ear.

Dad saw a psychic once. He was into that for like a minute when I was a kid. And he went and saw her and showed her a picture of me. The psychic said I might have tooth trouble in my life, and that if I was ever to be in trouble, I should go to sleep. If I went to sleep when troubled, I'd wake up with an answer. I've always remembered that. So I focus on the insides of my eyes and will my heavy heart to slow down.

The shapes inside my eyes intensify, go purple, pop and lock, rearrange and squirm. I feel it. I feel the sleep overtake me. And I'm so, so relieved.

Summer break is here! I flip the blue exam book closed after my AP History final, march up to Mr. Harrison's desk, place it in front of him, and wait to catch his eye.

"You're all set," he says, smiling at me. "Have a great break, you hear?"

"You know it," I say. "You too."

I just about sprint down the hallway toward the front door and all the way to my truck. Even the way the steering wheel burns my hands doesn't bug me, and I roll down the windows and blare the radio as I coast down Guadalupe the mile to my house.

We meet up at Betts's house for some Madden, and his dad takes us for pizza rolls at Nello's for dinner. They start talking about a Madden tournament and staying up all night, and I glance down at my phone. Betts notices.

"You got somewhere to be, Maximo?"

I shrug. "Gotta help my mom," I say.

Zay-Rod acts like this is an act of treason. "First night of break, dude," he says. "What the hell?"

"If I wanna have a break, gotta take care of Rosa first."

"Momma's boy," Betts says, and I say, "At least my mom's not a—" and then I remember Mr. Betts is sitting right there, and I stop talking in a hurry, prompting a mischievous laugh from Zay-Rod.

Mr. Betts laughs too. "That's fine," he says. "My wife is a prostitute."

Betts is like, "Dad!"

And we all laugh, and the fact that I'm begging out of our first-night-of-break Madden fest is momentarily forgotten.

The notification comes at 8:05. Just an address, near ASU. My heart flutters. I've met dudes from the gay app before, but this one is different. There's something that just seems right about it. He's chill. Funny. Said some shit about man buns when we messaged that actually made me laugh, and I can count on one hand the number of times a dude has made me laugh on there. I'm gonna meet him. Kick off the summer before my senior year with my first ASU kegger. Maybe we'll click?

I'll see you there, I text.

Not if I see you first, is his response.

I grin because he seems like a mischievous kind of guy, and I like that. Maybe boyfriend material? I'd be good with that. It's so damn hard to find someone. I'm not friends with the LGBTQ kids at school because I'm not out, because of baseball. One n ten was not for me, and while I can get into BS West with my fake ID, there's all these dudes there giving me shade, acting like their shit don't stink. I don't have the time for that.

I tell Rosa I'm off to Betts's place for some Madden, and she's busy reading Isabel Allende's The Japanese Lover *and tells me to have mercy on those other boys. I walk out with thrilling shivers dotting my arms and legs. I've never lied to Rosa before about something this big. I've never had to, and I'm not even sure I have to now, but it feels like it adds to the excitement to make this a Max-only adventure.*

The party is out of control by the time I arrive at ten. Shirtless dudes running around with Super Soakers and thump-y music blaring and girls dancing up on each other in tight tops and skimpy bottoms. I can smell the alcohol as I walk in, and part of me wants to turn right around because I've never walked into a party alone before. Always had my boys there, even with BS West, which Betts dug because he could mack on the straight girls hanging with their gay buddies, and they were all like, No thank you, please. *It was pretty funny.*

Thankfully it doesn't take long to spot Kevin. His blue faux-hawk gives him away, and he gives me an uneven smile and a tiny wave from across the room. When he speaks, his mouth closes crookedly, and that adds some additional quirk to his look. I like him immediately.

As we walk toward his dorm, my heart pulses in my ear.

I ask him, "Do you have protection?"

He tells me to relax. He's only been with five guys. This logic eludes me, but Kevin is older, more experienced. I defer to him.

I am shirtless in his bed. It's like Kevin is two people. One at the party, and one ever since we left. Ever since it's seemed like a done deal, I guess. At the party he talked fast and seemed overeager to please. Now he seems almost cocky in his attitude, and we don't say much. And when we do, it's not—not what I want. At all.

He stands at the foot of his bed, his shirt off too.

"Wanna smoke up?"

I shake my head no. I don't know exactly what he means, which makes me feel stupid. It's like I missed a class in Hooking Up 101. Weed? More than weed? I don't know, but I am not interested in finding out. A few beers is enough for me, and I've heard enough of my mom's diatribes about how Mexico has been ruined by America's hunger for drugs. Not gonna be part of that.

He takes out a pipe and a tiny wooden case and he pinches a bit of greenish-looking stuff and puts it in the pipe hole and lights up. He inhales heavily, holds it in, exhales. Pot for sure. I try not to take in too much of the smoke. Then he shakes his head, over and over, regarding me like I'm some sort of prize he's won.

He says, "Are you my dark-skinned boy?"

My esophagus fills with something slushy. "Um."

"Are you my Arabian prince?"

I'm like, Are you for real? My jaw tenses, because he doesn't laugh, or say "Just playin'." He means this, or thinks this is acceptable, a normal thing to say. I want to say something, make a joke at least about *how fucking stupid that is, how ignorant. But I don't want to kill the moment. I'm too curious to see what's next. When the room has been silent for so long that it feels like my not saying anything is a form of consent, I say, "My mom was born in Mexico City and my dad is from Indiana."*

He rolls his eyes. "Oh, come on. Don't be so sensitive. It's a fantasy, okay?"

I feel my shoulders tense and my face heats up. Nope. This is not me being too sensitive. And suddenly the quirky, talkative guy from the party has been replaced by this asshole I don't like at all.

I sit up and look away. "I'm gonna jet," I say.

I'm about to turn my legs to the side of the bed and stand when he jumps on the bed next to my feet, thumping into me slightly. He smirks. I stare. He sits on my legs.

"Nah," he says. It's half a statement and half a question, and I don't answer because I'm so shocked that he's just sat on my legs. I'm, like, bigger than him. By a lot. I remember thinking: Amateur hour. *He may be older, but he's never gonna get it, because this is some basic shit, stuff you don't do. Anyone with half a clue would know that.*

Then he inches up until he's sitting on my calves, pushing down in an uncomfortable way. I have to laugh. He doesn't laugh. I'm waiting for the camera. He's punking me. This isn't happening.

But I don't move. It's like I can't. And at the same time a part of my brain is thinking: Move, Max. Get the hell up. Get out of here. This is stupid.

I don't know why I don't move. It's like I can't. Not like he drugged me, but like the brashness of his actions has frozen me. His stare is boring into my eyes, and I avert mine. I think of alpha dogs. How sometimes Chihuahuas can be alpha over Great Danes. It's weird but it's true.

Kevin tweaks my nipple. I don't like it. I should punch him, I think. Pin him. Pick him up by his armpits and put him against the wall and stare him down 'til he apologizes. I don't.

He leans in for a kiss, and all I'm thinking about is that he called me Arabian. I don't kiss back but it doesn't stop him from kissing enough for both of us. I feel dirty. I hear voices. Voices from people in my life. My dad. My mom. Random shit like this joke my dad told me once about George Bush thinking that Brazilian is a number, like bazillion. This time my mom got food poisoning on shrimp.

He reaches for my shorts and I say, "Naw, dude."

I am not looking at him. I am not watching. He is intent on getting me naked, and I don't know this feeling. I don't get it. I can't understand why I'm still here. Because that means I want it, right? I'm bigger and I don't leave.

And then it's like I do leave my body, but only in my brain. My body stays put, frozen, and I float to the top of the room. I see the rest from up there. I do.

I become keenly aware of the dandruff in Kevin's faux-hawk. I see Kevin's tired, glassy eyes for what they are, and I feel this odd compassion for him, as I'm a rag doll and he is doing things to me, things I don't want. I want to hug him. I want to tell him it doesn't have to be like this, that there is a better way, which is a hilarious thought to have, and I know that, and yet I think it anyway. And time stretches like bubble gum, and loses its taste, like bubble gum, and I find myself repeating this litany as I watch the thing happen, from above, as I watch and feel nothing, nothing I should feel.

I'm not here. I'm not here. I'm not here.

I do not move. The whole time. I do not move. I do not look at him. We could be pushed up against each other on the bus. It is the most personal yet most impersonal experience of my life, and I know, as it's happening, that this is not normal.

And after, as Kevin goes down the hall to clean up in the dorm bathroom, I recline on the single bed, and an emptiness settles into my chest and breaks one of my ribs.

I feel it. A broken rib. Pushing in toward my heart.

And then Kevin comes back, and he collapses next to me, in silence, and I think that if he touches me, I'll scream. And yet I also want him to touch me. Is this crazy? Am I going crazy?

My eyes flash open, and I know. I close them tight. I don't want to know. I don't want this. But I know.

My heart pulses. I think of my dad. *Boys are not supposed to allow things into their bodies. You can be gay, but guys don't do that.* And I don't believe that, exactly, but some part of that stays with me, and I am filled with slush again and I cry out, which also boys don't do. I smile—it's always worked before. Just smile, Max. The pain cannot be stronger than a smile.

But it is.

"Max? You okay?"

It's my mom, right outside my door. I clench up and my heart pulses fiercely. I say something to my mom, and it's official. I am not ready for this to be anything, let alone official. I can handle this. I can handle it. I can.

"I'm okay," I say.

"You're moaning. Bad dream?"

"Yeah," I say.

"You need a glass of water?"

"Nah."

I listen as her footsteps fade away, and I breathe deep. Okay. Okay. I take a look at my phone. 4:33. Too early for this shit. And we have work in like a few hours, and now this, which is not real, not real until I decide it is.

Was I raped?

The idea makes me almost laugh. A smaller guy, just a year older. No. I stayed. I could've left. I stayed. Not rape. Just stupidity.

But then I think of the stuff we hear at school. No means no, which some of the stupider-ass baseball dudes translate as, "No means yes, yes means anal." Which wasn't funny then. And I said no. *Naw.* So is this like, rape-minus? Is that a thing? If you aren't overpowered, if you could have left but you didn't, you didn't because you were curious, maybe, that's not rape, right?

And I think of my dad, who saw that psychic, and who isn't wise, exactly, but is an adult, kind of. So without thinking too much I call him.

"Wha—Max? What's wrong? You okay?"

"Yeah. No. I don't know. Maybe."

He sighs. "Whataya need? Can you call back at like a normal hour when people are awake? Christ."

"Dad, is it, um, rape if one person says no but then doesn't leave when they could?"

"What?"

"Like the um, girl. Like, she says no, but the guy pleads with her, and she doesn't say yes, but she, like, freezes up like a rag doll. And he does—stuff—to her. Is that like rape?"

"What the — are you raping girls now?" Dad laughs. I don't. It's so not funny, and it's so something my dad would think is funny, because my dad is an idiot. Why did I even call him?

"No."

"So, are you researching rape now? At five oh-fucking-clock in the morning? Jesus."

And for the first time in my life that I am aware of, I desperately want him to put the pieces together. To get serious and have a clue. To ask me if I'm okay.

"Um, sure," I say, answering his question in a way that I'm sure will raise a red flag.

It doesn't. He laughs. "So the girl says no, and the guy doesn't stop, and she just lies there?"

"Yeah?"

Dad laughs again. "Dude. That's not even like illegitimate rape. That's garden-variety rape, kid."

My whole body goes numb. Have I explained it all the right way? It can't be. I mumble more words and then I can barely manage to press the button to hang up. But I do, because if any weird noise comes out of my body right now, Dad will make a joke, and the one thing I cannot take right now is a joke.

I shake, in bed. Waves of something syrupy run up and down my veins. That damn slush again. I feel myself underwater. I need to scream out the syrup. I cannot. I will wake up Mom. I will upset her. I cannot say anything about this, ever. To anybody.

CHAPTER TWENTY-SIX

JORDAN

I get maybe a little tad bit intense in the five hours between going to sleep and Max's arrival in the morning. In the shower, I find myself playing over and over again the moment when Max's truck will pull up, and I'll see his face, his eyes, and they'll tell me what I need to know.

For once in my life, it's gonna be good. His eyes will smile as big as his mouth, and we won't be able to keep our hands off each other as we set up for another lunch at ASU.

It's about all I can do to not scream "Hurry" when my phone shows 7:00 a.m. and he's not here yet.

True to form, he arrives five minutes late. What I love about Max is that he can do that and it's not a big deal. If I were even a minute late I'd be apologizing. Who am I kidding? If I were a minute early I'd be apologizing.

He pulls up and gets out of the truck, and my heart is beating out of my chest in anticipation of looking into his eyes, like Kayla said.

But when I look over at him to say hey, he's not looking at me. He mumbles, "What up, dude?" and gets right to work.

"You okay?" I ask.

"Tired. Didn't sleep well."

I laugh. "Why? You kiss someone utterly disgusting and were throwing up all night?"

He rolls his eyes at me. "Not everything is about you, Jordan."

I am speechless. Speechless. How the—what the hell?

I am so speechless that I actually don't speak for a bit. My insides feel like they are melting. Like everything good from yesterday has evaporated, and all the good feelings are gone.

I want to punch him, actually. Because you can't give someone something like that and then just take it away, can you?

Instead, I say, "We could use a few more lemons. You need anything at Safeway?"

He nods. "More garlic, and let me check the chicken breast supply."

I don't even respond, just get to work inventorying the rest of what I need—prickly pears, sugar, ice. I'm done. Not inventorying. I'm done because who kisses someone, knowing it's their first kiss, and then acts like nothing happened? It's like abuse, kind of, and I don't need abuse. I decide Max and I are definitely over. A lump forms in my throat about it, but I swallow it down. This is a big red warning sign. I can't and I won't do this.

Good-bye, Max, I think to myself. You'll be a work friend and nothing more from here on out.

I kick off my flip-flops and walk down the driveway to our mailbox.

It's early and the sun is just rising, but a full month of cooking in 100-plus heat, with no rain and low evening temperatures in the mid-80s, has rendered the white concrete of the driveway like an oven. Poor Dorcas is going to have to wait till tonight for her walk.

I feel the sizzle on the soles of my feet and I wince at the exquisite pain of burning skin.

I stand at the mailbox and pull out the mail that's been sitting there overnight. A bunch of solicitations and coupon booklets. I pretend to read them carefully, but really I'm allowing the singe of my toes to numb everything else in the world out.

Max climbs out of the truck and looks around for me. He waves me over. I don't want to go. I want to stay right here until my heels blister. But he keeps waving, so I slowly walk back over to the shade of the garage.

He smiles and looks me in the eye with kindness. I'm like, *Nice timing, asshole.*

"I'm sorry for the crappy good morning," he says, hugging me lightly. "Lots of crap on my mind today. None of it about you. You're the good thing, Jordan. You're like the one good thing. I'm sorry I did you like that."

I exhale, hug him tight and hold him close, stroke his beautiful black hair. "It's okay," I whisper into his ear. "Totally get that. I'm cool. We're cool."

"Thanks," he says into my shoulder. "I'll try not to shut you out when I get all whatever."

"Okay," I say. "Not a problem."

"Thanks."

He pulls away and I resist the urge to pull him back to me. I want more. So much more that it scares me. I scratch my elbow instead. "Can you tell me what's going on?"

He smiles that wide Max smile again. "It's nothing. Well, not nothing. Just. I don't want to talk about it, you know?"

"Sure," I say, too quickly.

"It's just stupid shit. Like, the world is a big place. We're just space dust. None of this means shit. Sometimes when I'm upset, I have to remember that." He crosses his arms over his chest.

"Sure," I say. He's right. Sometimes I get all freaked out, but in the end we're pretty insignificant in the grand scheme of things.

"Just know that you're not that problem, okay? You're the antidote. I can't imagine any person I'd rather be with today, okay?"

I can't help it. A smile bleeds out of me. "Okay," I say.

"You're my Jordan."

"Okay," I say, and the smile gets wider. "I like that. Okay."

CHAPTER TWENTY-SEVEN

MAX

I have a secret no one can ever know, and it's messing me up big time. The only way I can figure to stop being two totally different people is to go into superhero mode.

So I tell Jordan I have plans with my boys after work. I go home, head into my room, swallow everything else down, pick up my phone, and text Kevin.

Me: Hey

Kevin: Thought you were in ghost mode

Me: Sorry

When I type that, I feel bile rise up in my throat.

Kevin: Eh its fine you wanna hang out agin?

More bile. Like entering the back of my mouth now.

Me: Yeah

Kevin: Cum over

Luckily there is a trash can next to my desk. I lunge and vomit into it. The acid in my mouth burns like panic, like I can feel it dissolving my tooth enamel. We can't meet somewhere private, because I'm afraid of what Super Max will do to this kid. In public I can say what I need to say and at the end he'll still be alive and I won't be in prison.

Me: Nah wanna talk. You know Gold Bar?

Kevin: I'll find it. An hour?

Me: Yup

Kevin: Stay adorable

I got nothing to say to that one.

I arrive before him, order an iced tea, and grab a table by the window. My pulse quickens as I watch him saunter across the parking lot in a yellow tank top, his blue faux-hawk glistening in the sun. I hate him so much.

"What up?" he says as he walks in. He comes over and fist-bumps me. He smells like coconut.

"'Sup," I say back.

He gets a latte and when he sits down across from me, he smiles. The left side of his upper lip rises higher than the right side. "Food trucking today?"

"Yup."

"Makin' good money?"

"Pretty good."

"I always thought that would be fun. But not in the summer."

"Right. True."

"I'm taking classes. That way I can take out a loan and not work during the summer."

"Nice."

Kevin sighs. "Dude. Heavy lifting. You invited me here. Maybe you ask me a question now?"

I take a big sip of my ginger-peach tea. "What was that, the night in your dorm room?"

Kevin laughs. "What was what?"

"What happened between us. I mean, I know what happened, but, like, you know I—" The words get stopped up in my esophagus.

He smirks. "You what? Use your words, dude."

"Said no."

He laughs again and looks around. When he speaks his voice is quieter by half. "You were *sooo* nervous."

"Yeah."

"Sometimes a guy needs a little encouragement to get where he wants to go. You definitely wanted that."

I feel that slush again in the back of my throat. And these shakes that start in my legs, like when your teeth chatter after a cold shower, except my entire body. I push it all down. I command my body to stop, and amazingly it does. The chatters go away. The slush recedes. Super Max.

"Did I?"

Under the table, he nuzzles his knee up against mine. "Of course. You sure as hell weren't stopping me once we got started."

I am lost for words. I have none. I truly don't know how to make any sounds from my mouth. I stare at him, utterly confused. *Am I wrong? Was it okay?*

He smiles again, reaches over and flicks my cheek. "Look at

you, and look at me. In what universe could I get you to do any-thing you didn't want?"

He's right. And yet. It's like I froze. I travel back there in my brain. Him sitting on my legs. My legs wobbling under his butt. My brain and my mouth, kind of like now. Useless. What's wrong with me?

His face gets close enough to mine so that I can smell past the coconut to get a whiff of his sour breath. "I can tell when a guy is enjoying himself. You really were. Your eyes. Have you ever seen that passion look that a guy gives when he's, like, blissed? And it's not like you were soft."

I try to imagine that look I must have given. And I was hard. I know I was. That was like what was so crazy. How can something feel so good and so bad at the same time? Shit. Am I being, like, a snowflake? Too sensitive? I'm not like that usually. Maybe this is just, like, buyer's remorse? Am I making it into something it wasn't?

But didn't I say no?

No means yes, yes means anal?

"You're really intense, dude," he says.

"What?"

"Your eyes. They're beautiful. You're one of those guys who really listens and really thinks. I like that. It's so sexy."

More leg chattering. No. I put a stop to it. This time, it's harder. I try harder. Super Max, turning his powers on himself. I can control my own body.

"You want it again," he says.

"What?"

"I can tell you do." That uneven smile again, but this time bigger so I can see his bottom teeth, which are small, crooked, and uneven. "The quiet ones always do. C'mon. Come back to my room. I got weed. You ever done it high?"

Before him, I'd never done it at all. So no. There's so much he doesn't know about me, and he hasn't asked. And I'm a guy, so I should want that. No strings attached. Just fun, nothing intense. So why do I feel this way? What's wrong with me?

I know that nothing that comes out of my mouth now will do anything good, so I stand up, take my iced tea with me, and walk out. I feel his eyes on my back as I walk to my car, and this white-hot something pulses through my veins.

I slam the iced tea down onto the asphalt. It explodes, splashing red liquid onto my bare legs. I stomp down on it. Three times. Flatten the thing. I look back at the coffee shop. He's in the window, staring, mouth agape. I close my eyes, turn, and walk to my car.

I drive away so he can't get to me, all the way to the other side of the mall parking lot. Then I put the car in park, close my eyes, and think.

I don't want to feel bad anymore. I don't want to waste another minute on that guy. I can do this myself. Warrior up. I sit up taller and clench my stomach muscles, puff up my chest.

In a world where lesser mortals crumble, Super Max stands tall and says, "I'm the decider of my fate. I'm not a victim. Shut the hell up with all that victim shit."

I'm freakin' Max Morrison. I carried a dude through the desert in 120-degree heat. No skinny-ass, blue-faux-hawked dipshit has power over me. No way.

I start the car up, turn up the music, loud, and drive off, victorious. Mind over matter.

CHAPTER TWENTY-EIGHT

JORDAN

Things start to get crazy good on the truck. Beyond-my-wildest-dreams good.

Max gets on Instagram and Twitter and Snapchat and shows pictures of his various food concoctions, and suddenly we have regulars who say things like, "This time I gotta try the habanero-peach." The lemonade isn't the star, but something about ordering food outside while standing on the surface of the sun makes people of all different shapes and sizes say the same thing each time: "Let me get a prickly pear lemonade too. That'll cool me down."

A lot of other trucks take the summer off, I guess. To the victor go the spoils, or more like, to the fools who don't mind working on a scalding truck all summer goes the cheddar.

"Stop calling it that," Max says, when I remark that we got hella cheddar after the lunch rush slows down on a Wednesday afternoon. "I'm embarrassed for you, dude."

"Mo' cheddar less problems. I got so much cheddar I don't even care," I say, and he swats me on the shoulder and paints my face with habanero-peach sauce. Which is seriously delicious.

Hella cheddar, by the way, means our first day of netting a thousand bucks.

No. Really.

Like including our huge shopping to start the day, which cost us four hundred and fifty-three dollars. I keep a running tally in my mind, and when a girl in short gold shorts that let me see all her business orders a mango-cayenne chicken and adds on a frozen lemonade, we hit a thousand and two.

"Ding ding ding!" I yell after I give the girl change for her twenty and she puts a dollar in our tip jar. "You, my dear, are our thousandth customer!"

She looks at me with vacant eyes as I hand her three bucks back. "Free lemonade for you!"

"Cool," she says, monotone, but I don't give a shit, because I am feeling so . . . something. Grateful? For Max? Without whom this never would have happened? I'll have to look, but I'm pretty sure we have five grand now, and we're not even that close to our deadline.

When we close up, I wrap my arms around Max, which seems to stun him because he's Max, and he can go from super warm to uber distant in a heartbeat. But again I don't care. I am elated.

"We've done it," I say, kissing his ear five times in succession. "That was one kiss for every thousand. We have the money I need to save my house."

Max pulls back and looks me in the eye.

"For reals?"

"Yeah, for reals! I mean, I gotta pay you for today, but even after that we're up five grand already."

He breaks into a huge Max grin and then pulls me close. "Awesome, dude! I lose track not working with the register. I knew it was a shit ton today, but I had no idea how much of a shit ton."

I grab hold of his forearms and stare deep into his eyes. "We netted eleven hundred, seventy-one dollars, and fifty-six cents," I say, joyful shivers just dancing through my entire body. I hand him a hundred-dollar bill and say, "Bonus."

He stares. I stare. He starts laughing. I start laughing.

"No. No damn way."

"Damn way."

"Lunch?" he asks. "To celebrate?"

"Absolutely," I say. "Anywhere you want to go. On me."

Not even giving a shit that the truck has no AC, we go straight to our lunch destination. First we decided it had to be a new place. Then he suggested In-N-Out Burger.

I grimaced. "Oh my God I hate that name. Way too descriptive of the eating process."

He snickers. "Dude. You're so weird, dude."

Instead we wind up at the Angry Crab, which I've passed like a million times because it's just past school on Guadalupe, in the strip mall where Dairy Queen is.

"It makes a meal an activity," Max says, just about running toward the door. I can't run as fast, because (a) I'm Jordan, he's Max, and (b) I am cradling our cashbox. No way am I leaving that in our truck, even if we can see it out the window the whole time.

"You say that like having to work for food makes things better," I say.

He shrugs. "Don't you feel awesome about having worked to make all that money?"

I don't answer right away. Man. He's right. I feel amazeballs. Part of my whole thing with Kayla and Pam is that we have this aversion—allergy, almost—to hard work. I don't know if it's true for them, but honestly, after this experience, I wouldn't even want to win the lottery or something. Making honest money from a hard day's work feels like nothing I've ever felt before. (And yeah. There needs to be an asterisk after "honest," because the locally sourced thing is total bullshit, but still.)

Max orders for us. We get a pound of snow crab legs, a pound of king crab legs, and a pound of shrimp.

"Um, leave some for the . . . whatever animals eat shellfish?"

"Fuck that," he says. "We're celebrating."

And man, is it a celebration. The food comes out in these plastic bags with all this sauce at the bottom. The sauce is called Trifecta, and it's lemon and garlic and pepper, and Max shows me how to puncture the bag without getting sauce all over everything, and how to open the crab legs. Snow ones are not that hard, but the king ones are like a death struggle with a spiky creature that really does not want you to eat its flesh. At first I demur, because it looks painful. And it is when I try it. Super hard and ouchy. But when I finally manage to open one and I pull a hulking piece of crab leg meat just about the size of my forearm out, I change my tune.

"Nice," he says.

"Yeah." I dip it into the sauce and put it in my mouth and the taste. Oh my God, the taste. It's like eating a salty stick of tangy, spicy butter, maybe. So rich and sweet and . . . perfect. I almost cry. "Oh my God."

He cracks up. "I love crab legs more than I love my mom," he says. "And I love my mom a lot."

"I get that. And can we get, like, more? Do a crab leg flight?"

"Absolutely. We worked our asses off in that heat. We got the rest of the day to do whatever. You up for an adventure?"

I nod and nod and nod. No words are needed. Clearly nothing in the world would be better than more time with Max.

We park the truck in my garage, Max picks me up in his truck, and we do up the town.

First we go to a trampoline park. Trampoline parks are about the last thing I would ever do on my own, or with the girls. Sounds like a good way to lose a testicle, or at best get annoyed by loud, boisterous boys. But suddenly I am kind of a loud, boisterous boy, and we get on the mats and Max shows me he can do a three-sixty jump off the side wall, where he somersaults in the air and somehow lands back on his feet.

"Whoa!" I say. I know better than to try to copy it, so instead I chance a side jump, where I get next to the wall, jump, twist my feet so they bounce off the wall, and land back on the mat.

"Weak, dude," he says.

"Hey, I'm new."

"At everything," he says, and this makes me bounce away toward this area where I see some dodgeballs. I pick one up, cradle it in my arms, bounce back toward Max, who is trying his flips and all that, and hurl it at his head while he's not looking. It misses by about a foot and bounces away toward a young girl, who picks it up with a delighted squeal.

"What the?" Max says. "Did you just?"

"I did just," I say.

This time he leads us over to what turns out to be the

designated dodgeball area—oops. I mouth *Sorry* to the kid who is working the area and is frowning at me. He ignores me, probably because I am the most pathetic trampoline person in the world. And for once I don't really give two craps.

Max starts whaling balls at me and I have no dodging skills and I quickly remember why I hate dodgeball; those balls kinda hurt when they hit you in the stomach, you know? But unlike the horrifying experiences I had in gym class back in sixth grade, this time it's fun. I fall onto the mat a few times and bounce back up, which makes me giggle, and a few times I throw at Max and actually come close to him. One he catches with one hand, which is pretty impressive.

I'm covered in sweat, which is gross and suddenly not that gross. Everyone here is slick with the stuff, and everyone is smiling, and while I imagine the comments Kayla and Pam would make about how ridiculous I look, I let them go. Having way too much fun for that for once.

CHAPTER TWENTY-NINE

MAX

We Angry Crab, we trampoline, we go and check out the marsh-mallow café, where they make various kinds of s'mores.

It's all a blast, and I've never spent money like this before. By the time we're at the café, having our second s'more each—I try the Elvis one with peanut butter, chocolate, and bananas, and he goes with one with mint marshmallows and chocolate—we're drunk with power and starting to dream up ways to spend money.

"Rent a limo for a night? Go to dinner and a movie in a limo?" I ask.

"Go to dinner in it and then watch a movie in the limo," he suggests.

"Yes. That. We gotta do that. Live the high life."

"I always thought I was like that Lorde song," Jordan says. "Was wrong. We will be royals. Obviously."

"We'll franchise. Become food truck moguls," I say.

By the time I'm done with the second s'more, though, my stomach is done. Like I can't even imagine eating more food, and I can down some food usually. I pat my stomach and Jordan laughs.

"I know," he says. "Not even another bite. So what do we do? Call it a day? I guess we can do this every day after work if we want."

I laugh. He's right. I mean, I want to put some money away,

but when you start making hundreds each day, money begins to lose its meaning. We could totally make this a daily habit. But thinking about it, my insides cramp a little. Not from the food either.

"I think we're Donald Trump-ing," I say.

He makes a face. "Ew."

"Yeah. Ew. I actually think this is how you become the kind of person who puts his name in gold letters on buildings all over the world. You get increasingly immune to the good life."

"Yes! Exactly. It's like, Angry Crab was perfect today. But if we went every day, it would lose that."

"Right. True," I say.

Jordan demurely blots his face with a napkin, and I stare into space, thinking about how to be the anti-Trump.

"What was that called? Hooligan do-goodery?" I ask.

His eyes light up. "Yes!"

"You feel like doing one?"

"Sure," he says, and I watch as he sits up and I can tell his brain starts spinning. I shake my head.

"Nah. This one's my choice," I say.

I can tell he doesn't like giving up the control for about a nanosecond.

"Trust me," I say.

"Don't I always?"

I don't actually know where I'm going for our hooligan do-goodery when I get into the truck, but by the time I drive us to Jordan's and we get the food truck back and head toward the 101 North, I know exactly where we're going.

I park across the street from Tempe Beach Park along Mill Avenue, right where the steakhouse Monti's used to be before the rents got too high, right across from the old Hayden Flour Mill.

"More work?" Jordan asks, and even though he keeps a straight face, I can hear the slight irritation in his voice. "That's not exactly an act of hooligan do-goodery."

"Trust me," I say again, and in silence we do our prep work. For a moment I wonder if I misjudged him. I think this idea is awesome. I hope he will too, but I'm truly not sure.

We open the window, put up the awning, and Jordan grabs the whiteboard to write the menu.

"No prices," I say.

"No prices," he repeats.

"Hooligan do-goodery."

He shrugs and erases the prices and writes *Everything Free!* on top. He shows it to me and I smile.

"We're feeding the homeless," I say.

He stands there, motionless for a moment, and again I get afraid I've misjudged him. Then his lips curve up.

"Oh. Wow. Okay. Wow."

I nod, and I get off the truck and speak loudly.

"If you're hungry, we got food for you right here!" I yell. "All kindsa chicken, and fresh frozen lemonade too. Step right up!"

Mill Avenue, and especially the park, are known as the places homeless kids hang. For nine months out of the year, it's probably not the worst life, though obviously most people would prefer a place to sleep, but at least the weather's good. But in the summer, man. I wonder sometimes how the kids make it. I love me some heat, but at some point I get to go inside, turn up the air, and chill. These people don't get that luxury, and I'm guessing it's harder to make a living in the summer, when fewer people are walking along the street.

A haggard-looking, skinny kid with a backward red baseball cap and a few days of scraggly beard wanders up. I'm standing at the window with Jordan, and when he gets close I can see track marks on his right arm.

"Free? For real?"

"Whatever you want, my man," I say.

He looks at the menu. "Can I get two? One for my girl and one for me?"

"Sure," I say. "Which one?"

"I don't care," he says, and then he says, "Habanero. I like it spicy. But hers maybe mango-cayenne? Cayenne is less hot, right?"

"Yup," I say, giving him a smile, and I pivot back to the grill and get to work.

I hear the blender going as I work, and I look over.

"I'm just gonna start making 'em and handing 'em out," he says.

And that's what we do. When word gets out, a line forms, and I take a peek at the number of chicken breasts we still have — basically our inventory for tomorrow — and realize that this is costing us probably a thousand dollars.

We can make more money tomorrow. This feels amazing.

Some of the homeless people — who knows, really, if they're homeless or not — thank us profusely. But most of them just take the food and go on their way. It doesn't matter. By the end of the day, when Jordan hands out the very last frozen lemonade and we close the window, it's probably nine o'clock and we are utterly dripping with sweat. I wring out the bottom of my shirt and sweat drips onto the floor.

We clean up and the feeling in the truck is utter bliss. Like my chest could soar out of my mouth. Like I could jump a mile in the air and float on back down. I don't know if Jordan feels it too.

Until he puts the clean blender away, turns to me, and puts his mouth on mine.

"Oh," I say into his mouth.

Our soaked shirts merge. I feel his damp, skinny legs against my sopped, thick ones, and his cheek sweat mingles with mine. I feel his lips turn upward into a smile and he pulls back.

"We should do that. Every day."

"We couldn't afford to," I say.

"Well we should do it again sometime. I had no idea. With Kayla and Pam especially, it's like we're supposed to be numb and above everything all the time. Right there, feeding strangers for free? I felt, like, not above." His eyes tear up, and I have to look away because it's cheesy as shit, and damn it, I feel the same way exactly. "I mean, above in that we have the food and they need it. But also, in that moment? I felt like I could be homeless. And I won't be, now, because we're food truck moguls and soon we'll live in a mansion I guess. But I mean, I felt like I could under-stand what it would be like to put my head on a bench and sleep in this heat."

I sit on the floor and pull Jordan down with me by his shirt. The floor is sticky with sauce that's dripped off the chicken and probably some lemonade overflow, and I don't give a damn.

"Can I tell you something?" I ask.

He nods.

"I've been hanging with my buds—we call ourselves the Three Amigos—for the last three years. Other than baseball and family, that's what I do. And they rock. But it's nothing like this. These two times we've hung out after work? Best days of my life."

I find I can't look him in the eye when I say it. I study the truck from the angle of the floor. The dashboard up front looks like it's from some old, black-and-white movie, maybe. It's amazing we haven't stalled.

"Me too," Jordan says, and he puts his hand in mine. "I know two days is only two days, but when I'm with my wives—I call them my wives—it's like I'm always wondering how I come off. And I'm always doing what they want. I feel more like me with you."

I turn to him. He turns to me. We kiss once more, this time more tender, more deep. His breath is the tiniest bit stale, and I devour him anyway. I run my fingers through his sopped black hair, and he sighs a little.

"Same time tomorrow?" he asks into my mouth.

"Count on it," I say.

CHAPTER THIRTY

JORDAN

"Mom!" I yell. "Mom!"

I just about burst in the front door, and Dorcas, bless her heart, does her jump-up greeting, putting her paws on my stomach. I scruff her hair and she pants at me. Her breath is awful.

I know it's 10:30, and Mom could be asleep but probably not. I don't care. This is worth waking her up for sure.

It's not just pride about feeding the homeless. It's that I'm happy about Max, my—what is he? Is he my boyfriend? *My boyfriend!*—and I want to tell Mom. More importantly, I am dying to see her face when I tell her that we've already—*already!*—made enough money to pay the back mortgage, and at this rate if we work all summer I can probably pay a year in advance before going back to school.

Mom is going to be so proud! And yeah. Maybe I'm growing up this summer, but there's nothing quite like a proud look on Mom's face, and I guess also I hope it'll raise her spirits.

She's not in the TV room. There, next to her cell phone, are a few Twinkie wrappers on the kitchen island, a plate with sandwich crumbs, and a still-open bottle of mayonnaise. I run to her bedroom. The door isn't closed so I know she's not asleep.

But also she's not there.

Which is weird. I wander the house, wondering where in the

hell she could be. I don't remember the last time she was out this late. Without her phone too. I peer out the front window. Her car is gone. I hadn't noticed coming in.

I sit on the couch and text Kayla and Pam.

Me: So Max and I fed homeless people at Tempe Town Lake!

Kayla: Aww Jordan Teresa

Pam: You need like a sari

Me: You are. We like made over a thousand bucks today and we celebrated and then it was like we need to do something for someone else so we went and handed out food

Kayla: Your medal arrives tomorrow sweetie

Pam: And your sari

Me: Haha my boyfriend and I are better people than you

Pam: Have you even done the nasty yet

Me: Not yet.

Pam: Not yr boyfriend, doll. Kissing is like whatever. If yr not doing it? Nah.

Kayla: Gotta rule with Pam on this one. Not yr boyfriend. Sorry sweetie

Pam: Friend zone

Me: Thnks vry supportive

Kayla: Just keepin it real

I put the phone down. Fifteen minutes ago I felt as good as I'd ever felt. Now I feel like crap.

I text Max.

Me: My mom's not home

Max: Is that weird?

Me: Yeah a little

Max: You worried?

Me: Yah

Max: Want me to come over?

Me: Nah but thanks. I'll let you know. Had so much fun with you today

Max: <big smile>

Me: <me too>

Max: <smooch>

Me: Pam and Kayla said you're not my boyfriend and we're in the friend zone because we only kiss

Max: Sigh . . . fuck them. I am your boyfriend. And stop telling them our business

I squeak. Literally. Dorcas, lying at my feet, tilts her head like, *Huh?* I mouth the word "boyfriend" to her and she yawns. Clearly she does not understand the nuance of this momentous occasion. I have a boyfriend! When my fingers stop shaking, I go back to texting, making sure to keep it casual.

Me: I always tell them everything. Are Betts and Zay-Rod mean to you?

Max: Yeah but it's just trash talk

Me: I guess so but it was kinda like, why?

Max: I hear ya. Get some sleep, k?

Me: Nah gonna wait up for my mom.

Max: Text me when she gets there. Or if you need me. K?

Me: K. Thanks

I watch some *Kimmy Schmidt* and then some *30 Rock*, which is a way underrated comedy. I'm about to drift off to sleep when I hear the front door creak open and Dorcas scramble her paws against the tile as she runs to greet whoever it is.

My mom lopes into the TV room and drops her car keys in the plate where we put keys and loose change. She looks as tired as I feel. "Hey, you're still up," she says.

I sit up. "Hey. Where were you?" I say.

She pauses dramatically. "Oh my God," she says, rolling her eyes. "Worst meeting ever."

Of course! I forgot about her Wednesday night Gamblers Anonymous meeting. I give her a sleepy laugh because I've heard the stories. The way that some people will talk for like twenty minutes because they refuse to institute a time limit on sharing because it might hurt someone's feelings. I stand up, stretch, go to her, and bury my head in her shoulder, which I can tell surprises her because she freezes up momentarily before embracing back. She reeks of smoke, which is what happens at Gamblers Anonymous meetings because everyone is an addict and they all smoke like cigarettes are the new crack during breaks. But this time she smells even smokier. And it's really late.

"You do the meeting after the meeting?" I ask.

She rolls her eyes again and laughs a bit. "I don't know why I even bother. Gwen G. makes me homicidally crazy." She goes to the refrigerator, pulls out a chocolate pudding, grabs a spoon, and sits on the couch. Dorcas comes and curls up at her feet, and she massages Dorcas's stomach with the bottom of her left foot.

I sit back down on the couch opposite her.

"So, you know how I told you we were killing it, and you were all, 'Uh, sure you are'? Well . . . I have some news."

This gets her attention and she sits up and leans in toward me. "What? Tell me tell me."

"Drumroll, please," I say, and she approximates a drumroll, which makes Dorcas look at her like, *Bitch, please.*

"Well . . . I came home to tell you that I have the money. For the mortgage. All of it. We've basically kicked ass on the truck. We're pulling in, like, a thousand a day out there, pretty much."

Her face lights up. "No. Way."

"Yes. Way," I say.

She puts her hand on her heart. "We're really . . . You made all the back-mortgage money? Really?"

I nod, feeling so proud I could basically pop. "Really."

Tears form in her eyes. "Oh my God. Oh my God!"

"Yup," I say, warmth spreading throughout my body.

"You rock so hard."

"Well, me and Max. We rock, I guess. And, um, we're boyfriends now. I mean, he said the word, so, yeah."

"What? Oh my God! Jordan, this is all so amazing!"

I shrug like I don't care, but really it's the exact opposite. It feels like too much joy is in my life now, and my body can't handle it.

"We're doing so well we actually went and fed the homeless for free over by Tempe Town Lake."

Her eyes go wide. "Yeah, we probably need to talk about that," she says. "Let's not go crazy with the charity, maybe."

Something about her saying that makes my stomach clench, but the happiness in the rest of my body overrules it.

She rolls her head back dramatically. "You don't know how much — oh, Jordan. Thank you, Jordan. I am so proud of you. And so damn thankful."

The tears start to fall, and even though we're alone I look away. If it's like a week ago, or two, pre-Max, I would have gone over and held her. Now I'm just a little . . . I don't know. Not up for that, maybe.

"You're my savior. You're our savior. You have no idea how much I needed that news right now, Jordan. No idea."

I smooth my hair down in front of my eyes and half enjoy the knot that forms in my throat. And half wish that she'd stop. It's like I want her to be proud and thankful, but the tears are almost too much.

And then she starts to sob, and I feel frozen in my seat, and Dorcas jumps up and licks her tears, and it feels like I've played out this scenario a thousand times already, the one where I tell her it's all going to be all right. But I don't want to now.

Hoping she'll stop with the herstrionics and focus on me, I say, "Do you think it's too soon? To call him my boyfriend? I don't want to be the creepy guy who plans a wedding after two weeks and suddenly there's a restraining order against me."

She wipes her eyes and says, "This is a new start. Starting right now. No more thinking I'm the worst mother ever, because I'm going to be better. I'm going to do better. Do things. Like exercise and eat better and, that kind of thing. Will you hold me to that, Jordan? Can you help me be accountable? And call me on it. If you see me not doing right, will you just tell me? I really need that, okay?"

"Yeah," I say, feeling lost inside my chest.

"You're just the best," she says. "Thank you thank you thank you."

"You're welcome," I mumble, and in my mind I put a question mark at the end of the sentence. But I make sure she doesn't hear it.

CHAPTER THIRTY-ONE

MAX

"Well this should be a breeze," Betts says as he creates himself a golfer on the video game. "I mean, think of all the famous Mexican golfers out there. I think I'm pretty safe."

Zay-Rod reaches over and whaps Betts on the back of the head.

"Pat Perez. Lee Trevino. Nancy Lopez. Esteban Toledo," he says. "You're one ignorant motherfucker."

"Racist-ass idiot," I say. "What does ethnicity have to do with swinging a golf club?"

"Okay, okay. God. Sensitive people, the Mexicans," Betts says. He gets another head whap from Zay-Rod for that one.

"You know, instead of swinging pretend golf clubs, we could actually go out to Kiwanis and swing real baseball bats," I say. I'm not tired of video games. I just have a lot of extra energy and this is not doing it for me.

Zay-Rod says, "Not when it's over a hundred, dude. No way."

Betts agrees with Zay-Rod, so I give up and try to settle into the game and the AC.

"So what if I said I have a boyfriend?" I ask, while Zay-Rod creates his player.

"I'd say, 'Duh,'" Betts says. "It's not like you spend every second with your food truck boy. Who's on top?"

"We haven't—" I say, and again I'm flooded with this screwed-up feeling that I push away. I really don't have the time or energy for that shit. Ever.

"Come on," Betts says. "You spend the night out, and somehow you suddenly have a job with a gay boy on a food truck the very next day."

"What kind of job?" Zay-Rod asks. "Hand? Blow?"

He and Betts high-five.

"God, why do I hang out with idiots?" I ask.

"Yeah. We're the idiots. Not the guy who gives away a thousand bucks' worth of food," Betts says. I told them about the feeding the homeless thing. They were, um. Not impressed.

"Next time you do that shit, text us," Zay-Rod says.

"Which of you smells like day-old stinky cheese? Jesus. There's a thing called a shower?" I say.

Betts farts.

Zay-Rod farts.

"Jesus," I say. "Toxic."

We play the first couple holes in silence.

"I think you'd probably hate him," I finally say.

"Who?" asks Betts.

"Jordan. Food truck boyfriend guy."

"Why? Is he Mexican?" This is Betts again, and this time he shrinks back before both me and Zay-Rod pop him in the head from opposite sides.

"Because he's . . . kinda . . . emo-ish. Kinda feminine."

Betts snorts. "So the fuck what? My girlfriend is feminine."

"Right, like you have a girlfriend," Zay-Rod says.

"Well. If I did. She'd be feminine, okay?"

"I don't care if he's whatever," Zay-Rod says. "You like him?"

"Yeah," I say.

"He treat you good?"

"Yeah."

"Who cares? Invite him over."

Betts says, "Yeah," as he drives off the tee on the fourth hole.

As I think about Jordan meeting the Amigos, a shiver goes through my body. Me meeting Pam and Kayla was one thing. I'm good with the ladies. I don't know if Jordan is good with the boys. I doubt it. It took him awhile just to learn how to talk to me.

"Nah," I say. "I think I'll pass."

"Seriously," Zay-Rod says as he sets up his tee shot. "Don't be ashamed of him. For reals, Maximo. We wanna meet the guy you're whatever-ing."

I laugh. "Um. Yeah. He's not the one I'm ashamed of."

Betts slaps me in the head, and I grin.

CHAPTER THIRTY-TWO
JORDAN

We take Friday off to paint the truck.

It's time to change the name and change the image. It's not that I don't like the name my dad picked exactly; it's just that it doesn't feel like it's ours. We spent a couple hours texting on Thursday night, trying to decide on a name and a design.

> **Me:** So . . . name ideas. Go.
>
> **Max:** Um . . . Boom Chicka Wow Wow
>
> **Me:** Oh my God no. Chicken Littles?
>
> **Max:** We're not that little
>
> **Me:** Just trying to think of puns I guess. As they say, there are no bad ideas. Except Boom Chicka Wow Wow
>
> **Max:** Dude. Don't be hatin on the Wow Wow
>
> **Me:** Chick something? Chick-Fil-B?
>
> **Max:** Haha
>
> **Me:** Chick Trick? Chick Flick?
>
> **Max:** Meh
>
> **Me:** Boom Chicka Wow Wow?
>
> **Max:** I like it. Who Gives a Cluck?
>
> **Me:** Haha better

Max: Cluck U?

Me: Even better. I kinda like that. Cluck Truck? Max and Jordan's Cluck Truck?

Max: I like that I got top billing

Me: Insert sexual innuendo here

Max: Haha

Me: Poultry in Motion?

Max: !!!!

Me: Yeah?

Max: We have a winner

Since I came up with the name, and since he is the self-proclaimed "visual artiste" of our little team, I let Max come up with the design for the truck. He chose purple with yellow lettering and he spent hours watching YouTube videos about truck painting while I slept, because I'm a delicate flower and need my beauty rest.

He arrives at 5:00 a.m., while I'm still in bed, and texts me to get my ass going because it's supposed to hit 108 this afternoon. Also there's a 10 percent chance of rain late, so better to get it done early.

I go outside pre-shower (but not pre-tooth brushing), in an old tank top that doesn't drape particularly well on my skinny-ass chest, and he's leaning against his truck, looking like a superhero in the early-morning sunlight. I hurry over to him and lean in and nuzzle his neck even though we're outside and nosy Ms. Carpenter is probably peering through her blinds, watching us.

He's assembled a large cloth over the driveway, holding it down at the corners with big rocks. Two spray painters are ready to go, and he's placed several canisters of purple, yellow, and white paint along the grass.

He holds out his hand and I place a hundred-dollar bill in it, because I promised to pay him back. He shakes his head and I add another bill. He shakes again.

"Five," he says.

I grimace. That's a lot of cash. But it's already done, and I feel like it's time to unveil Poultry in Motion.

We back the truck out of the garage and I get my laptop out, open Spotify, and play a chronological '80s playlist that begins with the Psychedelic Furs and the B-52s, and goes all the way through T'Pau, the Bangles, and ends with Janet Jackson's "Rhythm Nation." I wait for Max to notice and compliment me on the music; it doesn't happen. Instead, as we spray purple over my dad's beloved chicken cartoon, we talk. A lot.

"Do you ever wonder what goes on behind the doors of your neighbors' houses?" I ask.

Max laughs. "Creepy, dude."

"I don't mean it creepy, though. More like, isn't it amazing that we're all, I don't know."

Max doesn't say anything for a while. He's picked up a paintbrush and is concentrating all his energy on the bottom left corner of the truck. "We're all what?" he finally asks.

"Connected, maybe? My dad used to have a favorite poem and he'd recite it, which was funny because he wasn't like a real poetry kind of guy. I don't know that I even really got it until recently. Last night I was tossing and turning a lot, and the poem came to my mind and it really made me think."

"You really like poems, huh?"

"Yeah. Do you?"

"I liked the one you wrote. But seriously? Like in class, with Whitman and Frost and Langston Hughes and all that? Nah."

I start spraying over the chicken's angry face, and say a silent good-bye to my dad's creation. "Why did you like mine?"

"I guess 'cause I could feel it. It made me understand you better and shit."

"Now that's poetry," I say.

"What?"

"Language. I like when language is funny or surprising, I guess. 'It made me understand you better and shit.' I like it."

"Just 'cause I added 'and shit' it's a poem?"

"Not a poem. Just. Double meaning. Please don't make me spell it out."

Max stops painting and looks at me. "I have no idea what you're talking about."

I roll my eyes and lower my voice. "Because 'shit' could be a noun or a verb. Sorry. I know that's gross."

Max cracks up and goes back to painting. "Wow. You think that's gross. Glad you don't hang out with my buddies."

We let the Human League and Berlin be our soundtrack and we barely take breaks, even after the sun rises and starts to broil our exposed limbs. About two hours in my mom comes out, looking like she hasn't showered in a few days. She salutes and takes a look at our work with her hands on her hips.

"Oh I love a project," she says.

"You want to paint with us?" I ask, hoping she will. I want her to get to know Max. I want her to see how mature I'm getting, making big decisions like changing the name without even asking her anymore.

She looks at the car and then back at me. "I'd love to but I'm doing that thing where I live better," she says. "Remember what I said a couple nights ago? I'm now a person who does things. Normal things. I'm going to the gym. Proud of me?" She strikes a pose.

I grin wide. "Go Mom," I say. "I'm really proud of you."

She puts her head to the side, turns her left leg in, and lifts up onto her heel as if she's bashful. "Thanks," she says. "That means a lot to me. Today is the first day of the rest of my life, and other clichés."

I laugh. So does Max. She walks over to her car and curses when she touches the door handle, and then again when she gets in and touches the black leather steering wheel. She starts to drive off, then stops and rolls down the passenger-side window. "You look so handsome, Jordan," she says. "You're becoming such a handsome, strong young man. And by the way, can you pick up some plain Greek yogurt later? I'm gonna start doing protein shakes again."

I nod and shade my eyes because she's stopped at an angle where I'm looking right at the sun to look at her. She drives off.

Max says, "You have an . . . interesting relationship . . . with your mom."

"I guess," I say.

"She treats you like you're the adult. Also that handsome stuff . . . creepy, dude."

A shiver goes down my spine despite the heat. "Whatever," I say. "I'm sure everyone's relationship with their mom is weird to other people."

Max shrugs. "If you say so," he says.

We paint in silence, and I can feel pressure in my jaw from clenching. Why would he say that to me? Who is he to judge me and my mom? I rant in my head a bit, but I so don't want to fight. So when Max says, "Truck's coming along pretty good, don't you think?" I nod and say, "Yup."

Once both sides and the back are a shade of purple that makes me think of grape soda, Max takes out stencils and says we need to let the paint dry before he can do the lettering and the design. We go in and flop on the couch with two heaping glasses of ice water. Mom has left empty Go-Gurt containers on the table in front of the couch. Three of them. Cotton candy and melon berry flavored.

"Is your mom six?" Max asks, and I laugh but really my entire torso twinges at the comment.

"Yes. My mother is six. I'm negative twelve."

"I've never in my life heard of an adult eating Go-Gurt. Or known that they make a cotton candy flavor."

"Well, you learn something every day," I say.

"Does that flavor come with an insulin pump?"

"Okay!" I yell, surprising myself. "Got it. My mom is an infant and I have a weird thing with her. Got it loud and clear. I'm a freak."

Max moves closer to me on the couch. He's drenched in sweat, as am I. He hugs me from the side. "You went wide there, dude," he says. "I'm just messing with you."

"I know, but."

"I like messing with you."

"Okay," I say.

"Because I like you. But I don't have to mess with you. If you want to be serious, you just say, 'Be serious' and I will. I like having deep conversations with you."

I pull back and steal a glance into his eyes, and then avert mine from his. "You do?"

"Yes. And I'm sorry."

He kisses me. My whole body goes numb in his arms. I want to stay this way forever. With Max kissing me and being serious with me, and it being a Friday afternoon and us alone at my house on the couch, with no boundaries, where anything can happen. I feel like I could get addicted to this. I whimper into his mouth, and I feel his lips curl into a smile.

"Better?" he asks.

I nestle my head in his wet shoulder. "Better," I say.

"You know what I'd really like to do?" I shake my head no. He says, "Draw you."

I laugh, because who the hell would want to draw this. He doesn't, though, and this warm feeling races through my bloodstream. Max has that impact on me. A lot.

"Uh, sure," I say, as casually as I can, while my mind is screaming: *HE WANTS TO DRAW ME! HE WANTS TO DRAW ME!*

The other food truck folks have all sorts of comments for us when we arrive at the Gilbert Farmers' Market on Saturday morning and unveil Poultry in Motion.

"Did a fifth grader paint that?" Burrito Truck Guy says.

"You changed your name? Did you do a DBA form with the state?" asks Popcorn Guy.

The lady from Chip's Potatoes says, "You should have hired a pro."

Max and I just look at each other and roll our eyes.

"Everyone's a critic," I say as we do our prep work.

"We're getting so many hits on social media right now," Max says. He announced the name change last night. "We'll outsell them all combined."

I have to stay busy cutting lemons so that I don't attack Max then and there. I am so, so, so ready for us to do more. We make out a lot, but for a dude bro, Max has been pretty slow to take it to the next level. I figured he'd be the fast one and I'd be slower. But on the couch yesterday, when I started bringing my hands lower, he stopped me. I know he says he's into me but maybe he's lying? Maybe it's just words so he doesn't hurt my feelings? I dunno.

And we do outsell everyone. Max's cloud eggs and bacon is a huge seller, and my lemonades do a brisk business too. We get into one of those rhythms where we're just flying around the truck, doing our thing, and time is going by and we barely even feel the extraordinary heat of the grill and the outside combined.

Also we talk dirty. It's an idea I came up with while we painted yesterday. I told him that Pam, Kayla, and I used to text "Ride the light-rail" when we meant doing sex stuff. Just in case Kayla's dad, who can be a little nosey, got a hold of her phone. He'd probably wonder why she had so many long conversations about whether she was ready to take the light-rail to Phoenix with Shaun from Chess Club. Max thinks it's a funny idea.

I start it. "You give any thought to riding the light-rail?"

He totally cracks up while scraping off the grill. "Um. Yeah. It has, um, crossed my mind."

"Me too. I'm trying to be a gentleman. But I really want to try the light-rail."

I go back to take the next order. An older white guy with a ponytail orders one and one—a cloud egg with bacon and a lemonade—and as I take his money, I call back, "One and one all day. How many times have you ridden the light-rail?"

Max yells up from the grill, "Once."

"Once more than me," I say as I hand the guy back his change. "Was it . . . fun?"

"Not really," Max says. "I mean, it should have been. Got in the wrong car."

I have no idea what that means, so I yell back, "Lots of home-less people?"

Max cackles. "Hella homeless people."

The ponytail guy says, "I love riding the light-rail. I'm kind of an aficionado."

"Oh yeah?" I ask, and below the window I kick Max's foot and he kicks mine back. "What's your favorite part?"

He grins. "Trying to get away with not paying," he says, and it takes everything I can to not die laughing.

Max turns around and smiles at the guy. "You ride with friends or alone?"

"I mostly travel alone, I guess."

"Been there," I say, and Max and I laugh and the guy laughs in that polite way people laugh when they don't know why some-thing is funny. I feel kinda bad for making fun of the guy, but yeah, when he leaves, I have to whisper, "As a first order of business, cut off the ponytail. Then someone might want to ride with you" to Max, who elbows me in the ribs.

The next person in line is a middle-aged Latino guy with a clipboard.

"You got a license to run this thing?" he asks.

"I do I do," I say.

He pulls his wallet out of his pocket. "Food inspector," he says. "Can I come aboard?"

Max hears this, and he says, "Can you give us a minute to get through this line?"

The guy frowns. "No. Got a call this morning. If you're not doing things by the books, I'm here to shut you down."

I think, *Who the hell would want to shut us down?*

He comes on and inspects our food prep area. He makes a few marks, and I try to see what he must be seeing. I have cut-up lemons I haven't thrown out yet, and some prickly pear cut open and ready to go on the counter next to the blender.

"You wash this after every use?"

"Yes," I lie. Since there's only one kind of lemonade, I tend to wash it once every few hours. Maybe that's not enough? Shit.

He makes another mark, and then he observes Max and the grill.

"Separate areas for the eggs and the bacon?"

"Yes, sir," Max says. I'm not sure, but I think this is a lie. Luckily, there's no major mess on the grill right now, nor are there any grill markings that would betray Max's story.

The guy looks at the four rows of chicken breasts next to the grill. "How long you keep these out before you grill them?"

"Less than fifteen minutes," Max says, and he pulls out a meat thermometer and stabs into one of the breasts. He turns his head sideways and reads it. "Thirty-nine exactly. Which is two degrees under what's allowable."

The guy makes another mark, and I can't tell if the marks are good or bad. "Let me see your license, please."

I go up to the dashboard and pull out what I have — our food handling cards, the truck's license, the truck's registration. He shuffles through them and stares at the license.

"It says Coq au Vinny," he says.

"That was our name. Up until yesterday. We re-painted and re-branded," Max says.

"You have a DBA form?"

"A what?" I ask.

"Doing business as."

"Um," I say, and I remember Popcorn Guy. Asshole. He must have called in and told the inspector. Why would anyone do that to some kids who are just trying to make an honest buck?

He fills out a form, rips it off the pad, and slaps it down next to our cash register.

"Fifty-dollar fine," he says. "And you're out of business until you get one."

I'm about to argue, but Max pulls on my sleeve and I close my mouth.

"How long will that take?" Max asks.

The guy shrugs. "Beats me. If I see you out here, or anywhere, again without a DBA, the fine will be five hundred. You hear me?"

We both nod in silence. A heaviness enters the pit of my

stomach as he leaves. We turn on the fan and close both the service window and the back door.

"This isn't good, dude," he says.

"Thanks, Captain Obvious."

"No. It isn't good because we have a refrigerator full of thawed chicken breasts. Like hundreds of them. We've been selling easily two hundred a day, so I figured . . ."

"Yeah," I say. "I get it. How long will they last?"

"A few days, tops. But the ones here have been thawed since Thursday, and you don't want to re-freeze them. Tomorrow at the latest for about a hundred."

"Shit," I say, doing the math in my head.

"Bad time to have just put out five hundred on paint," he says.

I sit on the filthy floor and put my head in my hands and think about what to do.

What would my dad do in this situation? He was always good in a crisis.

I have no idea.

"Sorry, dude," Max says.

"You feel like being a scofflaw?" I ask.

He laughs like I'm joking. I'm not. "How many food truck inspectors do you think there are?" I ask.

"I have no idea."

"Well, let's look it up. If there's like, one, how dangerous could it be?"

He shakes his head. "Dude," he says. "I dunno."

"Well, a week ago I had enough money to pay the back mortgage. Now I'm short. We can't stop now. I had to pay you and for the paint, plus us being idiots and living big those couple nights."

"So we'll get legal," he says. "C'mon, dude. I'm not doing illegal shit. My mom would kill me."

"Maybe just the thawed chicken? 'Til that's gone?"

"Where would we go?"

"Well, wherever we go, it should be where no other trucks are," I say. "And it should be legal. And you shouldn't put it on social media, because they're probably tracking us now."

Max says, "Trampoline place in Tempe?"

I smile. "I knew you were a badass."

He rolls his eyes. "We'll see."

It turns out it's not that easy to just park the truck at a location in Phoenix in the summer and expect foot traffic. We park in the trampoline parking lot, which may or may not be legal, and lots of kids go in and out but almost no one stops at our truck. We sell a couple frozen lemonades to a mom and her daughter as they leave, but as far as chicken goes, we get shut out. I guess jumping up and down while eating spicy chicken is not recommended.

We close up and Max says we should try the escape room place in south Scottsdale. We get there, though, and there's literally no place to park, as it is right on Scottsdale Road.

"We could do Zorba's," I say, pointing in the direction of the infamous dirty bookstore.

He laughs. "Good plan."

"Can you think of any place where there would definitely be people?"

He gets on his phone and surfs around for a bit. Finally, he says, "D-backs game?"

Having never been to a Diamondbacks game, I have no idea if this is a good plan or not. But I'm getting desperate. I'm afraid we're gonna waste hundreds of dollars of chicken if we don't find a location in the next day or two.

So we park in front of Talking Stick Resort Arena, a couple blocks west of Chase Field, as the streets closer to it are cordoned off. We face the sidewalk and soon we're doing a brisk business with people heading to the ballpark for an afternoon game, not wanting to eat the horrible food there—their words, not mine.

"Two habanero all day," I yell back to Max, about an hour into our stay there. A police officer walks up.

"Do you have a permit to be here?" he asks.

I freeze up. "Do we need one?"

He frowns. "Yes you need one. Get moving."

I nod, finish the order we're on, apologize to the other people in line, and we close up and jet.

As Max drives east on Van Buren, back toward home, we try to look at the bright side.

"At least we sold some," I yell up from my seated position on a cooler in the aisle behind him. My words are carried away by the open passenger-side door.

"I guess," Max yells back, and I hear the words more clearly than I expect. That's when I realize we've come to a stop. I look out the window. We are not at a light.

"Shit!" Max yells. "Shit shit shit."

"What happened?"

"Poultry is not in motion," he says.

Max has to turn off the truck as we wait to be towed. We sit there in the stagnant heat, watching cars go around us. Most of the drivers give us the finger as they go by. As if we're just taking a rest in the middle of two-lane Van Buren Street.

"This is where the no-tell motels are," Max says.

"You mean like hookers?"

"Yup."

"Firsthand experience?" I ask, and he punches me lightly on the shoulder.

"Got some shit to figure out," Max says, and I realize that this is karma. Our hubris. I celebrated too early. I have no idea what this will cost, but suddenly more money is going out than coming in, and who knows how long it will take to make the truck legal and drivable again.

"That we do," I say. "Gotta look up homeless shelters for me and my mom."

"Don't say that," Max says, but he doesn't contradict my statement either.

CHAPTER THIRTY-THREE

MAX

A fairly accurate recording of the first-ever meeting of me and my Amigos and Jordan and his wives. In the style of a play, because Jordan is rubbing off on me.

Max: You made it! Hey!

Pam: Did you think we'd die getting here? Get struck by lightning? A meteor? Yes we made it.

Jordan: Chill. I think he was just saying hi.

Pam: Don't tell me to chill. You chill. Bitch.

Max: Okay. So . . .

Kayla: Hi, sweetie. [*Hugs Max*] We have heard so much about you recently. Including the obvious lie that you are not doing the nasty with our husband.

Jordan: Kayla!

Pam: I mean, for real. Sure. You're not fucking. That makes total sense. Right.

Max: So . . . um, Pam, Kayla, meet my buddies. We call

this guy Betts. Real name Ron Betts. You choose what to call him, or better yet just ignore him because, well, you'll see. And this is Xavier Rodriguez. Goes by Zay-Rod in these parts.

Pam: Hey.

Kayla: Hey.

Betts: What up.

Zay-Rod: What up.

[*Awkward silence lasting perhaps twenty seconds . . .*]

Max: So . . .

Jordan: You keep saying that.

Max: Someone's gotta say something.

Pam: So awkward. This is why I don't make new friends. So it doesn't feel like this ever.

Kayla: Yeah, THIS is the reason you don't make new friends. The ONLY reason. Nothing about your personality.

Pam: Bitch, I will throw you in the dryer and put you on spin cycle. Bitch, I will haunt you all your life and terrorize your children.

Zay-Rod: [*Laughing*] So you are basically us.

Pam: What?

Zay-Rod: You're us. Jordan is the misfit [*points to Max*], she's the one with all the privilege who thinks she's all that [*points to Betts*], and you're the hot one.

Max: Hey!

Jordan: Hey!

Kayla: Hey!

Betts: Hey!

Pam: Hi!

Betts: Privilege my ass. Straight white men are the new minority.

Max: Why are you so stupid?

Pam: Why haven't I seen you around?

Zay-Rod: I seen you.

Pam: Yeah?

Zay-Rod: Yeah.

Kayla: Does this mean I'm stuck with this idiot?

Betts: I'm not an idiot.

Kayla: You're not NOT an idiot.

Betts: True.

Zay-Rod: You like to hang out?

Pam: Depends.

Zay-Rod: On?

Pam: [*Smiles*]

Kayla: Jordan, you need to stop this before it starts, and she doesn't listen to me. Tell Pam she cannot get with this boy because you're with his friend and that leaves me with this guy and he's not viable.

Betts: What? How am I not viable? [*Flexes his biceps*]

Kayla: [*Pointing with a finger and then circling with it in Betts's direction*] Um. This.

Betts: Oh please. Like you're so hot.

Kayla: No. You. Didn't.

Pam: No. You. Didn't.

Betts: What? You just said the same thing to me.

Zay-Rod: Read the room, B.

Betts: I'm telling you. Straight white men are the new oppressed class.

Max: He was dropped on his head a lot when he was a kid.

Zay-Rod: And he continues to fall on his head which is why it's so misshapen.

Max: Oh snap.

Betts: At least I'm not . . . [*Pauses, looks around, stomps a foot*] Damn it. I got nothing.

Kayla: Aww, poor baby. [*She goes behind him and rubs his shoulders*]

Betts: Oh. Okay. New strategy. Um, I'm a loser baby . . .

Kayla: [*Laughs*] Better, yeah. I cannot take that bravado stuff. Makes me nauseated. I like a man who knows he's less than.

Betts: Oh I'm less than . . .

Kayla: Yeah, but this is never, ever, ever going to happen, so maybe just stop trying? No offense.

Betts: [*Rolling his eyes*] None taken.

Pam: So question . . . Who here buys that these two are not having sex on the daily?

(Only Max and Jordan raise their hands)

Betts: Sure.

Kayla: I know, right? They should embrace it. We're all sexual beings.

Betts: Yep.

Zay-Rod: Yep.

Pam: Yep.

Jordan: But, um. Okay. So we're taking it slow? Because there's more to life than sex?

[*Everyone but Max and Jordan make a sound that connotes disbelief*]

Max: He's not lying. Why are you so up in our business anyway?

Pam: We're not. We just like the truth, is all.

Kayla: Exactly. Here you have all these friends who love you exactly as you are, and you can't even be real about having sex.

Betts: He's so repressed. Won't tell us anything.

Kayla: Oh my God! He's your Jordan. Do you give him makeovers and pep talks when you find his dildos?

Jordan: Kayla!

Max: Wha? This is, um. Information.

Jordan: [*Turning the color of an eggplant*] Pre-dating you, and can we not discuss this please?

Betts: Nice. So Maximo is the guy?

Pam: The guy?

Kayla: [*Play slaps him*] What is wrong with you? They're both guys. Are you one of those boys who thinks if you're penetrated you're no longer male? Because that's fucked-up.

Pam: True. And what about you?

Zay-Rod: Leave me outta this. B you're on your own.

Betts: Nice loyalty.

Kayla: You were this close to being passable, but that misogyny shit knocked you down five pegs.

Betts: How the hell is that misogyny? Do you all live in crazy town?

Zay-Rod: B, think back a couple minutes. Strategy, dude.

Betts: Oh, right. [*Puts his head in his hands*] I'm a useless man. . . .

Kayla: Insincere.

Pam: I know, right?

Betts: I can't do or say anything right.

Kayla: [*Back to massaging his shoulders*] Now we're getting somewhere.

Betts: I will stop talking now.

Max: Good choice.

CHAPTER THIRTY-FOUR

JORDAN

The girls and I debrief at the Chandler Mall food court.

"Zay is smokin'," Pam says, as she picks at her usual Panda Express junk.

"He goes by Zay-Rod," I say.

"Whatever. He's hot."

Kayla is off her diet and is eating a chocolate chip cookie from Panera for dinner. "How come you get the hot one and I get the one I'm not interested in?"

Pam shrugs. "Don't hate me because I'm beautiful. And anyway you have Shaun."

"That's not gonna happen," Kayla says, pouting. "He was absolutely, one hundred percent leading me on, which, if you think about it, is ironic because two years ago I would have totally ignored him in the hallway."

"Which speaks highly of your character," I add.

"Well, yes. But really we're talking about the social order here. And speaking of which, I feel like there are gonna be two couples and I'm gonna be stuck with Ron Betts, who is . . . basic."

"Basic dude bro," Pam says, slurping her soda.

"Agreed," I say. "Is Max?"

Kayla shakes her head. "That boy is quality. You need to keep riding that."

"I'm not—"

She smiles in a way that tells me she's somewhat kidding.

"So let me run something by you," I say.

Neither girl stops chewing in any way that connotes, *I'm listening.* I go on anyway.

"I'm working on this poem. I've been thinking about the connections between people. That Max and I have gone to the same school for all these years and we didn't even know each other until some crazy coincidence that he happened to walk by the food truck when my mom was melting down."

Kayla suppressed a smirk. "Did we know that?"

"I think so?"

"Lydia Edwards in *Super Fragile House Widows of Chandler.*"

A bubble forms in my throat, and I swallow it. "So anyway, a big coincidence leads us to meet, and now, I don't know if he's like my forever boyfriend, but he's important in my life. And maybe you and Zay-Rod? I dunno."

"I'm not even tryin' to—" Pam says, but a look in her eyes tells me she's thought a lot about it since the other night when the six of us got together.

"So connections. How does it all work? Is there a God that does this, or is it all just coincidence? And like the movie *Sliding Doors.* Did you see that? Gwyneth Paltrow gets on a subway, and in an alternate universe she doesn't, and her life is drastically altered either way."

I have so much more to say, and I know this is a stretch. I knew it when I started talking. But that's probably why I did. Because I feel like with Pam and Kayla, I'm forced to play this character. The GBF. Gay Best Friend. Campy and snarky and all on the surface. And I know that I'm not just that. And neither are they. I've known both Pam and Kayla for a long time, and while the moments have been few and far between, they've happened. I like them. I want more of them.

"It's summer," Kayla finally says.

"Yes . . ." I respond.

"I don't do ideas in the summer."

Pam says, "I'm with K. Save that shit for fall."

I'm used to trash talk, but for some reason this hits me hard in the chest. Like a sucker punch. I clench my teeth and avert my eyes so I don't say something I can't take back later. They don't seem to notice my reaction. Kayla kind of looks at me for a second and I wonder if she's going to apologize. But then she doesn't. At all.

"Let's do another makeover," Kayla says. "You're not as white as usual. Probably because of the food truck and you being outside so much. Plus we need to find you food truck chic."

Pam says, "Yes. That."

I stand then, because I'm so not in the mood.

"Pass," I say.

Kayla laughs. "Pass? You can't pass."

"Queer card," I mumble, but I'm over it.

She says, "Overruled. White girl card."

And for once in my life, I say no to Kayla.

"Overruled. Human," I say, barely choking the words out. "Taking an Uber home. Bye."

I ignore texts from Kayla and Pam as I wait for the Uber. While I wait, I get a crazy idea. I tell the driver to take me to Whole

Foods instead of home. I know it's expensive, but enough is enough. The Go-Gurt episode really bothered me. I need to help Mom eat healthier.

So even though we're at a money deficit with the truck I buy loads of fruit and vegetables, and stuff like unsweetened almond milk, and boneless, skinless chicken breasts and things I can use to make a marinade, because I've been watching Max for the past few weeks and we have a grill and I'm going to use it from now on. I don't buy anything frozen. I don't buy her cereal or snacks. Just real food, and when I wait for my Uber home, with my two bags of groceries that cost $115 (I know, right?), I feel good about myself.

There are texts from Pam and Kayla.

Pam: K, so . . . we talked about it, and you get a pass on being RUDE because we were bein kinda shitty. Sorry. U okay? We're worried about you. Your different.

Kayla: I'm sorry too, sweetie

Me: Thanks. I love you. Sorry for walking out. I'm changing and I kinda like it, ok?

Pam: That's cool

Kayla: Yup

Me: Thx

Kayla: And your really not having sex and hiding it from us?

Me: I would not do that. Srsly

Pam: Cool. We'll stop messing with u about it

Me: No you wont <smiley face>

Kayla: (After sending a meme of an actress dramatically blowing a kiss) Prolly not luvu

Me: (After sending a meme of an actor catching a kiss) Luvu

Pam: (After sending a meme of a big woman kissing a camera lens, leaving a lipstick mark) Luvu

I smile in the back of the Uber. I'm growing up. I'm asserting myself with Kayla and Pam. I'm gonna start taking better care of my mom. It's all good.

When I get home and start unpacking groceries, Mom is on the couch, watching *House Hunters* with a Diet Pepsi and a Twinkie. Meal of champions. Dorcas is on her lap. So much for her being a person who does things.

"Ooh, Whole Foods," she says. "Food truck stuff? How fancy."

"Nope," I say, opening the refrigerator and putting everything away. "This is for us. Like the Greek yogurt you wanted. I thought I'd go the next step. More vegetables and fruit, less prepared meals and crap."

She laughs.

"Why are you laughing?"

"That's really sweet, but. You don't get to decide what I eat. I don't like vegetables. You know that."

I shut the refrigerator. "You said you were going to do better. I'm just trying to keep you accountable, like you asked—"

"Vegetables are awful," she says. "They grow in dirt, Jordan."

I crack up. "We should sell that slogan to the vegetable lobby."

"Seriously," she says. "I'm not doing green stuff. There's only so much change I can take, okay?"

She takes a bite of her Twinkie, and a twinge of something goes through my chest. "That crap will kill you," I say.

She exaggeratedly lies back and rolls her eyes back into her head like she's becoming a corpse. "Well hurry up Twinkie," she says.

"Mom," I say. "That's so not funny."

"Oh my God!" she shouts, and I am stunned frozen. "I get it! You're perfect. I'm a total fuckup. I am so far below acceptable and there's about zero chance that will ever change. I get it, okay?"

The energy in the room shifts, lightning fast. Dorcas barks and scurries out the dog door, like she feels it. I stare at my mom with my mouth open. Words do not come out. I don't even have a coherent thought of how to respond to that.

She sighs dramatically. Herstrionically. "Forget it," she says. "Forget I said anything. I'm not me, okay? I'm not myself. I don't remember the last fuckin' time I was myself but it was no time in recent history."

She closes her eyes, throws the remaining bites of the Twinkie down on the plate in front of her, and stands. "Excuse me. I just need to—" And she walks away toward her bedroom. Moments later, I hear her door close softly.

I stand, stare toward the hallway, and then sit down in her spot on the couch. It's still warm from her body, and instead of her usual blueberries and shea butter scent, it's just a little sour, like yeah, no shower today for sure. How do I fix my mom? How do I do what my dad asked me to do?

I flash back to when I was the big one-three. First wet dream, first boy crush, last of my guy friends before they all decided I was too weird. Dad's been in the hospital for a month and I'm not allowed to see him too often because he's in rough shape, I guess. She's not her chatterbox self either. It's always been normal for her to flop down on the couch next to me and tell me about her ingrown toenail, or how Dr. Mohler, her dentist-boss, farted while giving some lady an exam and they all just pretended it didn't happen. This is the first time in my life that she's not saying stuff, and I know whatever's going on with Dad is bad. Real bad.

I'm sitting in the blue-walled kitchen on a stool, my feet up on the Formica countertop.

"Off," my mom says, headed for the refrigerator. "You're coming with me today." She grabs a jar of pickles. Half sours. Our favorites.

"Where?"

"To see Daddy. He has some things—" she stops speaking, puts an entire pickle into her mouth, and walks down the hall to their bedroom. That's the extent of our conversation.

It's been just a couple weeks since I saw Dad, but when I walk into his room at the hospital he looks like he's been photoshopped. Like someone came and added deep, puffy bags under his eyes, and erased about 40 percent of his chest bulk, and wrinkled his arms, which are now painted grayish white. I can't stop staring at him.

I sit down next to his bed and he reaches a freakishly frail hand out and touches my leg.

"Hey J-Bird," he says, his voice encrusted with slurry, it seems like.

"Hey Daddy."

"You keepin' everyone in line while I'm down for the count?"

"Yes," I say, ashamed that, no, I'm totally not. If that's my job, I'm really failing.

"Remember. You get extra points if you take care of your mom and keep her happy."

"And the points have no monetary value," I say, stealing his punch line, and he smiles, and he puts his head back and stares straight ahead. We sit like this for quite a while, and suddenly he's sleeping, which, oddly enough, makes me feel relieved. Because as much as I want to hear my dad's voice—gravelly as it is right now—for eternity, this way I don't have to think about what I should say. I'm so selfish.

His hand remains on my leg, and I allow myself to close my eyes too, and imagine my dad throwing me a Frisbee when I was eight, and his utter bemusement when I totally whiffed trying to catch it, like missed it 100 percent.

"So you're not an Ultimate Frisbee guy," he said, and I shook my head and stared at my feet, and he came and put his arm around me. "Everyone needs to find their own game," he said. "And sometimes . . . sometimes the game isn't even a game."

I don't know how my eight-year-old mind got this from those words, but in that moment what I heard was that my dad knew I was different, and as much as he was a cowboy sort of guy, with a fuzzy walrus mustache and a cowboy hat and Wrangler jeans, I'd never be any of those things, and it was okay with him.

After about an hour of him napping, he awakens with a start and says, "What time is it?"

I look at my phone. "Four thirty," I say.

He looks confused. "Morning or night?"

"What?" I say. "Night. Afternoon."

"What day is it? Tuesday?"

"Um. Saturday," I say.

He turns his head away and stares straight ahead. "Oh."

"Just in case there's a test," I say. It's something he says all the time.

My dad takes a deep breath and turns his frail neck to look at me again. "There's a test?"

I laugh, because this. This is what I miss. Dad joking with me. But he keeps looking at me, like he's waiting for an answer.

"Yup," I say.

He slowly turns his body until his stick legs are over the side. "Well let's get going," he says.

I sit straight up and try to push his legs back onto the bed. "No. Dad. No. We're not going anywhere."

He looks so confused. His face. Like he has no idea what's going on. "But there's a test."

"I was kidding, Dad," I say, but now his face is contorted into a mask of pain, and he starts to wail.

I've never heard this noise coming from my dad the cowboy. I don't know what to do.

"Mom! Mom!" I call. She's been sitting out in the hallway. I hope.

No one comes. "Help!" I scream, above my dad's wails, and I start to cry too.

A nurse comes in, and then a second, and they help my dad get back into a more comfortable position, lying down with his legs on the bed. And then my mom comes in, and she must have heard, or someone must have told her, because she looks stricken, panicked.

My dad says, "How to give your father a heart attack," and he won't look at me. I need him to look at me. He will not. Or cannot. I don't know.

Mom puts her hand on my back and says, "Let's get you out of here," and I stand and she leads me away from the room.

I never see my dad again. "How to give your father a heart attack" are his last words to me.

And I think maybe it's my fault that he died. That maybe he just needed rest and that his fragile heart and his aching lungs needed stillness, and me riling him up with my stupidity was the last straw, and that's what did it.

My mom cries for eighteen hours straight. Nothing can stop her during the service, or after, and I can hear the sobs from my room even with her down the hall and my door closed. And I think that I am broken, because I have no tears. I try to push them out. I feel sad. I feel nothing too. I don't know how to feel anything and I take out a pen and paper and write a poem that I think my dad may have liked.

Because to me you're the sun
I cannot shine without you
And all of our memories
They're all that I ever do
Because I can't forget your smile
You know it's all I ever see
You see I can't forget your smile
Now you've become a part of me.

I know now that it's a terrible poem, but it was real at the moment, and I put it away and just having it in my pocket made me feel like Dad and I had a secret.

And at home, things got bad. And when Mom falls onto the bathroom floor and starts screaming and writhing, I pick her up, and when she tells me that no one will ever love her again, I tell her that someone will. That I do. That I'll take care of her, and she's like a little girl and her hands are bigger than mine but somehow look tiny as I take her to her bed and tuck her in.

And when she closes her eyes I go to my room and I close the door and I go to my bookcase, and I tip it over and it shatters into two pieces, the top clattering into the far wall. She never comes in to check about the commotion. She never mentions it. I leave it there for three days but Mom acts like it isn't there, so finally I just pick up the busted bookshelf and carry its two pieces out to the shed in the backyard, where they still sit, untouched, as it was Dad's shed, and when something goes wrong we don't look for tools; we go to the phone and call the handyman.

And I am always sorry I tipped over the bookshelf.

And I'll never do anything like that again.

CHAPTER THIRTY-FIVE

MAX

With the truck still out of commission, we assemble the posse of six for a little Third Friday fun. We start the night out by eating as a group at one of the communal tables at Short Leash, which makes awesome gourmet hot dogs and puts them in naan bread.

I get the devil dog, which has red pepper, green chilies, sriracha, onion, cheddar, and jalapeños. It's the perfect mix of spicy and savory. Betts of course gets the most disgusting thing on the menu. It has smoked Gouda, bacon, peanut butter, BBQ sauce, and Cracker Jacks. He eats like a caveman, and Kayla makes a big show of getting up and moving as far away from Betts as possible. Betts reacts by chewing with his mouth open.

"They have a food truck," I say.

Jordan says, "I saw that. You ever think about doing something with hot dogs?"

"Totally. We should re-paint and re-name the truck," I say, and Jordan cracks up. It's day six of us being without a food truck, and we just found out yesterday that the license will be ready on Monday. The truck, though, needs some love, according to the guys at the shop my mom helped me find. It's gonna cost about two grand, and it's gonna take another full week before it's ready.

"I think we can expand off chicken, though," Jordan says.

I nod and sip my soda. "Sure. As long as we have the chicken options front and center. Yeah."

Pam rolls her eyes and says, "Our friends have gotten weird and boring," to Zay-Rod, and he nods.

"I know, right? You know they have a food truck? Haven't heard that five trillion times."

Pam laughs. Jordan curls his lip down like his feelings are hurt.

He says, "You are."

Pam kisses him on the cheek. For effect, Zay-Rod kisses me on the cheek too, only he does it after rubbing mustard on his lips, leaving a mustard stain.

"What is wrong with you?" I say, wiping it off. "Did your momma not love you as a child?"

Zay-Rod takes his fingers and rubs mustard on my forehead. Betts slams his fist into the table, because he's enjoying this, and because he's an idiot.

We finish up, pay, and wander down Roosevelt. Third Friday is this thing Phoenix does on the third Friday of every month, where they open art galleries downtown, food trucks show up, and it's like a mini-festival atmosphere. A lot of kids from school do it. It's an opportunity to drink beers out of paper bags and the police don't bug anyone unless you get out of hand.

"Are we really outside? Purposefully?" Kayla asks as we saunter past the church where people go in and listen to this famous choir as they practice.

"Wimp," Betts says. "You stay inside all summer?"

"Basically," she says. "Do you not do that? That's like Darwin Award–level idiocy."

"Oh good, I get to be called an idiot again by a chick."

She swats him in the shoulder. He grabs his shoulder in mock agony. She swats him in the other shoulder, and I can actually see the slight grin she's trying to hold in. Maybe they won't be a couple, but I'm kinda glad they're starting to dig each other.

Meanwhile, Pam and Zay-Rod are going the other direction. They're quiet, just sort of walking together. Both looking at their phones. Both with serene expressions, as if they're just minding their own business. It does not take a genius to know they are texting each other.

I nudge Jordan and watch the picture of our friends doing their collective things. He nudges me back.

"This makes me happy," he says.

"This makes me feel sorry for your friends."

He laughs. "This makes me feel sorrier for your friends."

We pass a woman who is drawing a mural on the sidewalk in turquoise chalk. I turn to Jordan.

"Hooligan do-gooder?" I ask.

His face lights up. "Yes!" he says. Betts and Kayla and Zay and Pam have kept walking, and we're fine with that. We can find them later.

"You got a poem?"

He looks so happy. That makes me smile. Jordan has changed quite a bit from the emo dude I met a month ago. He radiates now, and that makes me feel good. I'm Super Max. I have the power to transform people.

He flips through his phone. "I sent myself one yesterday," he says. "I think it doesn't totally suck."

"People love poems that don't suck," I say, and I tap the woman on the shoulder and ask if I can borrow some chalk. She smiles and hands me a variety of colors and points to the ground next to her, inviting me to join her in making the street beautiful. I thank her, kneel down, and touch the sidewalk. Even though it's nighttime and the sun has been down for a couple hours already, the concrete is hot hot hot. I can touch it for like five seconds and then I have to pull my hand off. That's how powerful the sun is.

Jordan kneels down and says, "Did I tell you about that poem my dad liked?"

I remember something about that while we painted the truck. I nod.

"So basically I looked it up. It's by Seamus Heaney, this famous Irish poet. Can I read it to you?"

I nod, and I sit on the hot concrete, savoring the heat emanating from the ground through my shorts.

He reads:

"A rowan like a lipsticked girl.
Between the by-road and the main road
Alder trees at a wet and dripping distance
Stand off among the rushes.

There are the mud-flowers of dialect
And the immortelles of perfect pitch
And that moment when the bird sings very close
To the music of what happens."

I look up at him. He's staring intently at me.

"I like that," I say. "I don't get it, but I dig it. I wanna draw the trees."

Jordan shakes his head. "I haven't read you my poem yet. That one influenced mine."

"Oh," I say, and for just a tiny sliver of a second, I'm uncomfortable. Because people are gathered around now. I am sitting on the ground, ready to draw, and they listened to the poem Jordan read, and it was good. What if Jordan's poem isn't? Will I have to lie to him and tell him that it is?

Jordan's eyes read fear, and I realize he's reacting to me saying, "Oh." So I smile wide, swallowing down my own stuff.

"Go for it!" I say. "I wanna hear."

He smiles tentatively, and I give him an encouraging nod. My boyfriend the poet. It's cool, really. I dig it.

"I call it, 'The Music of What Happens.' After the last line of the Heaney poem."

He reads.

"Down the street from me
Ms. Carter douses her head
The shower pulses
And spits her sins down the drain

Next house over, with the red plastic Adirondack chairs
Mr. Simmons cries while eating waffles
His sink bone dry
Dishes with dried-up barbeque pork and oatmeal pile high

Mowing the front lawn next door
Jimmy Fowler dreams of Jenny Carmichael
And her fantastic tits

Mr. Torres in his two-story mini-palace
Sits on his bathroom throne
His waste meeting Ms. Carter's sins somewhere
Under Carriage Lane

Here and there
We
Eat blueberries out of a ramekin
Chat with strangers about the sex we won't be having
Read fake news about the end of the world
Peer over our shoulder at the pimple on our back
Check our breath for rampant bacterial stench
Straighten the family portrait, the one where Kim grimaces
for some unknown reason
Dream of a better street
Ignore the sewage below our feet—
Which shows that we are human, and that's the worst—

And soon there is a knock on Ms. Carter's door
She answers, her hair in its final bun, her smile pasted on
Like a child playing with Elmer's
And the man asks
Can I climb your palm tree

And knock off the dead fronds

And she nods, because he is saving her life

And she says, as if it's nothing, 'Sure.'"

People clap. Jordan blushes. I tear up.

He's beautiful. My boyfriend is beautiful. I don't understand the whole poem, but there were so many images, and I think I get it in general. The way we're all connected, like he said when we were painting the truck. It tingles up my midsection, that I am truly connected to this guy. To my friends, even though they're, you know.

Even though, yes, this bad thing happened to me. And Kevin is a bad person. A user and abuser, as my mom would say. But not everyone is bad. Jordan would never hurt me like that, and in that moment I realize we don't have to go slow anymore. He's not Kevin.

I stand and go over to the woman with the chalk. She's stopped and listened, and she is beaming up at Jordan too.

"Can I borrow a navy blue?" I ask, and she searches for one and puts it proudly in my hand.

"Your boyfriend is a real poet," she says, and I nod.

"Thanks," I say. "He is."

I go back and start drawing a white ramekin. I close my eyes and picture how the ones we have in our kitchen have these ridges on the side. Then I start adding navy blueberries inside. I shade them with just a touch of black, like a shadow.

Jordan sits down next to me and watches. I look up and there are Betts, Zay-Rod, Pam, and Kayla, watching me. I look in Betts's eyes. I wonder if he thinks this is hilarious and he's gonna mock me one day, like he mocks Zay-Rod's poetry.

But his eyes aren't mocking. It's more like he's seeing me for the first time. And in that moment, it's like I see the dude for the first time too. He's more than the guy I trash-talk with. He's my buddy. I think maybe I trusted Zay-Rod could be, but I wondered about Betts.

I smile at him. He smiles at me. I draw blueberries.

CHAPTER THIRTY-SIX

JORDAN

Max: U up

Me: Yup. My mom didn't come home again

Max: Shit. She didn't leave a note?

Me: Nope. it's like three nights this week

Max: U wanna do something

Me: <smiley face> What do u have in mind

Max: Get yer mind outta the gutter <smiley face> I'll pick u up in 5.

Me: It's 1:06 a.m.

Max: Thank you captain obvious. Wear gym shorts

My heart flutters at the thought of a late night with Max. This summer. First time in my life I've been alive, really. I love it. Even with my mom's . . . whatever. Even with me needing to make money to keep our house. I always thought I couldn't do stuff. But I can.

Mom is who knows where. I'm pretty sure she's been staying out all night, because she came home this morning at around 7:30, looking like a total mess, her hair pasted to her forehead and unwashed, her normal sweet smell replaced with a bitter funk that made me wince.

I have no fucking idea what's up. There's nothing I can do about it, and I've given up on trying.

As I step outside I have to laugh.

There's something about the feeling of being in an outdoor sauna at midnight in late June that just takes my breath away. Like I can't imagine how the sun can generate so much heat while it's not even up. How my body can shiver from the shock of the temperature while just stepping out into the darkness is a mystery to me. And Max loves this shit. I will never get that.

"You ready?" he asks as I get into the passenger seat. He doesn't have the AC going—of course he doesn't. He's Max.

"Ready as a person can be when he doesn't know what he should be ready for," I say, and he revs up the truck and pulls onto Carriage Lane and heads north. He grins.

We pull up to 24 Hour Fitness, which is literally less than a mile from where I live and in a strip mall on the way to school, yet I've never even seen it as it's tucked away on the side. He puts this purple fob up against this red light and the front door automatically opens, and we are hit with cool air. Thank the Humble Baby Jesus. If it was another AC-less Max Special in here, I was going to turn on my heels and walk home.

My last workout was never. I have never really thought it would be great to have big muscles, or more like, even if I did once or twice think, *What would it be like to be all pumped?* my curiosity wasn't strong enough to overrule my general disdain for lifting things for no apparent reason. That's the thing about bodybuilding, I guess. You have to really want it.

The gym is totally empty. No workers, no exercisers. Purple walls and rugs, the antiseptic smell of cleaning product. The lights are bright for this time of night, and a Korn song I can't stand is playing lightly on the sound system—not loud enough to be annoying but loud enough that I wish it were almost anything else.

Max heads over to this corner where there are these multi-colored weights with handles on them, a bunch of big, bouncy balls, and a stainless steel apparatus with what appears to be three stations: some pulley system with weights and a steel handle, a rope hanging down from another machine, and a platform that appears to be adjustable, set high enough that I'd have to jump up to get onto it.

"We're doing Tabatas," he says. This means nothing to me, so I nod. He fiddles with his phone. "I have this app that helps us. My theory is jump in to the deep end before your brain tells you not to."

"I think that's how people drown," I say, and he gives me a dirty look. He pulls a black mat down and puts it on the scratchy-looking purple rug, and then grabs a large black ball that looks like the basketballs that kids used to hurl at my head back in fifth grade before I figured out that I should probably come up with a nagging shoulder injury so I could skip gym class. Extra study hall every day? Thanks, fake bum shoulder! He puts the ball down and it makes a surprising thump. Then I see that it says *20 lbs* on it, and my eyes go wide. He sees this and he grabs a slightly smaller one that says *15 lbs* on it and puts it down next to the other one.

"Is there a one pounder, maybe?" I ask.

He doesn't answer. Instead he shows me what we're doing.

"It's twenty seconds on, ten seconds rest. Four different

exercises. You'll start with the throw down." He shows me how it's done, squatting down, picking up the twenty-pound ball, lifting it over his head, and then slamming it down onto the purple rug with a loud thump. It's not the kind of ball that bounces. Then he squats again and does it again.

"Twenty seconds. The app counts down the last five seconds and you get a beep when you're done. Then you come over to the rope." He shows me the rope(s), literally. It's a circular rope pulley, and he starts pulling down on it as fast as he can. It actually looks kind of fun. He shows me that we'll do a forward grip and a backward grip on the rope pull, and in between, we'll do what he calls "burpees."

Burpees seem basically like God's way of punishing you for wanting to get into good shape. You start with your hands over your head, you fall into a squat, then kick your legs back to a push-up position, do a push-up, then pull your legs back into a squat, and then you jump up to the start position again.

Max will start with the forward grip rope pull and I'll start with the ball slams. Twenty seconds on, ten seconds rest, and then right to the next exercise. Four sets of all four, or eight minutes.

It actually doesn't sound that bad. If you think about it, some of that time is resting, so it's not even staying active for eight minutes. It'll be fine, I decide.

He presses a button and a succession of beeps sounds, and then he says, "Ready?"

I say, "Yup."

The final beep comes and we go.

The fifteen-pound ball is heavier than it looks. My legs shake as I pick it up in a squat and try to stand. Then my arms shake as

I lift it over my head, and it slips from my hand. It glances against my forehead, not entirely pleasantly, and it slams into the ground with a huge thump.

"Ow," I say, and Max looks back and stops what he's doing.

"You okay?" he says, smirking.

My face reddens and I look away, pissed. He's started me too high. He's used to this shit. I can't do this. I have negative muscles. Like the utter absence of strength or strong tissue. I'm skinny and I'm weak, and I've always been that way, and I'm in way over my head, and suddenly I realize that.

"I'm fine," I say, averting my eyes.

We start again, and this time, I am able to avoid giving myself a nearly certain concussion by gripping the ball tighter. But I also find out just how long twenty seconds is. It's like an hour, basically, when you're exerting yourself. I had no idea. When the five-seconds-left warning beeps sound, I am insanely grateful. When the final beep sounds, I say a prayer of thanks to gay Jesus.

Then I find out just how short, conversely, ten seconds is. When you're out of breath and having to go to another work-station. I've barely grabbed the rope when the automated voice says, "Go!"

Pulling a rope is hard work. I would be worthless in a boat-yard or a warehouse or wherever it is that people pull ropes for a living. This is not exactly a surprise to me, but nonetheless it sucks for the fifty hours it takes for twenty seconds to go by.

But it's nothing compared to the burpees. Who the hell would have guessed that a simple five-step exercise could be so awful? I do three of them and my lungs are screaming for relief. Another one, and I consider staying down until the beeps start. And when they don't, I wobble to my feet and do a fifth, cursing out Max for throwing me into the deep end of exercise.

The second set is awful. By the third set, I feel like I might have a heart attack. And when it's time to slam the ball for the fourth time, some six minutes into the eight-minute drill, I squat down, try to pick up the ball, and fail. I collapse onto the scratchy purple rug, hoping to die.

Max doesn't stop, and when it's his turn to slam the ball, he does it so close to my head that I wince. And I hate him for it. For being so insensitive to what it feels like to be knocked out. For not giving a shit that I am a hard-core failure at this and every other thing in my life.

Some silly trumpet horns sound when the eight minutes is up, and Max crouches down next to me.

"You okay?"

I'm still trying to catch my breath. "Uh-huh," I say.

He laughs and shoots me a Guy Smiley smile. "I promise. This gets more fun when you do it more often."

Fuck you too, I think. A couple hours ago, we were so connected. Reading poems and him drawing on the sidewalk. This Max feels like a stranger.

He takes me to this thing he calls a leg press next. You sit back with your legs angled up and your feet against this platform, and you load weights on a bar on top of it. Max adds two really heavy-looking round weights to each side. "Forty-fives," he explains, and I'm good enough at math to realize he's about to lift a hundred and eighty pounds in the air with his legs. My throat tightens. I definitely can't do this, and I'm going to have to tell Max.

But he's busy grabbing different accoutrements. He brings over these huge flat rubber bands, and he attaches them, one to the chair apparatus where you sit, and one to the bar on top of the platform.

"This makes it really burn," he says, looking all excited, and I try to match his excitement but I fail. This is just not . . . me. Not my thing.

He sits down, grabs the handles near his hands, twists them, and I guess that releases what the platform is resting on. His large quads tighten and pulse, and he lowers the platform until his knees are pushed up against his chest. Then he exhales with a grunt and pushes hard, and his legs straighten out.

Max is . . . impressive. But of course he is. He's perfect. And that's annoying. The rubber bands expand as he stretches his legs out, and contract as he allows the weight to fall close to his body.

"This would be a great rubber band flick trick," I say, imagining flinging a big rubber band across the room. He gives a charity grunt without looking at me, and keeps pushing. He does nine, then ten, then eleven, and finally twelve, and for the final three, his growls like a bear. A bead of sweat drips down his forehead, barely missing his eye.

"Yes," he shouts as he twists the handles back to catch the hundred-and-eighty-pound platform.

He stands and I curl into myself, afraid.

He puts a hand on my shoulder and squeezes. "We'll start you real light. I started light too."

I don't say anything, because the voices in my head are not nice ones. Not toward me, and not toward Max. I could be asleep now. I could be anywhere but here, proving to my first boyfriend that I am utterly unworthy of boyfriend status because I am the Wimpy Kid from the *Diary of.*

He pulls the big circle weights off and stacks smaller weights on each side. He tells me they are twenty-five pounds each, and I am entirely uncertain that he understands who and what he is dealing with. Still, I sit down and mimic what he did, well aware that the platform is likely to fall on me when my legs collapse.

Instead, when I push up after twisting the handles, I find I can do it.

"Oh!" I say, like someone pinched my butt.

He laughs. "There ya go," he says.

Bringing the weights down is easy, and from the scrunched-up position, I figure out that the rubber bands probably make this about twice as hard. And I don't mind. My legs can lift the weight, and when they start to burn after number eight, I smile a bit, because I am lifting weights. Me.

"Come on," he says, as I push a ninth time.

I grunt and push.

"Go go go," he says, staring down at me.

I meet his eyes and I push and it's a little embarrassing because it's so . . . intimate. Me trying hard and staring into his eyes. Also it's a little sexual.

"Push, push, push," he chants on number twelve, and I feel the sweat dripping down my face, and I feel the tent forming in my red gym shorts.

When I stand up on my tired legs, I linger close to him because something has changed in me. I feel . . . different. Like even though it's light weight, nothing like what he lifted, I did it. I finished the set. It feels awesome.

He loads more weight for my second set, and for my third, he goes with the big forty-fives on each side. I start to say something but he interrupts me.

"You can do this, Jordan," he says. "I saw how easy the fifty was. The seventy wasn't that hard either. You can do ninety, I promise."

I'm not sure, and I avert my eyes, once again afraid I'll let him down. But I get into the position, twist the handles, and jump into the deep end before I'm ready.

My legs burn right away. It's intense. A growl comes out of me followed by a whimper, while he tells me to push push push. By the sixth push, I can barely feel my legs anymore, and it feels blissful.

I can do this. I can do this. I can do this. These are words I've never said to myself before, and they make me feel like crying I am so happy. He sees it in my face, because he breaks into a sexy smile.

"Adrenaline," he mutters, and I don't give a fuck what it is. I just feel . . . different. Awake. Powerful. I want more of this, now. I hold his eye contact and keep up my pushing rhythm.

"Come on, come on," he shouts as I strain with everything I've got on nine.

"Ahhh!" I whimper involuntarily, and then I close my eyes and give it everything I've got.

It comes with a grunt that sounds like it comes from some other boy. Some boy with a shred of confidence. A kid who finishes what he starts and is capable of stuff. I straighten my legs and find myself nearly hyperventilating. Max grabs the platform like he's going to put it into place, like I'm done.

I'm not. I take my knees down to my chest, all the way. My skinny legs are shaking something fierce. I squeeze my eyes shut, I feel the sweat dripping like my forehead is crying, and I push like my life depends on it.

My legs straighten. All the way. It's a little bit beyond what I can do, but I straighten my legs, I twist the handles, and the platform drops with a metallic thump.

I laugh and roll off onto the ground, totally spent.

"All right!" he says, and I know he's not patronizing me. He bends and leans over me, and when I open my eyes, his dark eyes are smiling into mine. "That was amazing!" he says. "Amazing!"

I feel new. Like maybe how those kids feel when Dr. Phil sends them to Outward Bound and they complete all the crazy tasks. My legs feel like they won't ever hold me up again, but I lifted ninety pounds. With a rubber band to make it harder. I can't believe it.

We stare into each other's eyes for a bit, and I laugh, and he laughs, and I am utterly turned on, and I don't know if he is, but I am like, wow. Pumped, I guess. He lifts me to my feet, and I say to him, "Bathroom," and he helps me walk my wobbly legs to the bathroom, his strong arm behind my back and draped over my shoulder. Our bodies are so close and I smell his sweat and I want this moment never to end, ever.

He stops at the door. I am the one who drags him in with me.

"What?" he says, and I don't answer. I slam the door behind me and pull him toward me and mash my mouth into his and now it's his turn to whimper.

I've never felt so sure about anything in my life before. Like I'm possessed with some boy demon, and I decide, then and there, that if this is working out, I will do it every minute of every day of my life.

I push my chest against his and lick his lips and he groans and he pulls me closer in to him, and our sweat mingles into something funky and beautiful that I want to taste. I pull my mouth from his and lick his chin and his jaw and he squeezes my butt and I knead his shoulders and I need him in a new way.

"Not here," he says, pulling slightly away. "We'll get arrested."

I pull him closer. "Don't care," I mumble.

He laughs. "Okay now, tiger," he says. "I have a better idea."

"Definitely call me that," I say, still breathless, and he takes my hand, and even though the workout just started, he walks me out into the brilliantly scathing early morning Mesa air.

CHAPTER THIRTY-SEVEN

MAX

Mom is fast asleep when I bring Jordan in the front door. I can hear her snores coming from her bedroom, all the way out in the family room. For a little lady, she snores loud.

I open the patio door, take Jordan's hand, and lead him out to the pool.

"Is this okay with your mom?"

I nod. It basically is. Not that she'd want to walk out and see us, but like she said: There's lots of users and abusers out there, and Jordan is neither. He's my boyfriend, and having sex with your boyfriend is nothing to be ashamed about.

If only my body agreed. I'm shaking. I hope Jordan can't feel it through my hand.

I decide I'll tell her in the morning, and I hope she won't be mad.

Facing away from Jordan, I strip off my gym clothes. Part of me wants to watch him watch me strip, and wants to watch him take his clothes off too. But another part is feeling shy and tentative, very un–Super Max, and if I look at him, I'm afraid he'll see it in my eyes.

When I'm naked, I turn toward him and dare to look in his eyes.

They are . . . alive. I've never seen Jordan like this. A little wild. It scares me a little even. I like it.

He pulls off his shirt. I've seen this before, in the desert that day. No definition yet. I don't need definition. He's perfect. His nipples, small, perky, and brown, stand out against his lily-white skin. He's got a basic farmer's tan, which is adorable on him, like his arms and lower legs belong to a different person than his trunk.

Normally I'd jump in, but it's almost two in the morning and I don't want to wake up Mom. I take his hand and lead him to the steps. We walk down into the water together. The cicadas are buzzing loud, which makes it sound like the nighttime is sizzling. The water is warmer than the air, which is to say it's like a hot bathtub.

The moon gives me his basic shape, and I run my hands down his beautiful, alive body. He does the same to mine. I pull him close and sit him on my legs with him facing me. We kiss hard, like something on Animal Planet when two male animals are fighting for dominance. I kiss and then lick his bony shoulders, I bite his neck lightly and he whimpers. His hands are all over my chest, and then around my back, pulling me closer. I feel like laughing, and a little relieved, maybe, because the last time I did this it wasn't anything like this, and maybe I've been scared that I'd never feel this kind of good. Like Kevin took something from me, because it was my first anything.

I had no idea that working out would awaken this whatever in Jordan. It's scary and sexy and I want to be inside him, and I think we're finally going to do that, and my heart pulses with excitement and my chest shivers with fear.

The unknown. What if it's not good? What if it's really, really good? What if it's perfect? The thing moms don't tell you when they give you the talk, and the things dads definitely don't tell you, when they're telling you about stuff, is how scary sex is. When I talk about it with Betts and Zay-Rod, we definitely don't talk about what it feels like to be, like all out there, with your desires as uncovered and obvious as possible. Every inch of my body feels chilly and alive.

Jordan jumps off my lap and picks me up so that my legs are on his. He reaches for my butt and squeezes and I freeze just like that night with Kevin.

I dry heave.

Without even meaning to I push backward and do a dolphin jump, my chest and then my midsection above the water.

He jumps up and down, bounding toward me.

I submerge until my feet touch the bottom.

I scream water.

I scream out something that I didn't know was in me.

When I'm all out of air, I burst to the surface, wipe my eyes, and Jordan is watching me, a concerned expression on his face. That just makes it worse. I want to scream again. My body is shaking and shivering despite the hot water, and I gasp and leap toward the side of the pool. I pull myself half out of the pool, I lean forward, and I punch down. Onto tile.

The pain explodes in my knuckles. White-hot fire that reverberates up my shocked arm.

I yell in agony.

Jordan is up and out of the pool in like three seconds. I hear the screen door open fast and slam shut, and I put my head in my hands and sob. I cannot control the tears. I can't control anything. I can't I can't I can't.

I don't know how long later it is when the patio door opens again, and my mom's voice belts out, "Max? Max? Mijo, what happened?"

Her hand is on the back of my neck. I am led, naked, to an Adirondack chair. I am dried off a bit with a towel. A cloth is wrapped around my bloody fingers. Shorts are slipped on me without my doing anything. And I know as certain as anything I've ever known that I need to talk about this.

CHAPTER THIRTY-EIGHT

JORDAN

"I think I was raped," Max says.

"What?" I yell.

"What?" his mom yells.

She puts her arms around his shoulders and rubs. I sit on the concrete. I'm in my gym shorts but I didn't have time to put on my shirt. Max is shirtless too, and there's something especially naked about him, like I've never even close to seen before, with tears rushing down cheeks that are always so dry and typically raised in a wide, blissful smile.

"I think I was raped," he says again, and then his mom is leading him inside, and I'm following, and part of me wonders if I should give them privacy, and the other part? No way. I'm his boyfriend. I should be here.

She sits him on the same part of the couch where he sat a few weeks back, when his mom talked to us about making the truck legal. I sit on the love seat again and make sure I'm fully facing Max.

He hugs his arms to his chest. He's about to start speaking when his mom does the strangest thing. She pries his tight fingers off his biceps, first on one side, then reaches over him and does the other side too. His arms fall to his sides.

"Defensive, closed posture," she says. "When you need to do the opposite right now, mijo."

Max takes a deep breath.

"It was the night I didn't come home," he says to her. Then he turns to me. "The night before I met you at the farmers' market. I met this boy online. He invited me to a party. I went. Went back to his dorm room."

"This at ASU?" she asks, her tone sharp.

He nods. "He started saying weird things and I just wanted to jet. He sat on my legs and it was almost like funny, because he was this scrawny little dude. But I froze up. I said no. But he just kept going and then it was like I wasn't even there."

"You dissociated," his mom says.

He shrugs.

"People dissociate sometimes in situations like that. It's not your fault, mijo. Not your fault." She sits close to him and hugs him from the side, hard. Tears fall down his cheeks some more.

"It just happened and then it was like, I stayed? I think maybe I felt too dirty." He shakes his head. "I'm so stupid. How do you sleep in someone's bed after that?"

"Did he . . . penetrate you?"

Max averts his eyes to the floor. Finally he nods.

"Did he use protection?"

He shakes his head, and his mother exhales.

"Dios mío," she mutters.

More tears from Max, and then she starts to cry, and I feel numb and distant sitting across from them, so I tentatively move to Max's other side, aware he might go nuts again. He doesn't. I put my head on his shoulder and this makes him cry harder.

"Sorry," I say, looking into Rosa's eyes and pulling my head away.

"No, no," she says, and she motions me back. "That's what he needs right now. Please do."

I put my head back, my cheek and ear resting on his large shoulder, and I watch the tears fall from this weird side view that's almost surreal. And it is a bit surreal.

I never thought of Max as even possibly being a victim. And I have questions. Like how does a person freeze up in a situation like that? But thinking that just makes me feel bad because I know it's a real thing. I just haven't experienced it. So I turn and kiss his shoulder many times like an apology for thinking a terrible thought like that.

Rosa, meanwhile, is holding onto him tight from the other side, squeezing and purring in his ear warm assurances that it's all going to be okay. That she loves him and she doesn't blame him and she will be by his side through all of this.

I have this incredible, awful, sad realization. That if this was me, if I'd been raped, and this was my mom, I'd be hugging and consoling *her*. She would make this all about her. No question in my mind. That makes me need to close my eyes because it's like a dagger stabbing at my chest from the inside.

"We need to go to the police," Rosa says.

Max shakes his head. "No. Nope. No."

"Why not, mijo? The boy committed a crime."

"I can't. I won't. Nope."

She sighs again. "We'll revisit that. But what we really have to do is go to the ER right now and get you an HIV test. All the STIs. You had unsafe sex."

My body goes numb. What? I want to rewind. All of this. To have gone to my house, not his, where there is no pool. Where none of this would be so. I want an alternate universe where this nightmare isn't. Back further, beyond that. Before this happened to Max.

But in that alternate universe, we never meet like we did. We never run the food truck like we did. He's not my boyfriend. This is inconceivable to me.

Which would be better? Max avoiding this and us not meeting? Or him having the pain and us meeting? My head spins. Unanswerable question.

It's 3:18 a.m. as Max's mom gets in the driver's seat of her Ford Focus, I get in the back, and Max gets in the passenger seat. We drive in silence to Banner Desert Medical Center, the strip malls appearing and disappearing like a terrible mirage.

What if Max has HIV? Could he really?

No. No damn way.

Or of course damn way. Because life has always been shit and why wouldn't this happen? Maybe it's happening to him because my shit life has bled onto him. I should never have come into his life. I'm bad luck. It's my fault.

This thought makes me laugh a little. Max and his mom turn back, a little surprised by the outburst.

"Sorry," I say. "I'm amazing myself by making this about me even a little bit. I am truly the worst human being."

Max's mom reaches back and scruffs my knee. "Hardly," she says. "This is hard for you too. For me, also. I want to batter that asshole's brain in."

I've never heard little Rosa curse before, and I realize I really like her. Max has told me enough so that I know her foibles, but to me, she's really what a mom should be. Warm, kind, in charge, real.

We sit in the waiting room, the three of us, after Rosa and Max check in. Then they take Max back, and Rosa and I sit there in silence for a bit. She reaches for my hand and holds it. Her hand is warm and slightly damp.

"Thanks," I say.

"Thank you. I'm so glad you came and got me. This is too much for you to deal with on your own. Max is gonna need some help. A counselor, probably. Get some of the anger out."

"I didn't even realize," I say, and a tear falls again. "I'm so wrapped up in me that I somehow didn't notice—"

She shushes me. "Enough of that," she says. "You're a person. You did your best and it was plenty. I'm so happy Max has you."

This makes me smile. I blurt out, "Will you be my mom?" And then I shrink back, because I love my mom, and I don't mean that.

She smiles wider and laughs a bit. "Not so good on the home front, huh?"

"My mom's okay," I say, my shoulders automatically tensing.

Rosa smiles at me but I can tell her mind is elsewhere, as it should be. "You need anything, you just let me know, okay?"

I nod. I'm fine. We're fine. Somehow it'll all be okay.

The doctor comes out and calls Max's mom in. I am left alone to think about all of these things.

What if Max has HIV? Would I stay with him?

Yes, I realize. I would. I'd take care of him if I had to.

What if Max doesn't really like me and he was just in a weird place because of the rape?

That I couldn't handle, I don't think.

By the time they come out, hand in hand, it's 5:14 on

Saturday morning and I'm a mess. I've decided Max is going to break up with me because he doesn't really like me. And I know. I'm making this about me. But I don't know how to not do that.

Until I see his face, and then it all goes away, and I stand and I hug him hard, and he hugs me back, hard.

In the car, Max explains to me what's up.

No he probably doesn't have HIV, which causes AIDS, but it's not impossible. The window period to be sure is three months, but after one month, which it's almost been, it's 95 percent. That test was negative. I breathe a huge sigh of relief.

Thanks to his mom, who insisted he get vaccinated, he doesn't have HPV. He may have any number of other STIs, and those tests will come back soon. Anything he has would be curable, though. Or at least manageable.

"I'm here for you," I say, and I glance up and see his mom's mouth curl into a weak smile. "Whatever you need, I'm in. Okay?"

"Thanks," Max says. "That means a lot to me."

His hand is wrapped pretty tight with ACE bandages. Not broken, he explains. It might impact his cooking for a week or so, but we're not gonna be cooking much this week anyway, since the truck is still in the shop.

"I want to get you in to see a counselor who deals with sexual assault," Rosa says.

Max shrugs. "We'll see."

"No 'we'll see' about it," she says. "Required."

"Maybe," he says.

Rosa shakes her head. "I'd say you got that from your dad, but maybe that's just a man thing? I remember your uncle Guillermo did the same thing when I tried to get him to see a counselor. What is it with you men and not talking?"

Max turns to me like I'll be on his side. I am on his side. Just not about this. "I think it's a good idea," I say. "You punched a pool tile. A perfectly innocent pool tile."

This makes him laugh a bit. Then he stops laughing. "Can I be real?"

"Yes," Rosa and I say, simultaneously.

"Half of me doesn't believe I was raped. Like, I get about consent and all, but I was . . . I don't know." He runs his hands through his hair.

"Were what?" Rosa asks.

"I can't do this," he says, his voice exhausted. "Talk about this."

"Mijo? You have to. Really. Me and your beautiful friend back there? We're gonna be on you to talk about it."

He sighs, exasperated. "Can it be rape if you didn't hate every second of it, while it was happening?"

His mom takes his hand and wraps her small hand around it. "Absolutely, mijo. It must be confusing. I think that's very normal."

"I don't know," Max says.

"Did you say no?"

He nods.

"Did you at any point say anything that changed your answer?"

He shakes his head.

"You see, that's not okay. Doesn't matter if you're a boy. Or you're bigger. That's not okay. Hear me?"

He nods again, and soon I can see from the side his face cringing again, and I hear him sniffling, and I lean forward and put my arms around him from behind.

"I'm so glad you told us," I blurt out. "That's really awesome. It makes me like you more, okay? That you would tell us. That's like really strong."

I hear him take a deep breath. And then he says, "Fine. Whatever. Can I just say for the record, though, that I'm done being vulnerable for the day? I hate it so much."

Rosa puts her hand on his shoulder and squeezes.

"Good luck with that. The world will make you vulnerable. If you're acting like you're not, that's what you're doing. Acting."

CHAPTER THIRTY-NINE

MAX

It's later that morning and I'm in my room. I pick up my phone.

Me: U there

Kevin: Hey what up, u left in a hurry the other day, figured you hated me

Me: Just confused but I'm getting over it. Wanna meet?

Kevin: Maybe

Me: C'mon <smiley face> Wanna see you again

Kevin: Your like bipoler

Me: Lol am not

Kevin: Are so. Just come here?

Me: Cartel

Kevin: U want coffee or u wanna hook up?

Me: Lol both

Kevin: Okay whatever an hour?

Me: See you then

It's not that easy to get my mom and Jordan off my back. Jordan has stayed around, just hanging out with us, which is nice but I'm really truly done talking about my feelings. I could tell he saw a window open up and he liked it, but let's be real. That window isn't gonna stay open. I'm Max, and that's not me.

"I just wanna take a drive," I say.

My mom frowns. "Why don't you stick close to home today?"

"I need some air. Maybe go to the gym?"

"I'll come," Jordan says.

"I dunno," I say.

Jordan and my mom share a look.

"Can I just have like five minutes to myself please? An hour, tops."

"I'm worried about you," Rosa says.

"Me too," Jordan says.

I come over and stand between them and put a hand on each of their forearms. "Trust me. I'm okay."

Mom finally relents, and as I go to my room to get ready, she asks Jordan to stick around for a second. I can't help but feel a little pissed off. A guy doesn't want pity and to be treated like a baby. Doesn't matter what happened to me. Treat me like the guy I was before you knew, right?

I park at Cartel, my heart pounding. I need to deal with this my own way, and yeah, I know it's in public. But I'm doing it in public because in private I'm afraid I might hurt the guy. I gotta use my words and just say what I need to say, and that'll be it. I'm not calling the cops. I'm telling him that he hurt me, that he won't hurt me again, and that if he knows what's good for him, he'll make sure guys say yes in the future. And that's it.

Kevin is sitting on the second of four square wooden benches in a horseshoe formation, facing away from the back door. It's perfect, because it's dark and while there are people around, they're mostly wearing headphones. I see his forehead first, and my throat tightens involuntarily.

"Hey," I say, sitting down next to him. Leaving a little room in between us.

"Hey," he says. He has a coffee. "You gonna get one?"

"Nah," I say, and he laughs.

"Um. Okay . . ."

"Wanted to talk to you again," I say, and he starts to stand up. I pull him back down by the shirt. "Nope. You're gonna listen this time. Just shut up and listen."

He looks super uncomfortable, and he's looking around like he's afraid and hoping there are witnesses.

"I'm not gonna hurt you," I say, careful to keep my voice low as I hear someone sit in the next bench over, like right behind where we are. "I just need to say something."

"Fine," he says. "Say whatever. I really don't care."

"You . . . raped me," I say, my voice catching when I say the word, real soft so no one else can hear.

"That's just. Wow," he says. "I . . ."

"Shut up. Really. Just shut up. I told you no. You don't get to decide what no means. It's called consent. I'm not gonna like call the cops. I just want you to know that I know now that you raped me."

"Wow," he says.

I sit up tall so that he remembers that I'm bigger than him. He shrinks ever so slightly.

"I got an HIV test and it's negative, so that's good. I don't know if you gave me anything else."

"Maybe you gave me something," he says.

"Yeah, no," I say. "You're the only person, asshole. I've done that with."

He smirks. "Right. Of course. Sure. Whatever you need to tell yourself."

"You could get in trouble anyway, dude. I'm seventeen. How old are you?"

"None of your business, dude. And that's so lame. I'm still a teenager. I'm not some creepy old guy taking advantage of a young guy. Grow up. Take a little responsibility for your actions. You were there. You're a big dude. You could've stopped me. You didn't want to stop me."

I don't know what to say to that, and for about the millionth time in the last four weeks, I wonder if he's right. Maybe I did want this. Maybe I'm being a big old baby—

"You did it because you were horny, and you're no better than anyone else, even though obviously you think you are. You're a horny dude, which makes it weird that you're so frigid." He laughs. "I figured you'd be more chili pepper and less . . . I don't know."

My head pulses. "What?"

He shakes his head and laughs. "You look Mexican, but really you're a white guy with dark skin," he says.

"What does that even mean?"

"You're supposed to be passionate. You're the opposite. You're actually bad in bed."

The fist glances off his chin. The bone-on-bone crack is gratifying, but also surprising.

Because it isn't my fist colliding with Kevin's jaw that creates that sound.

"Ow," Kevin says, shocked.

I look to my left and there is Jordan, staring at the back of his hand like it's operated without his consent. Everyone is staring at us, eyes wide.

Kevin's hand is squeezing the center of his chin, like he's popping a big zit. His mouth looks funny.

"Jesus. You misaligned my jaw, what the fuck."

"He what?" I ask.

"It's a thing that happens," Kevin says, his mouth sideways, and in that moment I realize for the very first time that he's a person. A bad one, to be sure. I'd never do what he did to another person. But it floods me that this person who hurt me has a mother, and probably wore braces, and they probably hurt sometimes.

"Go. Now. You fucking rapist piece of shit," Jordan says, making his hand into a claw. "Next I claw your eyes out." He says it calmly, and I am putty at his slender feet.

The guy runs. People go back to doing what they were doing, like they didn't just watch my boyfriend punch my rapist and misalign his jaw.

I just stare at Jordan, my unlikely, shocking savior, and part of me feels humiliated that I needed saving, but a much bigger part feels so grateful he'd hit someone for me. I try to give one of my smiles but it's beneath something else and all I can do is stare into Jordan's beautiful face.

"You followed me here?"

He nods. "Your mom asked me to."

"Wow," I say, and the shaking is gone. I find myself smiling.

We walk back out into the sunshine, his arm around my shoulder. I put mine around his, still stunned.

"See you at your house?" he asks, getting into my mom's car.

"I didn't know you drive," I say.

"I don't. I couldn't tell your mom. It was actually kinda hard to get here. I never learned. I winged it."

I shake my head and open the passenger-side door of my truck.

"We'll pick that up later," I say, and he nods. "I don't want you to die."

"Kindest thing you've said to me today," he says, and I kiss him on the lips.

"Thanks, by the way."

"Hey. I'm as shocked as you are," he says, shaking out his hand.

We drive, and I'm thinking about users and abusers, like my mom says. The time my dad swung me around by my feet and I got hurt, and how he told me to man up. Who came up with that?

Who came up with all those rules and ideas about how a guy's gotta be?

Kevin said he expected a chili pepper. Why say that? Why is it okay to say shit like that to other people? I would never say something like that. That's some fucked-up, racist shit.

And with white folks, why is racism my issue and Zay-Rod's issue, but not Betts's?

With my white friends, I'm always half-Mexican. They never say I'm half-Irish. Never say I'm half white. Like I'm tainted halfway away from standard. It's like when I was a kid and I thought vanilla ice cream meant no flavor, like it was the base of all the flavors. But vanilla is a bean. Like chocolate is a bean. Like cinnamon is a root. All roots and beans. All flavors. There is no base. No ice cream without a flavor.

I glance over at Jordan in the passenger seat. His profile. His slight nose. It's the nose of a guy who would never use or abuse me. And I wouldn't use or abuse him, either. I grab for his hand.

"Ouch," he says, and he shakes his hand out again.

I crack up. "Sorry."

"God. You're always apologizing," Jordan says in this funny voice, and I realize he's imitating me. It's a fucking terrible imitation, and I smile, and I almost throw it back at him by emulating him saying "Sorry" again. But then I don't because I realize: He isn't sorry. Nope. Not anymore.

CHAPTER FORTY

JORDAN

"What is that thing?" I ask, pointing a crooked finger at the ball in my lap as Max drives us to Carriage Lane Park. It's two days after the punch, and we're hanging out midday because we are still a few days away from getting the truck back.

"That thing is a football. You did know that, right? We don't need to drive you to a hospital because you have managed to go through seventeen years of life without knowing what a football is, do we?"

"Aren't we in some sort of health-care crisis where they don't have enough beds or something? Do you really think a hospital would take me in because of that?"

He shrugs. "They should. That's just un-American, dude."

I roll my eyes. "Oh my God. That's not a thing, Max. You don't need to know what a football is or, like, where to stick it to be American."

He grins, parks the truck, and jumps out onto the broiling asphalt of the parking lot. As I slowly get out, he twirls the football high in the air and catches it just above his head. I glance out at the greenbelt between the parking lot and the canal pathway, where I usually take Dorcas in the mornings when it isn't insanely hot out. It's empty, not surprisingly. We are the only freaks out in the middle of a June day.

"Look alive!" Max says, and a heavy ball smacks me in the chin.

I open my mouth and narrow my eyes at him. "I know you did not just do that to me."

"Sorry," he says, smirking. "I'm used to friends who, you know, look alive."

I kneel down and pick up the still-spinning ball. I stand and whip it at Max. I throw it sideways because that's how it's in my hands. He catches it easily.

"I hate you," I say, smiling.

"God I love late June in Arizona," he says as we walk toward the large, empty green field next to the basketball courts. One woman is walking a dog toward us from the pathway, and when she sees it's me, she waves and unleashes her dog.

"Because you're crazy," I say as the pit bull runs up to me, white tail wagging like crazy. It jumps up to greet me. I scruff the dog on the top of the head. "Hey, Rufus! Sorry, boy. No Dorcas."

"Did you ever tell me why she's named Dorcas?" Max asks as the dog runs back to its owner and we walk on toward the center of the huge greenbelt area.

I roll my eyes. "My mom. Went through a religious phase right after Dad died. Right when we got our goldendoodle. So a biblical name for our dog. As God would have wanted."

He flashes a smile. "Amen."

"So how does this work?" I ask, hoping the answer is, *We throw the ball once and then go home.*

He spins the football up in the air and catches it. "It's very complicated. We draw up plays. Ten of them. Then we memorize them. And we run them in order until they all are perfect."

"It's sooo hot," I whine.

"Kidding," he says. "It's a ball. We throw it to each other." He tosses the ball at me, and this time I violently thrust my hands up and catch it.

"Woo!" I say. "I got it!"

"Later we'll buy you a medal."

I narrow my eyes at him and take a deep breath. I decide to just tell him. "For you this is normal, I guess. I have never, ever caught a ball before. Of any kind. Ever."

"How is that possible?" He puts his hands up and I throw it sideways again. It wobbles and falls well short of him even though I am just ten feet away.

"I grew up petrified of this kind of thing. Or maybe just the people who did this kind of thing. They all wanted to punch me in the chest and call me a sissy."

"Wow," he says. "Can I show you something?"

"Anything, cowboy."

"Gross," he says, and I mock pout.

He shows me how to hold the football, putting pressure on the lacing mostly with his middle and index fingers. I take it from him and copy him. He nods, takes it back, and waves me away. I wave back.

"No. That means run. I'll throw you the ball."

"It's sooo hot," I whine again.

"Just five minutes and I promise we can spend the rest of the day inside. Doing anything you want."

"Anything?" I ask, and I give him a tentative look. I honestly don't want to push him given what he's been through, but I have to admit: I'm curious.

He tips his head as if to say, *Oh good. Sexual innuendo. My favorite.*

"Yes," he says, and he waves his hand toward me again. "That means 'Go out for a pass.'"

"Oh, um," I say, momentarily confused. Then I turn and run a bit. About five seconds later, I turn around. Max tosses me the ball. I flail my arms up and my hands grab at the ball. It hits off my palm.

"So close!" I say, a little excited, actually. "Throw it again!"

I pick the ball up and throw it to him the way he showed me, with pressure on the laces, the small end facing him. It spins out of my fingers and goes right to him.

"What the?"

I have no idea how I did that, and a tingle climbs my spine. "A boy likes to be mysterious," I say.

"I guess." He throws another, and this time I really concentrate and zap my hands up like a Venus flytrap or something. The ball nestles between my hands and stays.

"Yes!" he says, and he runs over to me. I'm just standing there, looking at the ball in my hands, amazed. He puts his arms around me and hugs. I tingle some more; also the sun begins to feel like it's going to make me faint.

I say, "You know? I don't hate this. I mean, in the heat I do a little, and I don't love it like the working out thing. But I could totally do this sometime. Play football catch."

"I'll take you up on that. And by the way? Not everyone who grew up doing this wanted to punch you." He kisses me on the lips. I kiss him back, and we walk, hand in hand, back to his truck.

I ask him to take me back to my house, and when we arrive, I lead him to my room, and on the way I realize he has no idea about my '80s bordello. Shit.

Then I decide, fuck it. He knows me. This may be the weirdest thing about me. Maybe not. Doesn't matter. We're solid. He'll be okay.

He exhales wildly when he sees it for the first time.

"Dude," he says.

I laugh. "Back in eighth grade I convinced my mom to take me Goodwill hopping. We bought everything '70s and '80s that would fit in a bordello."

He actually bends over and clutches his stomach, laughing. I watch him, unsure, but soon I realize I'm not the joke, exactly. I start to laugh and he glances up, sees me laughing, and comes over and sweaty hugs me.

"Oh my God," he says. "This is seriously—I don't know, dude. I kinda love it."

"Do you?"

"I love it because it's you. Would I love it for me? Hell no. Hey, is that a record player?"

I nod, and he goes over and picks up the arm with the needle. "I've seen these online. Badass."

I go to my shelf and pick up *Beauty and the Beat* by the Go-Go's, take out the album, and put it on side one. As "Our Lips Are Sealed" starts up, I hand him the jacket. He stares at the five women wrapped in bath towels, who are covered in face cream.

"You really love this stuff," he says.

"This is everything," I say. "They should have stopped making music after this."

"The Go-Go's?"

"Everyone. This one was nineteen eighty-one, the first year of the last decade for music."

Dorcas, who must have been asleep because she didn't greet us at the door, comes up to Max with a yellow stuffed-animal bird in her mouth. She always brings people her toys. He pats her head.

I point at my desk chair. He sits, and I sit at his feet and pull off his sneakers.

"What are we—" he asks, but he stops when I pull out the bottle of red nail polish. "Um. No. Absolutely not."

"Come on," I say, as the guitars for "How Much More" start up. "For me?"

He frowns. "Do we need to?"

"Look. You owe me this."

"For real? This?"

I change my tone and my posture, looking up at him with demure eyes. "Well . . . I mean, if you say no, then no is the answer. But . . . I'd like to."

He can't help but crack a grin. "Fine," he says.

"Yay!" I say.

I start by filing his pretty gross nails. I have never actually done this before. It's not like it's something I love to do, or even want to do that much. I think it's more that I want him to let me do it to him. Once his toes are filed, I start with his big left toe. I apply a layer of cherry-red polish. It looks pretty against his dark skin.

"Do you do this? Like, with your foot?"

I shake my head. "Nah. Not my thing. Kayla tried it on me once. Decided it was part of the Gay Best Friend package. I was like, whatever."

"So why did you want to do it to me?"

I shrug. "Kind of like the football thing, maybe? That you'd do something you don't want to for me, maybe?"

He leans forward and puts his foot down. He scoots toward me, leans down, and kisses me on the lips. Then he looks deep into my eyes and says, "Anything for you."

I blush, and he smiles wide.

CHAPTER FORTY-ONE

MAX

I choose the pool as the place to tell Betts and Zay-Rod what's up.

Mom's at work and we're a day away from having our truck back. The Amigos are hanging out on mesh rafts that keep them half in, half out of the water, and I have two noodles under me, holding me up as I sit.

"Kayla loves me," Betts says, and I snort, and Zay-Rod snorts, and Betts splashes us in response. "She does. This is how it works with me. Girls act all annoyed, but the Betts system is in effect and fully deployed. You just watch."

"Sure," I say. "She loves you like I love snakes. She loves you like a menstrual cramp."

Zay-Rod laughs. "She loves your ass like a canker sore."

Betts makes this dramatic scoffing noise with his tongue. "Watch and learn, dudes." Then he points to my foot. "You have one red toe."

I roll my eyes. "Jordan," I say.

He laughs. "Yeah. That girl Karen did that to me once."

Zay-Rod paddles over to the side of the pool and grabs his iced tea and takes a swig. "Jordan is nice," he says.

It's actually the first real comment either of them has made about him, and I've been wondering if I should take that as a sign.

"Yeah?" I ask.

"Yeah. His poem was good," Zay-Rod says.

"He's okay. He hangs out with hot girls," Betts says. "That's like the one good thing about gay dudes. They bring the chicks. Except present company, I guess."

I jump off my noodle, pounce on the side of his raft, and flip it. Betts comes up splashing, and then holds his breath, swims around me like a menacing shark, and then goes under me and lifts me up onto his shoulders. As he stands, I raise my hand in the air like I'm a rodeo cowboy. He stays up for a few seconds, then dunks and lets go of my calves. I swim away.

I sit on this little alcove seat in the deep end, and I savor the feeling of the broiling sun on my shoulders.

"So I gotta tell you something," I say.

Zay-Rod says, "You pregnant, dude?"

Betts says, "Nah, Max is the guy."

And for once, I say, "Cut that shit out. Seriously."

"What?" Betts asks.

"That. That one of us is a girl and one is a boy. That's fuckin' bullshit. We're both guys. That's what gay is. Two guys."

"Okay," Betts says, jumping back up on his raft. "Sorry. Didn't know that bugged you."

"It doesn't," I say, half lying. "It's just. When you always give me shit and nothing is ever serious, it gets old. Also I have no idea if you're being serious."

Zay-Rod says, "That's what we do. That's what you do too, dude."

"Well, yeah. But maybe we could be serious once in a while too?"

It's quiet for a bit, and my heart sinks. I count on the Amigos. So much. I don't want to lose them. I'm about to take it back when Betts says, "Sometimes it bugs me that you guys think I'm stupid."

"Wow. Look at the time," I say.

He laughs a little. "Nice."

"Kidding," I say. "I don't really think you're stupid."

Zay-Rod says, "Me neither. I mean, you're not an intellectual and you don't like a lot of book stuff. But you're smart in other ways. You're good at math. You come up with good jokes and shit."

Betts keeps quiet for a bit, and then he says, "Thanks."

"I got raped," I blurt.

The pool goes quiet. Betts and Zay-Rod both sit up and look at me. The look is one of, *Tell me you're joking.* I slightly shake my head.

"Jordan?" Betts asks softly.

I shake my head again.

"What happened?" Zay-Rod asks.

I feel weird, talking about this in a pool. I glance over at the turquoise Adirondack chairs where my mom and Jordan took me a few nights ago. I leave my seat and swim over to the steps. They follow, and we shake excess water off as we exit the pool. The tile around the pool burns our feet as we walk over and sit down in the plastic chairs.

"What happened?" Zay-Rod repeats.

I need to take a moment to look both my buddies in the eye. This is something we've never done before, and I need to know they can take it. They both hold my eye contact—first Zay-Rod, then Betts. So I take a deep breath, then another, then another. And then I tell them everything.

"Shit, dude," Betts says.

"You okay?" Zay-Rod asks.

I shake my head. "Not really. I mean, yeah, I'll be okay. But I have lots of nightmares, and when Jordan touched me around that area, I freaked the fuck out."

Betts stands, walks over, and makes like he's going to sit on my lap. I laugh, because I just told him I got raped and what's the first thing he does? Invade my space. "Plastic chair, dude," I say.

He stands and he lifts me up by my shoulders, and he hugs me tight.

"I'm sorry, dude."

Zay-Rod joins our little huddle. It is, sex included, the most intimate moment of my life. They hold me tight, and I just close my eyes and breathe, thinking how glad I am they're my buddies, and wondering why I was ever afraid to tell them.

Zay-Rod asks, "Does Rosa know?"

I say, "Yeah."

He adds, "Jordan?"

I nod.

"Can I kill that dude?" Betts asks.

"Yeah," I say. I quickly correct. "No, actually. Jordan already punched him."

Zay-Rod pulls back. His eyes are shocked. "Seriously?"

"It was . . . surprising. At that coffee shop Cartel on University? Not the best punch ever, but it misaligned the guy's jaw."

Both guys are looking at me, shocked, and then Betts imitates a guy with his jaw misaligned. "Hi, I'm a rapist whose jaw doesn't shut right," he says in a silly voice.

Zay-Rod looks at me, holding in a laugh. I have to laugh myself, and that allows him to do the same.

"Too soon?" Betts says, pleased at the reaction.

"Uh, yeah, too soon," I say.

We wind up in my bedroom for hours, basking in the AC and talking. It's freakin' awesome. We never talked like this, ever. It's like my traumatic thing opened this door, and out poured all this stuff.

I tell the guys about how serious I am about this foodie stuff. That I love to cook more than maybe anything else. They're cool about it. I don't know why I've been afraid all this time to tell them. I mean, I guess this is a first, us talking for real. But the point is it could have happened much sooner if any of us had had the balls to try it.

And I think that's thanks to Jordan. I would never have done any of this if I hadn't met him, and if he hadn't showed me how to be real and serious with another guy.

Betts talks about what it feels like when his mom calls his dad an idiot in front of him, and how it scares him because he's a lot like his dad. And then he talks about how his dad probably deserves it, because he's so mean to his mom.

"I don't want to be that guy," he says.

I nod and nod, and Zay-Rod says he gets that, and all I can think of is how it must totally suck to have that in the back of his brain and then hear from us, his best buddies, about how stupid he is all the time. That never even occurred to me, that he had feelings.

Zay-Rod talks about how he's not over Hailie Thompson, who he dated sophomore year and was his first girlfriend. Also his first time.

"She was special. She's the one I'll always compare every girl to," he says, and Betts says that's like Shaundra Timmons for him.

All this time, I thought Zay-Rod was cool and emotionless about all girl stuff. Betts too.

They weren't. Not even close. All this time.

"That's why with Pam, I just . . . I don't know."

"What?" I ask. We haven't asked what was up with Pam, and he sure didn't tell. That's more Betts's thing.

"I like her, you know? She's smart and funny and sexy. She could be, I don't know. I don't want to jinx it."

"Sure," I say.

"And what about you and Jordan?" Betts asks, and it actually takes me a second to put down the wall that comes up without me even trying. Like part of me is programmed to say, "Mind your business."

"We're taking it slow," I say. "I mean. Not in terms of hanging out, but in terms of the other stuff."

"Sex," Zay-Rod says, and again, it's like I flinch. I don't want to flinch. So I swallow that response down and say, "Yeah. Sex."

"You think you'll be able to at some point?" Betts asks.

"I hope so," I say, and I get this shiver in my arms. What if I never can? What if Kevin ruined me forever? I can't think about that. I swallow it down.

"What do you think it would be like if I told the team? That I was gay? That I was dating Jordan?"

Zay-Rod says, "I don't know. Everyone likes you. Why would that make it different?"

"Yeah," Betts says. "It's like, it shouldn't matter. But with those guys, if you're a dick they'd probably give you shit about it. But you're the opposite of a dick."

"A vagina?" Zay-Rod asks. We all laugh.

My mom knocks on the door. "What are you boys up to?" she asks.

"Just hangin' out," I say.

She smiles. "Up to no good if you ask me," she says.

"I told them about what happened," I say lightly.

She smiles again and she sits down on the floor. She's still in her work clothes, and she crosses her legs. "Good," she says. "Secrets are bad for the soul."

Zay-Rod says, "We're working on telling each other our secrets."

"Good," she says again. "Teach this boy how to talk, please. He's just like his dad."

"Mom," I say.

She leans over and musses my hair. "Not in all ways. Just the talking one. And you're getting better."

We're ready to go, with our DBA form and a working truck, by Friday morning. We pick it up from the repair shop on Baseline, and it's still a steaming pile of crap, but at least now it drives when you put it into drive, and reverses when you want without so much shaking. And they put in a side window that we can see through, so we no longer have to drive with the side door open.

It puts us back a couple thousand, and after we pick up supplies at Safeway and head toward ASU for the lunch rush, Jordan tells me where we stand. We have about $1,200 in profits put away toward the $5,000 he owes. The deadline is next Friday.

"If all goes well and the truck holds up, we'll make it. But we really have to push," he says.

"Challenge accepted," I say, and I mean it. We're gonna make this happen.

We're like a well-oiled machine once we get going. I flip chicken breasts like a pro, and Jordan has probably picked up his pace on lemonades and on the ordering situation by 100 percent since we started. The line just goes on and on for at least two hours, and I lose count of how much we've sold pretty quickly and get in that work zone where I'm loving the heat of the grill and the challenge of what we're up against. Also I love that I'm doing it with Jordan. It's amazing how we've known each other only a month, and I already feel like meeting him has changed everything for me. I can't imagine my life without him.

"Two cayenne, one no tomatoes," he calls back, and with my nongrilling, still-slightly-sore-from-punching hand, I reach back and fondle his thighs below the window, so no one can see.

"What's that for?" he asks, smirking.

"Stuff," I say, and his smirk grows.

"Don't start what you can't finish," he says, and he flicks me on the upper thigh so I know he's joking.

"I think you might be surprised what I can finish," I say.

His smirk grows yet again.

We work both East Valley farmers' markets on the weekend, we do lunches at ASU, and it's about three in the afternoon on Wednesday, at the ASU lunch area, when Jordan takes an order, thanks the woman whose card he's charged, and then pulls me toward the back of the truck.

His eyes are so unlike the eyes I remember when I first met him, when he was so miserable and his mom was struggling so much.

"We did it," he says, and he jumps up and down.

"We did?"

"Taking out taxes, taking out your pay, even taking out the next shopping we'll need to do? We have it. The back-mortgage payment. We did it!"

I hug him tight. "I'm proud of you, dude."

"Me too!" he says. "Of us."

CHAPTER FORTY-TWO

JORDAN

"So what are we gonna do with all this cheddar?" I ask Max, as the Friday lunch crush dies down and we start our cleanup. I flash him the bills in my hand—maybe eight hundred more today. Every day has been at least solid in terms of profit, and this time it won't go to back mortgage, since I handed my mom that money on Wednesday night, which felt amazing.

"I told you already. Don't do that. Cheddar shit. That's not you, and that's not cute," Max says, and I laugh, because, yeah. Not so cute.

"We should like take a vacation. Take off without the truck for a few days. We've earned it. Ever been to Rocky Point?"

He snorts. "That's white people Mexico."

"All I know is they have good shrimp there. Fresh right out of the ocean. Back when my mom was normal and my dad was breathing, he used to take us down there some weekends. All I remember is shrimp and tomato juice out of the can. That's weird, right?"

Max rubs the middle of my back with his palms. "I still remember the first time I tried cream cheese. It was this time my dad and mom took me to Yuma, and we went to a bagel place, and Dad ordered me an everything bagel with cream cheese. I thought it was the best thing ever, and I thought it was only in Yuma."

"That's funny how we remember foods more than anything else."

He squeezes my sides. "That's why I love this. I mean, I love this for a lot of reasons, and I kinda saved your life and all." I poke him in the ribs and he grins. "But I love that we make memories. Someone we've served in the last few weeks will remember what we made for them for the rest of their life. And we don't know who or what, but I like knowing that."

I think about how true it is, and how, before Max, I never gave two shits about strangers. Other people were kinda just there for me and Pam and Kayla to make fun of. Now I see people more. More clearly. Not all the time, maybe. But I'm gonna try. To remember that they're basically like me, and I'm basically like them, and yeah. In a way I think Max taught me that.

"Me too," I say. "I like how——"

"Is Lydia Edwards here?" asks a man in a green T-shirt, holding a clipboard. He's standing at the order window. His shirt reads *Tylers Towing*. No apostrophe. Genius.

"No," I say. "That's my mom."

"I gotta take the truck," he says.

I laugh. "Um, no you don't," I say.

"But I do. There's a title loan out on it and no one's paid and we can't reach her. It's not yours anymore. Sorry."

He walks over to the passenger side and attempts to board, and I lunge over and hold the handle so he can't. "Wait. What?"

"I just told you. Not your truck no more. Tell you what. I'll give you five minutes to grab your stuff and get out."

"We're not giving you anything until you show us proof," Max says, and I nod my head, so glad he's here with me.

The man shrugs, walks back over to the window, and hands the paper through to me.

I read it. Max looks over my shoulder and reads it too.

The amount listed is $27,500. My mom's signature is at the bottom. The date is May twenty-seventh. Which would be the day after Max and I took over the truck. My stomach drops into my groin, and without even thinking, I crumple the piece of paper up and throw it at the guy.

He shrugs. "We have copies, so, yeah. Throw all you want, kid."

I look at Max. My throat goes dry. In his eyes I see resignation, which is so not what I want to see. I want him to have the answers. I want him to point out to me that this is obviously a mistake, because it has to be. Why would Mom take a loan out and not tell me, and still make me work the truck and give her money to pay off the mortgage? If she took out a loan, she must have paid it already. Right? Right?

But his eyes look sad, and in them I understand something that is unfathomable to me, and I swallow, look around the truck, and say, "Let's take the meat and cheese, at least. Can you call an Uber?"

He does.

As we watch Poultry in Motion get towed away, I feel almost nothing. I say nothing. Max reaches down and holds my hand, and he squeezes, but my hand remains limp. Everything feels numb.

We take the Uber back to my place. Mom is on the couch, eating Sweetos and watching an old cartoon. *Tom and Jerry*, I think. Tom is trying to bop Jerry over the head with a sledgehammer.

She doesn't turn when I come in. She doesn't stop chewing. She just yells, "Hey!"

I walk over and sit on the arm of the couch near her head.

"Mom," I say softly.

The way I say it seems to impact her, kind of. Like she pretends to keep eating but she slows her pace, and I can tell I have her attention.

I repeat it. "Mom."

"Jordan," she says, a little edge in her voice.

"You took out a loan on the truck," I say.

I see her throat constrict. She doesn't answer. Her eyes stay on the television.

"You did, didn't you?"

She closes her eyes and pauses the TV. "It's complicated, Jordan."

"Mom," I say. "Mom. What did you do? What's happening?"

She turns off the TV, but she doesn't sit up. She just stays staring at the set even though it's off. "It's bad," she says. "It's really, really, really bad."

"Mom," I whisper. "Tell me what's up. Tell me what you did."

She closes her eyes. "It's worse than you think," she says.

I sit, motionless, as she explains. I know Max is behind me, and I'm half-glad he's there, and half wish he weren't because someone else hearing it makes it more true, and I don't want it to be true.

I should have known. How had I not seen it? Denial is a funny thing.

Of course. My mom has gambled away all the truck money.

I feel like I've been robbed at gunpoint. I feel gutted. Like someone has come and taken everything I have, cut everything inside me out. I feel like I want to scream, but screaming is useless.

"The money I gave you for the back mortgage?" I whisper, because my voice is gone.

"I have a problem, sweetheart. I'm so so sorry. You have no idea how sorry I really am."

"Um," I say, light as a feather.

"Every time I leave Casino Arizona, it's like I get on the 101 and the shame is so deep that I just think, 'I should turn the wheel all the way left.' Slam into the guardrail. End this all. You'd be better off. Everyone would be. I failed. I failed at life, Jordan, and I know that, and I know it doesn't help you that I know that, but I want you to understand. I get it."

The voice that comes from my mouth is not mine. Someone else's. "Um."

"For what it's worth, nothing you could think about me is worse than what I think about me. The level to which I hate me right now? It's like, an insane amount, Jordan. I beyond want to die. Beyond, Jordan."

I don't even repeat um this time.

The rest happens really quickly. Too quickly. I don't have time to say good-bye. I don't have the words for it. I guess it's good that my mom gets that, because it would be worse if she cried. But also it's not enough. Time. Not enough anything. How do you say good-bye to your world in less than two minutes?

"So I'm gonna go," I say.

"Probably a good choice," she says.

I look back at Max. I want him to hold me. I want him to

never touch me again. These are not thoughts that go together. This is not a scene that goes together. It's all jumbled, disjointed. Unfitting.

I turn back to my mom. "Maybe we call nine-one-one?"

"Mercy," my mom says, and I have absolutely no idea what that means. I should have mercy? Call them because she's had enough? No idea. I just call, and tell them to come and pick up my mom because she's a danger to herself. I say this in front of her. She does not stop me or contradict what I'm saying. She looks small, and scared, and not mine. Not anymore.

I mouth *Bye* to her but the word doesn't come out. She isn't looking at me anyway. I focus on her profile. Her left eye, half-closed like she's wasted. Her expression oddly blank. Then I grab Dorcas's leash, which makes her run over to me. I leash her up, turn, and walk to the door. Max takes my hand and squeezes. My mom hasn't moved. She's not going to. I finally have to look away.

"You'll stay with us," he says, and I'm too far gone to say anything other than what I say.

"Thank you."

Ms. Gutierrez is standing in the doorway waiting for us when we get back from the house where I no longer live. Max must have texted.

She envelops me in an all-encompassing hug. I wrap my arms around her but don't squeeze. I can't cry. Bone-dry like the fucking desert we live in.

"I took the rest of the day," she says, holding me tight. She's dressed for work. "Of course you can stay here," she says, answering a question I guess Max must have asked her via text. "As long as you want. As long as you need."

"Thanks."

Dorcas shakes her neck collar as if to say, "I'm here too." Max's mom pets him.

"Of course you're welcome too."

I say "Thanks" again. I don't know what else to say, or how much I can just be normal right now, which I know they don't expect but it's kind of like, I don't know how to show them what's real right now.

She says, "Let's get you situated," and she leads me to the hallway where all the bedrooms are. I feel like I'm dreaming as I walk the hallway. In what used to be our house, my mom was in the main bedroom, I was across the hall, and the two rooms in between were storage. Here, Max is in one of those two rooms, and one is an office. Across from Max's mom's bedroom, the room that was mine at our house, is a guest room, painted bright yellow.

"This will be yours," she says. "So you have your own space. Okay?"

"Okay. Thanks, Ms. Gutierrez."

"Rosa," she says.

It's weird being here and trying to get through my head that I'm a visitor but not really. That I'm not going back home tonight, because I have none. It's strange to have one suitcase with clothing and toiletries and my backpack with my laptop, and that's it. It's like I'm holding all my possessions. I know I can go back and get more, but really, so much of the stuff that's in my room back home is things I don't use. I don't even want my '80s bordello room anymore. It's tainted, because it was Mom and me who bought all that stuff. It was another life.

Mom has probably been picked up from our house now, and who knows where they took her? It feels like the blood has been drained from my veins, and I'm so, so tired.

Rosa lets me get settled, and Max lingers in the doorway.

"You wanna call the girls? I can call the Amigos. We can do a swim thing here."

I shake my head. I don't want to see anyone. I love my girls but the idea of everyone pitying me is way too much for me right now.

"You wanna just hang out?" He sits down on my bed.

I nod, and Rosa comes back and tells us she's gonna do some work in her office unless I need her. When she walks off, I shake my head amazed at how not like my mom Rosa is. Lucky Max.

"So we'll just hang?" he asks.

"What I really want is my truck," I say. "Our truck. In some ways, I'm more pissed about that than I am about my mom."

He winces. "Really?"

I plop down next to him. "No."

"Yeah. Didn't think so. I miss the truck too. But that's your mom."

I think about the night I took her to Sweeties, and what she said when we were in my room. That I was great just as I am. And I think two things. One, how can I trust that now? Because when she said it, she knew that she was fucking us over and screwing up our lives. And two is how much I can't believe that as of this moment, I no longer live with her.

"She used to be so different," I say. "One time a couple summers ago, we did this experiment where we tried to cook an egg on the actual sidewalk in June." I laugh. "I have no idea why I'm telling you that."

He laughs. "That's cool."

"It worked when we put it in a pan."

"Nice."

"When my dad died, it was like my mom became real fragile. And yeah, she gambled, and then she went in this program for it. But she told me it wasn't that big a deal even when it was bad, and she told me she'd stopped, and I believed her."

"Yeah," Max says, and I'm glad he doesn't try to make things better, because he can't.

I'm thinking about how she made a point of telling me she was thinking about gambling but that she hadn't. And is that in some ways worse? That she tried to make it seem like she was honest, but she was lying? And how do you ever trust a person again after they gamble away your house? You don't, that's what. You don't. When I think that, the tear ducts fill up again, and Max puts his hand on my arm and squeezes.

"It's okay," he says. "You let me cry. I'll let you cry."

I crack up. "Permission granted," I say. "But nah. Too angry to cry. I want to burn something."

"I hear ya," he says, and I know it's not his fault, but momentarily I want to yell at Max, because no, he doesn't know what this is like. No one does.

"Tired," I say. I'm exhausted. From feeling all this stuff.

"Wanna take a nap?"

I nod.

He comes and puts his arms around me. I put mine around him, but I'm not feeling it. Too something. Like how I feel about him is behind something. A screen I can't break through. I pull him closer, too close for intimacy, because I don't want him to feel like I don't care about him. I do. I'm just the boy in the bubble right now I guess.

He kisses me lightly on the cheek, stands, and walks out of the room.

"You do you, friend," he says, and he leaves.

CHAPTER FORTY-THREE

MAX

It's kinda weird, but having my mom home from work is actually really nice. When she comes into the living room, Jordan is asleep in his new room, and I'm sitting on the couch, watching episodes of *Catfish*.

"Quite the day," she says, and she gives me a hug and sits down next to me.

"Yup," I say.

"How are you doing with all this?"

I shrug. "I can't make him feel better. That part sucks."

"You just have to give him time. This will always be one of the hardest days of his life, as long as he lives."

"Yeah."

"Just like you, when you were assaulted. You weren't ready to talk about it right away. Sometimes people just need a little time to stew in their juices."

"Sometimes I think I'm a superhero," I say, and my mom laughs.

"I know," she says.

"You know?"

"I know you a little bit, mijo. You like to think you can save people and make people better, and nicer. Your superpower is your smile."

I can't help but grin at that, and she does too.

"It's okay, though, if sometimes you don't smile and make everything better."

"I know," I say.

"Okay. I just worry sometimes. That you take too much on yourself. Other people can figure out their problems. And you have to take care of you."

The thing is, I don't know if people can. Figure out their problems. Would Jordan have gotten here, or somewhere like here, if it weren't for me? I don't think so.

Then this thought comes to me, and it makes me gasp out loud.

"What?" my mom asks.

"Nothing," I say.

She rolls her eyes. "Nothing," she repeats.

The thought is that no, Jordan wouldn't be here. But I wouldn't be, either. Without his help. Without my mom. Without the Amigos.

That feels like a profound thought. Cheesy as shit, but also simple and true.

"So you're not going to tell me?"

I shake my head. "No. But something else I will say."

She sits back on the couch and puts her legs across my lap and waits for me to speak.

"Thanks," I say. "For being you. For loving me. I know I'm a pain in the ass, but you're always there for me, Mom."

This reddens her eyes.

"Do you know that I basically told Dad I was raped? Before you. He made jokes. I mean, he confirmed that what happened was rape, but he, like, didn't say anything more. Or help me."

She sits up. "What?"

"Yeah," I say.

"What are you talking about? You told him and he didn't do anything?"

"Well, I basically called at like four in the morning after a bad dream. Because the dream made me wonder if I should say something to someone or if I was making shit up. I told him not me, but hypothetically. Like a friend. But who calls their dad at four in the morning and asks something like that without it being about them?"

She shakes her head, hard. Her face is creased and rigid.

"He didn't get it, I guess. It's not his fault—"

"The hell it isn't," she says, just about exploding, and I worry she'll wake up Jordan. "He's your father. It's not okay for him to hear that and not follow up. With me. Has he followed up with you?"

I shake my head.

"Damn it," she says. "He tries my patience, mijo. I hate to talk bad about your father, but the man needs to grow up."

"Well there ya go," I say, my insides tightening.

She nuzzles the side of my leg with her foot. "Sorry," she says. "I don't like to do that. That's your business between you and your father. But can I say one more thing?"

I shrug.

"You can call him out on it. If you want, I mean. It's up to you, and what kind of relationship you want with the man. But you're seventeen, and he let you down. You can let it go, or you can say something. That's up to you, mijo."

"Can I go back to my show now?" I ask.

She shoots me a look but then relaxes her face. "I know," she says. "It's a lot. I'll leave you alone."

"Love you, Mom," I say again.

"Love you too."

CHAPTER FORTY-FOUR

JORDAN

A monsoon rolls in overnight.

First comes the alarm buzzing all our phones. They sound five times and the warning from the national weather service appears. *Dust storm warning for all of Maricopa County until 3:00 a.m. tomorrow with reports of blowing dust along I-101 in Scottsdale. Blowing dust can reduce visibility to near zero in a matter of seconds, making driving hazardous. If you're driving, pull aside, stay alive.*

I'm in the guest room, pretending to be asleep on top of a beautiful, flowery bedspread, when it comes in. It's not unusual to get a few of these a week during monsoon season, but overnight ones don't come too often. I'm staring at the ceiling fan on the white ceiling above me, my arms above my head, my head cradling my hands, thinking about everything, and I get the urge to go outside and watch the storm.

The hot air smells of creosote and dust as I roll open the sliding door from the living room to the back patio. The one at our house creaks when you open it, but this one, not surprisingly, is smooth. Dorcas follows me out.

Our house isn't ours anymore, and there isn't an us anymore. I live here now, and I have a headache that could split my whole fucking face apart.

You don't see a dust storm come in at night. You hear it though.

You hear the winds pick up and whip through the palm trees, the fronds slapping in the breeze, and you see the lightning flashes, and seconds later the thunder rumble, and then the neighborhood dogs barking. Not Dorcas. She stands by my side as I look up into the invisible night sky that may or may not be blowing a film of desert dust into the pool I can barely see in front of me.

You're not supposed to go into a pool when there's lightning out. Everyone knows that. But not everyone's as totally over it as I am right now. I sit on the edge and dangle my legs, feel the bath-temperature water soothe my already hot skin. I kick my legs back and forth, making ripples.

"What are you doing out here?"

I hadn't heard Max slide open the door and join me. His legs are next to me, and part of me wants to lean my head against his knee, and part of me wants—I don't know. To destroy something beautiful.

I grunt. "Trying to get hit by lightning," I say.

"Awesome," is his answer. "Can I join?"

"Sure."

He sits down next to me and for a bit we just sit there and listen to the winds pick up and the sizzling sound of sand and dust we can't see zipping by our ears. Then he puts his hand calmly over mine and wraps his left thumb under my right pinky. I squeeze back to show I'm there, but I'm only half, or a quarter.

"I want to hit something," I say.

He doesn't respond, which is perfect. He doesn't grab after my hand when I pull mine away either. Also a good choice. My forehead is pulsing, thinking about everything. I'm so tired of thinking about it. This is why people do drugs. So they don't have to think. Or gamble, I guess. And you know what? As much as I don't want to think, or feel, I'll never fucking drink or gamble or anything, because if I ever made anyone feel the way my mom has made me feel, I would not be able to live with myself either. And thinking about that makes my insides hurt, because I love her still, even though she fucked up my life. Our lives. I can't even imagine the pain she is feeling because deep down I know she loves me, and yet she did this still. And I know that it's a disease and not a choice but right now that feels like blah blah blah. She cared more about spinning video slot wheels than she did about me.

Then he grabs my hand and stands up and I resist saying, "Let me go," but just barely.

"C'mon," he says. "Let's go hit something."

He texts his mom and we're out the door and in his truck. When he turns on the beamers, I can see the dust blowing brown in the black night.

"They say don't drive," I say.

"We're going like two minutes. Two turns. I think we'll survive."

He pulls into the road and I'm in no position to complain. Maybe we'll get hit and this will all be over.

He takes me back to 24 Hour Fitness. No cars are out front, which is good because I don't want to see anyone and I don't want anyone to see me.

And suddenly I'm inside, in front of a boxing bag. Black with red stripes. And Max is strapping black-and-red boxing gloves on my hands.

"I've never hit anything," I say.

He snorts. "Except Kevin."

"Well he deserved it," I say.

"This is my favorite way to get out the pain when I'm pissed. When some stupid kid tells me to go back to Mexico, or when Fabio Breen calls someone faggot at practice. I know I say that shit doesn't bug me, but. Sometimes it does, okay? So I come and I beat the shit out of this thing until I can hardly swing another punch at it."

I hit the bag half-heartedly. This is a dumb idea. When I said I wanted to punch something, I meant it as a metaphor. Someone from my AP Comp class ought to be able to understand a good metaphor when it appears before them in a dust storm at 2:20 a.m., but apparently my boyfriend is blind to figures of speech during monsoons. The dusty wind must obscure his vision and understanding of language.

"Come on," he says. "Harder. And punch flat. You can break your hand or wrist if you punch wrong. Make a fist and hit the bag flat with your knuckles, 'kay?"

"Not sure telling me to do something that might break my hand is making me feel more like—"

"Hit. The fucking. Bag. Jesus."

I hit it. Pretty hard. My bicep wobbles at contact.

"There ya go. Again."

I hit it again.

"Add a sound."

I hit it again, silent.

"Listen to me. Let the sound out, however it comes out."

I hit it again and emit this high-pitched squeal that would

make me laugh if it didn't carry with it my entire broken heart. And Max doesn't laugh either. Just says, "There ya go. Again. More."

And I hit and hit and hit, and I scream and then I pound and cry and it's not a classy, well-put-together cry like I'd want but a messy, snotty wail that comes with so many punches, I get dizzy throwing them. And I'm wailing on the poor punching bag and screaming my guts out, and I don't want to stop, ever. And sadness bleeds out of me. And grief. And fury. And missing Dad. And missing Mom. I'm sad angry sad angry and I hit and hit until I'm doubled over in fatigue on the scratchy purple carpet.

Max rolls up next to me and spoons me, and for a bit I'm just numb in his arms, spent. It feels . . . beautiful. I'm spent. I'm not that angry anymore. I mean, I am, but it's all been screamed and punched out and I'm exhausted and I start to laugh.

He laughs too. "Isn't that awesome?"

"Yeah," I say. "You're kind of awesome."

"I know, right?"

I elbow backward into his ribs and he rolls on top of me and he's smiling that wide Max smile and his dark eyes are peaceful and wise and playful and . . . everything.

And this time we don't go to the bathroom and claw at each other. We just lie there, looking into each other's eyes, breathing in harmony, and waiting for the next thing to happen.

CHAPTER FORTY-FIVE

MAX

"Hey Dad," I say.

"Broseph!" he yells into the phone. "What up what up?"

"Nothing," I say, lying. It's Sunday morning, and I've called him before I even went out to say hey to Jordan or my mom. My dad doesn't even know that Jordan has been living with us over a week now, and you know what? That's fine.

"I got a gig at Comedy Works in Denver! This is YUGE for me. I never played there before. Scouts and agents and shit like that. The cool thing is I get to do a greatest hits, because they haven't seen me up there. I get to bring back Axe body spray fails and the whole Bloomin' Onions shtick."

"Nice," I say.

"I feel like it's happening for me, you know? Like I'm a step away. I'm not *that* old. Larry David, Ricky Gervais. Both were older than me when they got their breaks."

"How come you didn't say anything when I called you about the rape thing?"

Dad is quiet for a second. "Wait what?"

"I called you at, like, four in the morning. Asked you a question about the definition of rape. Why didn't you question what that was about, Dad?"

It takes him a couple beats to answer. When he does, his voice is unsure. "I didn't—what was I . . ."

"Dad," I say. "You're my dad. Ask. You should ask."

More beats before he asks in a thin voice, "What happened, Max?"

"I was raped," I say, my voice cracking as I say it. My heart is pulsing crazy. "Like I said. The guy wanted to and I said no because he was a fucking racist fuck. He sat on my legs. I froze up, okay? I'm supposed to be strong, and I was even bigger than him, but I fucking froze!"

"Max," my dad says. I can't even describe what he sounds like. A little boy, hurt, maybe? Not anything like the guy who spun me around and wouldn't come to me when I smacked my head on the armoire. Who said that "pain doesn't mean that much."

"Yeah," I say. "So that happened."

"I just," he says. "Jesus. I'm not cut out for this. I don't know how to do this, kid."

My insides twist like a tornado. "Daddy," I say.

"I just . . . I can't—"

"I can't," I repeat. And I take the phone off my ear, look at the word "Dad" across the screen, and hit the red button to hang up.

Not sure what to do or what to think about my dad saying "I can't" to me, I warrior up big-time. I sit on my bed and think about Super Max.

In a world in which some fathers are assholes, Super Max stands tall. He doesn't need—

I stop myself. Fuck that. I've been doing that shit all my life. And you know what? This hurts. It hurts bad.

The phone rings. It's Dad. I can't. Like he said. I just . . . can't.

So I hide under the covers for a bit and think about my dad, and kind of give him a funeral in my brain. I think about the good times when he lived with us in central Phoenix. Going out to this awesome seafood restaurant that had an actual mariachi band even though the space was about the size of my room. And how we just laughed so hard, the three of us, because our ears were ringing and we couldn't hardly breathe it was so loud. Or when Dad took me to the batting cages, and how he was so proud of me for hitting the ball so hard. There were good times. But also bad ones, obviously.

I'm just about to start crying when there's a knock on the door. I dry my eyes and sit up tall. "What's up?" I yell.

"Just me," Jordan says.

"Come in."

He does, and when he sees my face, he sits down right next to me. "What's wrong?"

I shake my head. I'm about to say, "Nothing." And then I think about how that's exactly what my dad would tell me to do. And that's stupid. I have a chipped red toenail and I don't give a shit if Dad would think it made me less of a man. I don't care anymore.

I say, "My dad."

"What happened?"

I tell him, and the damn tears start up, and he holds me as I tell him about what it felt like to hear him say, "I can't."

"I'm sorry," Jordan says.

"It's not your fault."

"God, I hate when people say that. I'm not sorry because it's my fault. I'm sorry that happened to you, okay?"

I smile a little. "Okay."

"My mom can't either, if that helps. And I know it sucks royal testicle meat when your mom or dad can't."

I nod a bit. "Yeah."

"Anything I can do to make you feel better?"

An idea pops into my head. It's so different from my usual answer. Which would be, of course, "No, I'm good." Warrior up.

Instead I say, "Can I draw you?"

He freezes for a second, and then he moves his body into a side pose, his light green eyes all bedroom-y.

I crack up. "Easy there, Ryan Gosling," I say. "I want you to sit in a chair. I want to draw your face."

He's cool with that, and I grab my supplies, sit at the desk, and go and grab a second chair from the dining room. I sit him in it so that a little bit of sunlight bleeds into the room and lights up his face. I sit and stare.

"Make sure you get all the zits," he says.

I shoot him a dirty look.

"I used to be a child model. A before model, actually."

"Would you shut up?"

"What kind of way is that to talk to your model?"

That cracks me up, and I give him a serious look that he seems to understand, because he does, finally, shut up and stop putting himself down. We sit in silence, and I use a black pencil to trace a face. I notice as I draw him just how narrow his face is, which is one of the things I like about him. And yet, you know what's funny? That's what drew me to him, but now what matters is that he's Jordan. I realize that even if his face were rounder, like mine, I'd still be hooked. That's saying something.

I use a light green for his eyes. It's the first color I put on his face, and as soon as I do, the page lights up, just like the room does when Jordan enters it. I smile to myself.

"Tell me," he says.

I shake my head no. There's a level of cheesy I can't get to. That thought is something I think I'll keep to myself.

I use white pencil to pop his eyes a bit more, and then give his face some contour by smudging some white under his cheeks.

I look at him. I look at the drawing, which he can't see yet. He won't either. Not for a while, I don't think. It's too personal. What I think of him is too personal.

"What?" he asks again.

I can't tell him all that. But I can tell him something. So I put the drawing facedown on the desk and go over to him and put my hands on his face.

"You are so freakin' beautiful," I say. It's something I never, ever would have said a few months back. No chance. But now I can.

The color of purple he turns is almost comical. I stare at him, smiling. I'm trying to give him mental telepathy. To beam into his brain an important message. Which is, *Just take the compliment. I mean it.*

And the craziest thing is that for maybe the first time ever, he doesn't say the self-denigrating thing.

I think to myself: *Progress. We're both getting better. Well, that's something.*

CHAPTER FORTY-SIX

JORDAN

When Max finishes drawing me, he turns the drawing upside down and comes over to where I'm sitting and says, "You are so freakin' beautiful."

I giggle. Me. I'm beautiful. And hearing it makes me feel like I'm a giddy twelve-year-old schoolgirl, maybe, and that's especially embarrassing because I'm like this homeless kid and I shouldn't be feeling all giddy, and I know I turn super red because Max just stares at me and I can feel the color in my cheeks. And I have like a million Jordan-like comments, but I don't say even one of them.

I point over to the drawing. "Can I see?" I ask, and Max shakes his head.

"Pretty please?"

"Nope," he says. "I'm not ready."

I groan. "I want to see what I look like through your eyes."

I expect another no, but something about what I've said actually means something to him, I guess, because he goes over to the desk and slowly turns the piece of paper over.

I follow. And what I see shocks me.

He's drawn a boy with life in his eyes. Green eyes, the color of spring grass. A slight grin on his face. And the weirdest part: handsome. I stare and stare until the picture blurs. I say, "Wow," and he says nothing back, just lets me stare.

I'm staring at a drawing of a boy who is an actual being, like a . . . substantial person. Someone who makes choices and does stuff in the world. That's all I can say about that, because it's so weird to me. That I've never seen that in me before.

I hug him then, and I say, "Thanks. You're a freakin' amazing artist."

He whispers the words right into my ear. "Thank you."

And it's like we float into his bed and lie down next to each other, which feels like a little bit of heaven.

We talk about my wives, and Max says he loved how they were right there with me when I texted them about Lydia. They must have come over in like two seconds, and Pam brought me a Ziploc baggie of yellow candy hearts, because she knows those are my favorites, and Kayla showed me the unsolicited lewd photo Shaun from Chess Club had sent her that made her decide to ghost him, and neither of them tried to dress Dorcas without her consent, and mostly they just loved on me, which was exactly what I needed. It was so weird to have them in Max's house, draped across his mom's gray fabric couch and love seat like they belonged there. One thing Max doesn't know is that when he left for a bit, I actually talked to them about how I sometimes wish they didn't Gay Best Friend me all the time, and how it would be okay to be serious sometimes too. And then Pam hugged the orange throw pillow to her chest and was like, "I'll stop if you stop calling me one of your wives."

That hit me right between the eyes. I had never even thought of that before, and I started to get all "Oh my God, I'm so sorry," and she smiled, and shook her head, like, *It's fine, just saying*, and we didn't have to have a big, dramatic scene, which I guess is step one of me not playing the role of their Gay Best Friend (GBF), and them not playing the part of my Two Sassy Wives (TSW). So yeah. I guess that's progress. That maybe not everything has to be a joke, just because it started that way. It was kinda amazing.

And then my thoughts turn to my mom, and when Max senses that I've gone dark, he hugs me tight, and I willingly roll into his chest and let him hold me and put his strength into me, and I wonder if I'll ever be able to give him half as much as he's given me.

"I sometimes think we're like space dust," he says as my head is cradled in his chest.

"Like our problems are small, all things considered?"

"What?"

"I remember you said that once. That our problems don't amount to much."

Max is silent for a bit. "Wow," he says. "You really listen, don't you? No. I mean, yeah, but I guess I'm saying what you said with your poem. Like that's why we fit together so well. We were once particles of space dust, connected to each other, and then the Big Bang. And now all these millennia later, we've found each other. And Betts and Zay-Rod and Pam and Kayla. They were close by too, and now we've all found each other again."

"Like space dust?"

"Like space dust."

"Okay," I say. "I like that."

His mom sticks her head in the room and tells us she's going to church. She's all dressed up in a pretty, light blue skirt and yellow blouse. "You boys behave now," she says, smiling, and Max says, "You too," which makes her smile wide and wink.

We're quiet for a while. A truck rolls by outside. I'm thinking about how we need to find jobs. And also about how lucky I am to know Max. He's the best person I've ever met, and for some ridiculous reason, he's chosen me.

"It is pretty incredible," Max says again, shaking his head. "How a month ago I barely knew you, and now you're, like, here."

"It's just the music of what happens," I say.

"It's the what?"

"The Seamus Heaney poem, remember?"

"Oh yeah."

"My dad used to tell me this story. It's where that phrase came from in the poem. A story about the legend of Finn MacCool. He was this mythical Irish warrior. He challenged all these brilliant men to come up with the most beautiful sound in the world. One guy said it was a young girl laughing. Another said the bellowing of a stag. A third said the sound of a sword against a shield. No, Finn MacCool said. It's the music of what happens."

Max screws up his face at me. "What the hell does that mean?"

"I don't know," I say. "My dad liked the story. And I guess I like the phrase. 'The music of what happens.' It's maybe the stuff of life. Birds singing. Babies crying."

Max stretches his arms above him and then cradles his head in his hands. He says, "To me, it's maybe more like 'music' meaning 'harmony.' The harmoniousness of what happens."

"Everything happens for a reason, eh?"

Max shrugs. "If that's true, somebody up there has a hell of a sense of humor."

"It's beautiful, though. Your idea."

"You think?"

I say, "I think there's something really cool about the idea of sitting back and listening to what happens in the world, rather than fretting over it and trying to fix it. After all, if it's what happens, it's what happens. Right? I can't make what happens not happen."

"Unless that's part of the plan."

"You're really smart."

"You're really cute," Max says, and I blush like crazy. "You're also really interesting. I liked that about you right away. You say interesting things."

"Thanks," I say, and I'm thinking, *Man, I could get used to this thing where I don't think I'm a total piece of shit all the time.*

Max and I talk about tomorrow, when I'm supposed to go see my mom, who is in in-patient treatment in Phoenix. To be honest? I don't want to. It's not that I don't love my mom; I'm just not ready, you know? He says he'll help me pack up my things at my house, and I can't even really talk about that yet. It's the only house I've ever known, and it's where my dad was, and it's where my mom was, and I feel a little like an orphan here, which is something I don't want to tell Max or his mom, because I'm so glad they've taken me in. I like it here too. I just don't know if it will ever feel like home. If anything ever will, again.

Then we talk more about the rape. His counselor and what she said about the healing process. How when trust is violated, it's like you're left with an empty piggy bank. Building trust again, she said, is like putting big, fat nickels into the slot. They clank against the bottom, and that sound is jarring. But in order to heal, you have to keep adding those nickels, and soon enough, there will be coins to cushion the nickel's fall and make the sound not so grating.

I tell him that I don't mind the clank, and that I'll make sure I always remember that he'll hear a jarring sound even if I hear nothing. And I tell him that he can always tell me, and I will always hold him when he feels that way, and I will never judge him, and I will give him all the time and space he needs until the bank fills up again.

He doesn't respond to that, but I can tell the words mean something to him by the way he pauses and looks away after I say them.

Instead he tells me how his friends have been cool. I like those guys. I don't want to spend a lot of time with them without Max around, but that's more my thing than theirs. People just make me nervous, I guess. Maybe if I got used to them. After all, Max made me nervous once too. Man did he ever.

"But what about when there's no beauty in what happens?" Max asks after a long, languid silence. "When ugly things happen? What does 'the music of what happens' mean when it comes up against, you know. Bad things."

I swallow. I've been wondering this too. What "the music of what happens" means when the happenings are total crap. I want everything to be okay. For my mom. For our little family, such as it is. And maybe they will be, and maybe they won't, and I can't imagine a time will ever come when thinking about that won't slam me right in the chin.

I breathe for a while, and then I take Max's hands in mine and squeeze. He squeezes back. The chin pain fades, and another, very different feeling takes its place. It's like a full-body sigh, like a cool breeze through the hot desert of my life that tells me, *You are here*. It's new, it's different, and it's welcome, and I don't want to let go of his strong hands, ever. Dorcas jumps up on the bed and nestles between us, first up high so she can lick my right ear. Then she plops down between our legs. Total cock block, but I don't mind. If it feels like this, she can stay forever.

I don't know. I mean, it's not all beautifully harmonic, this world we find ourselves in. Clearly. There's shit music, and sometimes the melody goes away completely. There's silence and dissonant chords that cringe your ears. But the synchronicity of a perfectly created chorus? And the fact that you never know when one is coming? And that amazing feeling, the first time you hear a song and you know it's going to be with you forever?

I have to think that's worth everything.

"Hmm," I say, knowing Max is not a music person, and that if I said any of this, he'd only kind of get it, and us being on the same page is everything right now. I think about the half notes of dissonance, between what I hear and what someone else hears, and those moments where the world is so cold, and when someone reaches their hand out to you. In those symphonic, connected moments where another soul joins you and feels what you feel, and you can breathe again. Like right now.

"Yeah," he says, and we look at each other, and I don't know if we're singing the exact same tune. But I'll take his word for it.

Because for eternity I'd like to float around the universe on this bed, with this boy, with this dog. In this perfectly imperfect moment.

ACKNOWLEDGMENTS

Once upon a time, I set about trying to write a novel based on a young person who had been kicked out of his home for being gay. It was based on the painful, true story of a fan, and watching it happen to him touched me profoundly, as did his resilience in the face of adversity.

I followed the path where it led me, and this is that novel. Except it's not at all about a kid who was kicked out of his home, and Jordan, initially based on Reagan Stanley, has a totally different home life. I am not sure I'll ever be able to explain how *The Music of What Happens* came about, but I'd be remiss if I didn't start by thanking Reagan, who is brave, and who is special, and who told me about throwing dreams (in balloons, not condoms) and who says stuff like "Sweet Gay Jesus."

I also must thank my editor, Nick Thomas, who guided me as this book came together, and also Cheryl Klein, who was there at the start when I was figuring this story out. I have learned so much from both of you and I am grateful for all of it.

Oh yeah, and Linda Epstein! My agent. Who is hardly an "Oh yeah" in my life, but she will understand why I say that. Sorry and love you and thank you for your support.

Thanks to my Scholastic family. You folks have been so good to me, and I love working with you. A special shout-out to Arthur A. Levine. Thank you for your friendship and thank you for, well, my career.

To my husband, Chuck: You and I will float around on a soft, cushy, flying rug for eternity. I'd say I'm looking forward to that, but we're already there. Thanks for making my life so cozy. Thank you to my mother, Shelley; my father, Bob; my sister, Pam; my brother, Dan. You are my family, and I know that sounds like I'm saying the obvious, but I mean it in the greater sense. You are my people. I love you.

Karen and Sam: You have become my family too! I adore you.

Thanks to the amazing Doug Bland for reciting a Seamus Heaney poem over dinner one night. The last words of the poem became the title, and really it transformed the story too, bringing poetry into the fold.

Thank you to my readers: Lisa McMann, Kameron-with-a-K-Martinez, Josh Horton, Laurie Halse Anderson, and Joseph Chavez.

Gratitude to Staci Edwards, who allowed me to watch her draw, so that I could understand how that happens.

Much appreciation to Jonathan Willis from Traveling Cup, Mike Baum from Paradise Melts Food Truck, and Robert Coleman from Circle R Farm Food Truck, for letting me hang out and find out what it's like on a food truck in the summer in Arizona. Toasty! I appreciate you answering all my stupid questions.

Anthony Celaya at Dobson High School: Thanks for letting

me hang out in your classroom and pick up on the vibe of your students. "This I Believe" comes from you.

And never least, to my friends at The Mankind Project, particularly Steve Murphy, Steve Harrison, and Rick Isenberg, thanks for continued support and teaching me about men's work.

ABOUT THE AUTHOR

Bill Konigsberg is the author of four books for young adults, which have won honors including the Stonewall Book Award, the Sid Fleischman Award for Humor, the Lambda Literary Award, and the PEN Center USA Literary Award. Bill lives in Chandler, Arizona, with his husband, Chuck, and their two labradoodles, Mabel and Buford. Please visit him online at billkonigsberg.com and @billkonigsberg.

This book was edited by Nick Thomas and designed by Nina Goffi. The production was supervised by Rachel Gluckstern and Melissa Schirmer. The text was set in Adobe Garamond Pro, with display type set in trendhmsans-one. The book was printed and bound at LSC Communications in Crawfordsville, Indiana. The manufacturing was supervised by Angelique Browne.